PRELUDE TO FATE

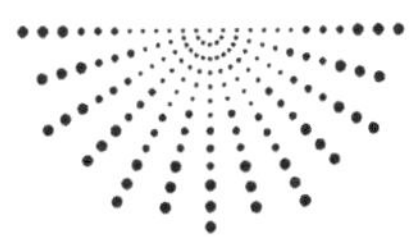

ROSIE CHAPEL

Prelude to Fate

Rosie Chapel

First printing 2018
ISBN: 978-0-6482797-5-4 (e-book)
ISBN: 978-0-6450738-8-1 (paperback)

Ulfire Pty. Ltd.
P.O. Box 1481
South Perth
WA 6951
Australia

www.rosiechapel.com

Cover Designed by Lisa Miller with Got You Covered

❋ Created with Vellum

From one crazy Roman history enthusiast to another,
Jackie, this book is dedicated to you with my love.

ACKNOWLEDGMENTS

To Melody, Amy, Lilly, Julie, Jackie, Paola and Maria –
you wonderful ladies keep me sane while I'm tearing my
hair out,
and panicking over… well… everything.
Your friendship and support mean more than you will ever
know!

To my Mum who suffers my first drafts without complaint -
thank you.

Heartfelt appreciation to Lisa Miller from Got You Covered
for my gorgeous cover.

My gratitude to Bill Thayer for his assistance with my
endless questions about Latin!
You would not think I have studied it - twice!

Thank you also to Graham from A Fading Street Publishing
Services for his editing finesse.

To my long-suffering husband, without whom, none of this would have happened.
would have happened.
I love you!

GLOSSARY

Author's Note:

The first time a word in Latin appears in the book, it is in italics. Although each one is explained within the text, here is a glossary, just in case!

Thereafter, unless it was an endearment or a greeting, I reverted to normal type.

lanista - manager/director of a Gladiatorial School
fossa bestiaria - the enclosure from where animals were released into the arena
domus - home
dominus/domina - master/mistress
cubiculum - bedroom
tablinum study/office
triclinium - dining room
medicus - doctor
salve - a greeting, like 'hello' (pronounced salwe)
legatus - the commander of the garrison
taberna - shop
mare nostrum - Mediterranean Sea

mi dilecte - my love, sweetheart, darling - an endearment

decumanus maximus - main road running east west through a Roman town

cardo maximus - the main street, which ran north to south through a typical Roman town

insula (pl. insulae) means island, but was also the name given to Roman tenements

stamen - horizontal threads on a loom - quite stiff in texture

trama - vertical threads on a loom - softer and more malleable than the stamen

thermopolium (pl. thermopolia) - ancient fast food outlet

popina (pl. popinae) - *a* local wine bar, whisk also served simple foods (often associated with gambling and pros-titution)

scholae bestiarum or *bestiariorum* - where the animals who were trained to fight were housed

bestiarii - the men who trained, and fought with the wild animals

spoliarium -where dead and dying gladiators were taken

saniarium - the treatment rooms for wounded gladiators

armamentarium - where the weapons used in combat were locked away

compluviums - opening above the atrium in a Roman house, through which rainwater fell and was collected in a pool (called an *impluvium*) underneath.

laniena - butcher's shop

mulsum - honeyed wine

calda - spiced wine (similar to modern day mulled wine)

ientaclum - breakfast

prandium - lunch

cena - dinner

tunica recta - straight, hem-less tunic worn on special occa-sions, such a marriage for girls and coming of age for boys

stola - a dress-like garment worn over a tunic. Characteristic of married women, it was considered a privilege to wear.
flammeum - orange coloured, rectangular veil
nodus Herculanus - an intricate knot in a belt worn by the bride, which represented virility and could only be untied by the bride's new husband
nova nupta - bride
toga praetexta - ceremonial toga
decumanus maximus - main road running east west through a Roman town

Prelude to Fate

PROLOGUE

NORTHERN TARRACONENSIS, HISPANIA
AD 14

"Lucius Caedicius! Lucius Caedicius!"

The shout went up across the garrison, startling a group of soldiers bustling around the compound. They stopped what they were doing to stare in astonishment at the man who, while continuing to yell, dodged around them at a fair pace — given he did not look to be in the first flush of youth.

About to step inside the stables, Lucius Caedicius Pacilus, upon hearing his name, turned to see someone haring across the quadrangle towards him. He squinted at the figure but dazzled by the bright sunlight, did not recognise who hailed him. Sighing with frustration, he paused and waited, rather impatiently. He had much to organise. Tomorrow, he would begin his long journey home to Emerita Augusta, more than a week's steady riding away, and there was still plenty to do prior to his departure.

The man all but skidded to a halt in front of him, and Lucius was surprised to see it was Vel, the elderly man he had saved scant weeks ago.

Smiling, Lucius greeted him. "Vel, how are you, my

friend? You are looking much better than the last time we met and have speed enough to put some of these laggards to shame." His eyes twinkled with mirth.

The man, Vel, grinned, remarking that he had never felt better, and that it would take more than a mere dunking to finish him off. The friends chuckled in recollection.

Almost two months previously, Lucius rescued Vel from a raging flood. The elderly man had been crossing the rickety wooden bridge into one of the neighbouring villages, when it collapsed, tossing him into the fast-flowing river, which was in full spate following heavy spring rains. Lucius, who happened to be standing chatting to some locals, witnessed the accident.

He reacted immediately, running along the edge of the river until he spotted Vel who was desperately trying to reach the bank. With no thought for his own safety, Lucius jumped in and swam to the hapless Vel who was tiring, the powerful torrent quickly sapping his strength. They were towed some distance downstream before Lucius was able to drag them both out, by which time Vel had swallowed half the river and was unconscious.

Lucius carried him back to the village, where he was met by the headman, and directed to Vel's abode. Willing hands helped Lucius strip Vel out of his saturated garments, doing what they could to get him dry and warm until their healer arrived to treat the lacerations he sustained from being thrown against the rocks. In his turn, Lucius was borne away to the headman's hut, where he was provided with dry clothes and a hot drink.

Vel had succumbed to a fever and, for a time, his condition gave Lucius grave concern, fearing his friend would die.

Not only would he lose a dear and esteemed companion, but also Vel was a champion of closer ties to the fort, encouraging the native Celtiberi to try to work *with* the Romans rather than against them.

The garrison had taken great pains to assimilate in this remote part of Hispania. The recent wars still rankled in the memories of many of the older generation, and Lucius, along with his fellow soldiers, had done everything in their power to maintain the precarious truce.

Vel and Lucius had been friends for over four years, the former acting almost as a father figure to the young soldier, who had been assigned to the isolated Roman outpost fresh from army training. Fortunately, the gods smiled on Vel and he recovered, albeit more slowly than anticipated. Lucius visited whenever his duties permitted and had informed Vel of his imminent departure a week ago, presuming their goodbyes had been said.

Now here he was, and almost quivering with what Lucius suspected to be suppressed excitement.

"This is an unexpected pleasure, Vel, what brings you here today?" Lucius asked as he steered his friend into the relative peace of the stables. He indicated Vel should take a seat on one of the wooden benches alongside the loose boxes and joined him there.

Vel took a breath and began to speak, "We have known each other but a few years, yet you have become like a son to me. Our improbable friendship has held fast through troubled times and knowing you has enriched my life. It saddens me that after tomorrow I shall never see you again, and I will miss our comradeship." He paused, as though collecting his thoughts. "We have a tradition in my village. If a child chooses to take a pilgrimage they are presented with a token. Something which we hope will both remind them of home and protect them in their travels."

Lucius felt a wry smile curving his lips. The various superstitions of these ancient peoples were not far removed from his own religious practices. He forbore to comment, it was clear Vel had more to say.

"I was not blessed with children, and the woman of my hearth died many years ago of fever. Then you came along, and our friendship revived something in me I thought long dead. Recently, you saved my life, granting me a few more years and is a debt I can never repay. I am honoured to have known you, Lucius Caedicius, and on this, the eve of your own journey, I give you a token of my undying affection and gratitude."

Vel handed Lucius a leather pouch.

Although small, it was quite heavy, and when Lucius tipped out the contents he was thunderstruck. In his hand, a large ruby, not quite an oval not quite a teardrop, something in between and, in the low light of the stables, it seemed to glow.

"Vel, my friend," he breathed. "I cannot accept this, it is too valuable." He tried to hand it back but Vel simply curved Lucius' fingers around the gemstone and pressed his hand.

"This was presented to me by the wise man of my birth village — I moved here when I was handfasted." Vel sought to clarify, at Lucius' raised brow "He said it would protect me while in my possession, that my ownership was temporary, and that the ruby would touch seven lives before it enters the keeping of the person for whom it is intended, whereupon it will become a treasured heirloom. My heart tells me you are the second recipient but, remember, we are merely guardians, Lucius, and you will know when it is time to entrust it to the next custodian."

Again, Lucius tried to return the gem, spluttering a denial. He did not wish to be responsible for such a costly jewel. Vel ignored his protests.

"We do not get to choose Lucius, this is our fate and Fortune will smile on those who shield the stone." His tones were both reverent and implacable. "Farewell, my friend. Keep it safe."

Distracted by the perfection of the ruby, Lucius turned it over and over in his palm. Then Vel's words registered, but when he looked up to say goodbye, his friend had gone.

Lucius hurried to the door of the stable; Vel was nowhere to be seen. Slightly unnerved, Lucius held up the ruby until the sun caught its facets, mesmerised by the tiny shards of red light scattered over the ground.

"So, I am to guard you, am I?" he murmured, feeling heat steal up his cheeks as he realised he was talking to a gemstone as though expecting it to respond. "I wonder what Fate has in store?"

CHAPTER ONE

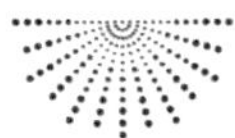

EMERITA AUGUSTA AD 37

The noise was deafening, the roar of hundreds, maybe thousands of people boomed around her. *Where was she?* Her mind wouldn't focus, everything was hazy, and the cacophony made it worse. Aghast, she became aware she was tied to something and a deadly foreboding ratcheted through her. She struggled to free herself, but the movement exacerbated her dizziness worse and, unable to help it, she vomited. Cackles of laughter reached her. *Why were they laughing? What was going on?*

Taking several deep breaths, she tried to concentrate, slowly opening her eyes onto the most terrifying sight of her life. She was in the arena, not in the seating area — actually *inside* the arena. A horrified moan fell from her lips as she looked around. There were several others in the same state of incapacitation as she. *What...?*

Desperately searching her mind for the explanation, she came upon a blank. She recalled being in her home — well, it was more a shelter really — on the edge of the town just inside the forest and away from prying eyes. The thunder of horses' hooves, the sounds of men shouting, her friends screaming, metal clashing. Peering out through the flap she saw three men coming towards her, and she had no chance of escape. A harsh voice yelled something at her in a tongue she recognised but his words made no sense, then nothing.

The Romans! That was who had done this to her, those *bloody* Romans. She thought herself safe. She lived on her own, away from the rest of the Vettones, on the perimeter of everything. She made enough coin to feed herself by selling woven cloth in the town. She created beautiful pieces and all the ladies of high status wanted her wares. She was always busy, she kept out of trouble and she did nothing to call the wrath of the Romans down on her head. So how in Hades had she ended up here?

The hot sun was high above; it must be around the sixth hour. She was tied to a stake in the arena at midday. That could only mean one thing. Executions! Biting off a crude profanity, she attempted to gather her scattered wits, but her head throbbed, and everything remained fuzzy.

Pushing herself upright, she stared across the huge circular space. The ground beneath her feet was covered in sand — the better to soak up the blood she presumed, cynically. Odd rock formations were spread around the arena and she could see people shackled to chains pinned to these rocks, and there were others, like her, tied to wooden stakes. All looked demoralised, heads sagging, and clothes shredded.

She glanced down and to her undying shame, noticed her own dress was ripped and barely covered her thin body.

Her humiliation was complete.

The roar went on unabated but as she listened, out of the random bawling came a sort of chant, whatever was going to happen was about to start. A strange smell began to permeate the air and she knew what she was about to face. A pack of wild animals. She inhaled deeply, detecting wolf and bear, maybe even boar, at which point she knew she was doomed.

She knew what the Romans did, how they loved to watch people being torn limb from limb by starving animals. Even with her gift — the gift she kept so well hidden in dread of precisely this kind of situation — she did not think she would be able to stop animals driven to madness by lack of food. Distractedly, she wished she was still unconscious, that way she would not know what was happening until it was too late.

Tears began to roll down her cheeks, what had she ever done to deserve this?

A tall man leaned against the cool stone at the entrance to the arena. He hated these spectacles but as a veteran soldier he was included in the company of men tasked with keeping the peace. Keeping the peace on a day like this? Ridiculous! The morning bouts had been fairly tame, a few injuries but no deaths.

This, the lunchtime *entertainment* never failed to turn his stomach. It was all very well killing on a battlefield, generally both sides had an equal chance to fight, they had weapons, tactics, and, for the most part, their numbers were balanced. Even gladiatorial combat had its place, participants carefully matched to give both a fair chance.

Shackling people to rocks or posts was not balanced or fair, it was barbaric and, to the veteran, worse than any crime committed by the victims, some of whom were not even criminals — just anti-Rome.

Sickened, he was about to turn away when he noticed a small figure at the far side of the arena. Blinking to make sure he wasn't imagining things, he recognised Lucia, the girl who sold those glorious pieces of cloth. He had purchased one for his mother.

Shock hit him like a punch to the gut. This could not be right. What had she done to warrant such treatment? Rushing around to where the *lanista* — the manager of the Gladiators' School — stood with his charges, the man barked a question.

"From where did you acquire these miscreants?"

"Ah, Gaius Rufius, good day to you. They were rounded up out at the forest this morning. A patrol came upon them and, because they are known to be part of a subversive faction, they were brought in. It was no more than good timing that we already had an execution planned for today's event," Marcellus Aculeo, the lanista, replied.

"In that case how do you know they are guilty? There has been no trial. Have we stooped to executing people on the possibility that they might be engaging in seditious behaviour now?" Rufius was perplexed, this did not sound right at all. Fair enough, most criminals never really had a proper trial, but it seemed rather precipitous to snatch a group of people, and immediately have them killed without offering any chance to explain or defend their actions to their accusers.

Marcellus shrugged, "It is not my job to question the Watch, Rufius. These malcontents were brought to me, and because the games already included an execution, I simply boosted the numbers. It adds to the enjoyment of the crowd, and I fail to understand why this bothers you."

"You think that slip of a girl is a malcontent, a subversive?" Rufius spluttered, incensed, nodding towards Lucia. "She weaves cloth. From what I have heard, she lives on her own and has never shown any sign of being seditious. You must release her."

The greying lanista shook his head. "Too late, Rufius, the animals are about to be freed. Anyway, what is one less Vettone? They are no loss."

Rufius gawked at the man; stunned he could dismiss life so callously. All the more inexplicable because Rufius knew Marcellus had seen battle also. Most men, certainly those over the age of thirty, in Emerita Augusta were either soldiers on active duty, or veterans. To kill without reason seemed iniquitous and made them as culpable as the criminals in the arena.

"Surely someone has time to save her?" Rufius countered. "It will take mere seconds to get her out. I agree some have been causing trouble, but to let a young girl die for no other reason than it is easier than saving her is beneath us."

"Why do you care so much?" Marcellus asked curiously, "she is nothing to you."

"She is a person, and an innocent person at that. An artist who creates the extraordinary from the mundane, adding a little colour to our humdrum lives. She is well known in the markets, and respected for her work ethic. Besides, she is scarcely more than a child. Does she sound like someone who is part of a rebel group?"

"Too late, Rufius," Marcellus repeated. "Forget her, she will be dead before you have time to think about it." As the lanista spoke, the roar from the crowd would have lifted the roof, had one covered the amphitheatre. Rufius could not believe it. He started to run into the arena but several guards — at a shout from Marcellus — stopped him, gripping his arms, and holding him against the chilled stone of the tunnel.

Rufius let loose with a string of expletives, calling into question Marcellus' family, his heritage and his legitimacy, which didn't bother Marcellus one jot.

Lucia, almost fainting from terror, frantically tried to break her bonds. It was hopeless, they were too tight. Whoever secured her to this post made sure there was no possibility of a last minute escape. The noise from the crowd reached hysterical levels as a pack of emaciated wolves slunk into the amphitheatre, snarling and drooling.

Lucia bit back a despairing wail, and the ground seemed to pitch and roll, fear overwhelming her. The creatures paused, getting their bearings, sniffing the air, inhaling the scent of their wretched victims. Slowly, they padded towards those prisoners closest to the *fossa bestiaria* — the enclosure from where animals were released into the arena.

Immediately the wolves moved away from the fossa, three bears were loosed, followed shortly thereafter by half a dozen or so wild boar. Lucia was sobbing now. To see your own death, to look into the eyes of the crazed beasts who would inflict that death was a savagery she would not wish on her most hated enemy. Neither, in her worst nightmares, could she have imagined it would be she who faced such a death.

Blood-curdling screams rent the air as the so-called entertainment began in earnest. Lucia was one of the furthest from the fossa and witnessed the trauma of those taken down before her, the beasts circling closer and closer. She would never forget the sounds, they would haunt her forever — suddenly realising her forever was less than half an hour.

She had one chance. Lucia let everything fade out, forcing herself to focus solely on the animals. For as long as she could remember she had shared an affinity with wild crea- tures. Her own tribe thought her some kind of mystic or at least under the protection of a deity — although in view of her current predicament, that appeared unlikely.

It was not that she could bend animals to her will, or

converse with them in the recognised sense — as some believed her capable — more she seemed able to understand and soothe them. If an animal was sick or hurt she was usually able to heal it; if any were beyond help, she could ease their passing.

Thrusting her fright aside, Lucia drew what she hoped was a calming breath, and cleared her head. The noise of the crowd became muted, as though she was hearing them from a vast distance. She stared out over the arena, silently calling the creatures to her side.

The alpha female of the wolf pack — resisting the summons, lifted her head testing the air, a low growl rumbling through her. Lucia ignored it, reaching out with her mind.

Her spirit connected with the bears and they dropped onto all fours, shambling towards her, at the same time as the boars stopped gouging at their prey — grunted, appeared to falter, and trotted meekly after the bears.

Last came the wolves. The alpha, surrendering to Lucia's call, padded regally across the sand, followed by the rest of the pack, the juveniles nipping at each other — to them this was just a game.

Soon all surrounded Lucia.

A hush fell over the crowd. Their anticipation a tangible thing, the sudden quiet almost as deafening as their roars. Rufius held his breath, his head refusing to accept what his eyes were seeing, his gaze fixed on Lucia who seemed to grow taller, her bearing now proud rather than defeated.

One by one, every single beast lay down, jaws caked with blood and flesh, panting a little from their exertions, but without aggression, and within seconds became as passive as lambs.

Lucia gasped, trembling with the effort. She had done it. She was not safe, she was not free, this was simply a reprieve, but for a moment she could breathe.

Rufius marched back to Marcellus. "The gods have smiled on Lucia, even the wolves lay down before her. Would you risk their wrath by killing her now?"

Marcellus was dumbfounded. Never in all his long years had he seen such a thing, and he was not prepared to anger the gods by flouting their very clear indication that Lucia should be allowed to live. "You must get the approval of the sponsor. If he agrees to her release, you will assume all responsibility for her?" the lanista demanded.

Rufius nodded. "I will take her into my home and she will be under my protection, but you must give me your word she is free. You will not seek her out to try to finish what you started." Rufius pinned Marcellus with a fierce gaze. The lanista nodded, and the two clasped hands firmly and shook. A soldier's agreement was binding. If the sponsor agreed, Lucia was saved.

Taking every care, Rufius walked into the arena, raising his hand to keep the audience quiet. He paused for precious seconds making eye contact with Quintus Antonius Valerius; procurator, sponsor of today's games, and a man Rufius knew relatively well. While he waited, motionless, he hoped his judgement of the man was correct. The official inclined his head, a slight smile on his lips. Relief poured through Rufius, and he continued steadily, but with haste across the arena towards Lucia.

The animal handlers followed at a reasonable distance. If the beasts decided to attack, they would not linger to save any but themselves. As he neared Lucia, Rufius called her name softly. She swung her head in his direction, and Rufius noticed her face was expressionless, her eyes empty.

"Fear not, Lucia. I come to release you," he said quietly, hoping she understood him. "Are you able to keep your friends placid while I remove your bonds?"

She nodded, biting her lip as he approached with a healthy degree of caution. Coming around behind her, he sliced the twine from around her waist, wrists and ankles. The threads falling away, blood dripping from where the restraints had scored her skin.

He could see she was trembling, but her mind held the animals quiescent. Rufius lifted her into his arms, presuming, correctly as it happened, her legs would likely buckle if she tried to walk from the arena.

Lucia held herself stiffly at first, until they were into the tunnel from where the gladiators entered, at which point she relaxed her mind, relinquishing her control over the animals. Her head lolled against his shoulder and she knew no more.

Wolf, bear, and boar slowly got to their feet, shaking their heads as if waking from a trance. The alpha wolf went to the stake and sniffed, then she turned and walked to the centre, her yellow eyes scanning the arena. Once there, she stopped and lifting her magnificent head, bayed — a long mournful howl, the unearthly sound sending the hairs up on the backs of the necks of each member of the audience. Then, as though released from a spell, they continued with their killing spree.

The crowd erupted.

CHAPTER TWO

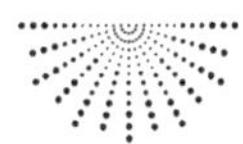

Oblivious to the commotion in the amphitheatre, Rufius was striding along the dusty streets leading to his home. It concerned him that Lucia weighed nothing; she seemed naught but skin and bone. Her hair, a rich, glossy brown, spilled over his arms, dark curls bouncing as he walked. He wondered, absently, what it would be like to run his fingers through it. He couldn't see her face for she was tucked against his neck, and he had to suppress a sudden urge to rest his cheek on her head. *Good grief,* he admonished himself, *she is a child, and you have been standing in the sun too long.*

Shortly thereafter, he reached his home, his *domus,* shoving open the heavy wooden door and yelling for his slaves. Two women scuttled into the atrium, jaws dropping when they saw what their *dominus,* their master, carried.

"She needs fresh clothes, food and water. Hurry!" he barked, aware his tone was less than polite, but concern for Lucia far outweighed his need to be civil. They fled to do his bidding while Rufius carried his burden through the atrium and along the peristyle courtyard to a small *cubiculum* next to his own.

Fortuitously, the bed was made ready for its next occupant, and he placed Lucia on it. She tossed a little but didn't wake, muttering something under her breath as she settled against the covers.

Seconds later, Flavia, one of his slaves, appeared carrying a platter on which lay flat breads dried fruit and some roasted vegetables. It smelt wonderful, and Rufius could feel his stomach growling in response.

"Thank you, Flavia. Please would you and Tullia fetch a bucket of warm water and some cloths? This woman needs to be cleaned, she has been in the arena."

Flavia gaped at her master although she knew better than to question his orders or his sense. Why on earth he would want to be bringing some miserable lowlife brat into his lovely home was beyond her comprehension, but she was not there to worry about such things. Flavia went to do his bidding, returning a little later with a pile of soft cloths, Tullia trailing behind carrying a large bucket.

Thanking them, Rufius stood aside while they began to remove the remnants of clothing still clinging to Lucia's body. Rufius noticed ugly bruises marring her tanned skin, anger gripping him at the thought that anyone, soldier or civilian, would deliberately inflict such damage on a child. When her clothes fell to the floor, however, it became blatantly obvious, Lucia was no child for, although petite, her figure was all woman.

Rufius backed away, suddenly uncomfortable, leaving Flavia and Tullia to minister to his guest. Advising them he would be in his *tablinum* — the study, which doubled as an office — and to find him when they had done all they could, he left the cubiculum, the image of the fragile young woman on the bed imprinted in his mind. Shaking his head trying to dispel it, Rufius headed for the tablinum, and submerged himself in household finances.

It wasn't too long before Flavia came to advise Rufius that Lucia hadn't woken, but they had washed and dressed her, and administered a healing balm to her cuts and bruises. Rufius thanked the slave, remarking that he would be along shortly.

Leaning back in his chair, he ruminated about the day, drawn back to the conversation with the lanista. What *was* it about Lucia that made him want to save her? Marcellus was correct, she was nothing to him, just another Vettone woman — well he thought her little more than a child. Was it simply that she didn't deserve to die or was it something else, something he could not articulate?

Unable to answer his own questions, and deciding he was being fanciful, Rufius shoved his musings aside, tidied his desk, and made his way over to the cubiculum where Lucia rested.

He paused at the door, studying the woman lying on the bed. She was tiny, he had never realised this. Every time he saw her at the markets, she was behind the little table on which she displayed her wares. He had always presumed she was sitting on something but, looking at her now, she could well have been standing. Making himself comfortable in the chair Flavia had placed at the side of the bed, Rufius observed his unexpected guest.

Lucia's breathing was shallow and her face pale. Not surprising really when he considered what she witnessed that day. The shock of watching people being torn apart would be enough to kill a person, to know you were also on the menu... Rufius could not finish that thought, it was too horrific. Without knowing why, he took her hand, and began to talk to her, trying to bring her out of her stupor. Lucia had been unconscious since he rescued her and in his limited experience, he believed this to be a bad sign.

"Lucia, please wake up, I would like to hear your story. Why are you alone? What happened to your family? How did you learn to weave such beautiful pieces of cloth?"

He continued in this vein, and when he ran out of questions, started to tell her about himself, for no other reason than it was something to talk about. He told her about the places he had lived, wars he had been part of, battles he had fought, and friends he had lost.

"We are not dissimilar, you and I," he told her. "It seems likely we have both lost people close to us and have had to fend for ourselves. Being a man, I assume my life is much easier than yours, but maybe we can help each other overcome the loneliness."

Rufius stopped abruptly. What was he saying? He did not know Lucia; it was mere hours since he rescued her. He was losing his mind. He didn't need a mistress or, worse a wife, considering himself too old and set in his ways for such nonsense, and certainly had no desire to be answerable to anyone other than himself. Ignoring the peculiar sensations Lucia evoked, Rufius went back to talking about inconsequential matters, willing her to wake up.

Hours passed. The household had eaten, and all save Rufius were in bed.

Lucia stirred. She came awake slowly, her eyes studying the room, her surroundings unfamiliar. She was so comfortable, never in her life had she slept on anything so luxurious. *She must be dreaming.*

A lamp burned in the corner, its flickering flame not bright enough for her to make out where she was. Turning her head, she saw a man sitting next to the bed, and she realised he was holding her hand. Lucia frowned, that could not be real — *definitely dreaming.*

She ached all over. Why would that be? She tried to recollect, but everything was blurry. She shifted onto her side.

The movement disturbed Rufius who was dozing. Bewildered, he sat up. *Why he sleeping in a chair and not his bed?* A diminutive woman was regarding him, her head tilted, the better to see him, and he was holding her hand. Memory flooded in. The woman was Lucia and she was finally awake.

"Lucia, do you understand me?" Rufius asked quietly. The woman nodded

"I speak your tongue, my father was a Roman soldier," she husked, the words dragged through her aching throat. "What happened? Why am I here? Who are you?" She hesitated, the man seemed vaguely familiar. "Wait, I have seen you before," she rolled it around, then it came to her, "you bought one of my pieces."

Rufius inclined his head. "Yes, for my mother. My name is Gaius Rufius Atellus. Lucia, can you tell me how you came to be in the arena today."

She gaped at him. *The arena? Why would she be in the arena?* "Was there a festival?" she queried.

Rufius' brow creased in concern. It seemed she could not remember, but he did not know whether that was a good or a bad thing. "Lucia, you were tied to a stake, left to be butchered by wild beasts, it was only your ability to calm them that saved you," he explained gently.

She lifted her eyes to his, and he sucked in his breath. She had the most incredible eyes, a sort of grey green, like moss on the stones at the river's edge, and they seemed huge in her pale face.

"Please, would you say that again?" she asked her voice quaking, holding his gaze while he repeated his words.

"Why? What was I…?" As she spoke, images began to fill her head, and she motioned desperately for the bucket Tullia had placed near the door. Just in time, Rufius held it under her chin as wave after wave of nausea hit her. Eventually she had nothing left and was able to control her need to retch, wiping a trembling hand over her mouth.

Rufius handed her a goblet of wine, it was quite acidic, but it did the trick, rinsing away the sour taste.

"I-I am so s-sorry," she stammered. "That was not polite, when you have been so hospitable."

"Lucia, please do not apologise. You were nearly killed today, you saw people being torn apart, which I suspect is enough to make anyone sick."

She leaned back on the pillow, staring at him in confusion. If she was tied to a stake, how was she here in this comfortable bed?

Rufius watched as several emotions flickered across her face. "When you calmed the animals, I persuaded the lanista the gods were smiling on you, and if I was not allowed to free you, they might heap their wrath on him. He did not warm to that idea, so here you are. He agreed you would not be sought out, and I agreed to become your protector." An odd expression darkened her eyes, but it was gone before he could read it. "Your wounds needed tending to and, as your clothes were cut to ribbons, a fresh tunic."

"Thank you, sir," she said, exhaustion clear in her voice. "I do appreciate it, but my head does not seem to want to work with the rest of me. Everything is muddled. I know I should check my home, my cloths and my threads. If you are my protector does that mean I can no longer live in the wood?" She was tiring now, her words slurring.

"We will discuss it in the morning. Sleep now, Lucia. You are safe here."

As slumber claimed her, Lucia smiled a sweet smile and

murmured something Rufius did not catch, so he just squeezed her hand, the hand he suddenly realised he had yet to relinquish.

Unwilling, for reasons he could not explain, to release his grasp, Rufius settled himself back in the chair and hoped to sleep out the remainder of the night. He surmised it must be already into the third watch; soon dawn would break. Maybe he could snatch sufficient rest to see him through what he knew would be a busy day.

He felt as though he had only just closed his eyes when he was catapulted awake by heart-stopping screams. Lucia was thrashing on the bed, presumably tormented by some inner demon; her sleep ravaged by whatever terror stalked her. Flavia appeared in the doorway, her clothes rumpled, and her hair tousled.

"Thank you, Flavia, it is Lucia. She is in the throes of night terrors. Go back to bed, I will take care of her."

Flavia grumbled something about inconsiderate guests and stumbled back to her bed. Rufius grinned after her. His servants were more friends than slaves. Yes, he had purchased them, but he could not manage on his own, he had no clue how to cook, and although he could clean he detested that particular chore. All his staff, as he preferred to call them, were treated exceptionally well and maybe this meant that sometimes they were not quite as respectful as they should be, and maybe he was rather more cordial with them than was appropriate, but it worked for his household, and for that he was very grateful.

Meanwhile, Lucia was shrieking in panic, words tumbling out of her mouth, but all were just babble to Rufius. It was probably the local Vettone tongue, but he did not have enough knowledge of their language to work out what she was yelling. Unsure how to break through her fear, Rufius lifted her into his arms and started talking to her. He didn't raise his voice, more he spoke in a kind of singsong manner, the way he recalled his mother crooning to him when he was a child.

Lucia continued to fight him, but slowly it seemed his voice was reaching inside her head. Eventually, her cries lessened, her hands stilled and at last she was calm. Rufius moved to lay her back on the bed but that seemed to alarm her even more, her slender fingers gripping his arms.

Nonplussed, and knowing they would not be comfortable in the chair, Rufius stood, carrying her over to the bed and, without letting her go, carefully settled onto the wooden frame. He lay on his side, tucking the fragile woman against his chest and, resting his chin on her head, tried to sleep.

The day was already in full swing when Rufius finally woke the next morning, the smell of food making his stomach rumble and he made to get up, only to find he was hampered by something. He felt peculiar, as though a weight was lodged against his belly and as he tried to move one arm appeared to be trapped. Blinking in the bright light, he tried to work out what was going on. This wasn't his cubiculum, where was he? Something shifted against him and he stifled a groan as whatever it was pushed against his full bladder.

CHAPTER THREE

A gentle sigh made him glance down, dark curls swam into his vision and he blinked again. *What on earth?* The events of the previous day rushed back; Lucia, the arena, bringing her here to his home, and her nightmares. She fitted snugly against him, as though born to do so and it was all Rufius could do not to kiss the top of her head.

Much as he might want to continue cradling her in his arms, his bladder had other ideas, so dismissing the impression as inanity brought about by lack of sleep, Rufius carefully slid his arm out from under Lucia's body, and crept from the room without disturbing her.

After he had completed his ablutions, spoken with the rest of the household and eaten the first meal, Rufius returned to check on Lucia. He carried a platter of food and a goblet of the sweet drink Ana, his cook, often made. Peering into the cubiculum he noticed, somewhat uneasily, Lucia hadn't stirred. Her breathing sounded laboured, and her face was sallow.

Frowning, Rufius mused over whether any of Lucia's injuries might be inflamed; it certainly would not be unexpected given the rough treatment she received. He would ask Flavia to take another look at her. Placing the platter on the small table by the bed, Rufius settled his bulk into the chair, and took her hand in his.

"Lucia," he spoke in undertones, "Lucia, it is time to wake, you have slept well passed the fourth hour."

She murmured something but did not rouse. Rufius had business to which he should be attending and knew he would have to make a report to his commander after the scene at the amphitheatre, but he was loath to leave Lucia. A sentiment he found hard to fathom, and as such chose to ignore.

Although a veteran, and technically answerable only to himself, Rufius, along with his comrades continued to behave in a soldierly fashion in Emerita Augusta. Hispania was, for the most part, peaceful, but pockets of resistance remained, especially along the trade routes. Not only did Emerita, in the province of Luisitania, sit at the crossroads of several major routes and the junction of two rivers, but also the town was not far from the borders of the provinces of Baetica and Tarraconensis. While an eminently suitable position, that same suitability left the inhabitants vulnerable.

The native Vettone peoples, despite being outwardly accepting of their Roman conquerors, periodically felt the need to stage an insurgence, to prevent said Romans from becoming complacent. Moreover, the Turduli and the Celtici, even the Oretani, occasionally joined forces with the Vettone to take part in lightning raids of the outlying farming communities, stealing what food or livestock they could — a common enemy making for strange bedfellows.

In a bid to protect trade either by road or river, the veterans of Emerita Augusta were never unoccupied. As with every such colony, army engineers were in constant demand to maintain roads and buildings. Emerita was typical of any Roman town. In addition to the usual market traders, street sellers, and hawkers, there were all manner of small industrial workshops spread throughout the town for metalworking, carpentry, and stonemasonry, not to mention those producing goods from leather, glass, and cloth, supplying the numerous tabernae — the shops. So far from Rome, they had to be self-sufficient. Transport of goods from the capital of Empire took many weeks and, perishable items were often spoiled — or appropriated by pirates and brigands — long before they reached the interior of Hispania.

As a result, Rufius' days were always busy, and he felt useful. Younger than most veterans, Rufius was discharged from the Roman army earlier than his term of service, following a grievous injury, which nearly ended his life three years previously. He bore the scars well, a slight limp the only outward sign of wounds inflicted. The army was his chosen career, and Rufius balked at being demobilised.

Uncharacteristically sympathetic, his superiors offered him the opportunity to assume the responsibility of those — veterans, civilians, and serving soldiers from the garrison — assigned to maintain the infrastructure of the flourishing town of Emerita Augusta. A conciliatory gesture it may have been, but since his arrival more than two years ago, Rufius had to confess he enjoyed his position within the town, which afforded him a little status.

Now he had this young woman in his house and under his protection. What was he thinking? Regardless of the foolhardy nature of his conduct, Rufius could not in all conscience have left Lucia to die. His actions meant a conversation with the procurator was in his future, but he was not perturbed. The two men enjoyed a cordial relationship, and Rufius knew Quintus Antonius despised the spectacle of violence as much as he. Moreover, Rufius would not petition an official in the manner he did, if it were not imperative.

Bringing his mind back to the current dilemma, Rufius surmised it was simply a matter of working out their living arrangements, as well as retrieving Lucia's possessions, presumably still in the forest. Despite the likelihood everything she owned was destroyed by the patrol, no doubt the young woman would want to see whether anything was salvageable.

These things were ran through his head, while Rufius observed Lucia. She was so petite, her tiny frame lost in the bed, itself not very large. Her hair, completely tousled, billowed around her elfin face, which remained ashen. Across her cheeks, Rufius noticed a slight flush — perhaps indicative of a fever. Was he correct in his assumption something was amiss? He needed the physician.

Going to the atrium, he called for Scaro, the young lad who ran messages, and asked him to find the medicus. Scaro scampered off. Rufius strolled into the street and along to the bakery three doors down, buying a sweet roll full of candied fruit, which he devoured while waiting.

Ten minutes passed, then Scaro appeared around the corner pulling on the arm of an elderly man. The young lad was dancing about in his need for the man to hurry to his master's bidding. The gentleman, whom Rufius knew to be Decimus Salonius Pacila — a friend and aforementioned medicus — was waving him off and shambling towards the Atellus house at his usual sonorous pace.

"*Salve*," called Rufius, raising a hand in greeting.

The medicus glared at the tall man. "What is so urgent I have to drop my food and rush to your house, Gaius Rufius?" he growled, his tones tetchy.

"My apologies, Decimus Salonius. Let me make amends and share my meal with you. I understand Ana is poaching fish today and I already smell roasting vegetables," Rufius invited, persuasively.

Salonius grumbled something, but Rufius' affable smile and the temptation of Ana's cooking was enough to mollify, and he nodded grudgingly. "Thank you, Rufius, I should be glad to accept. Now, where is this woman of whom young Scaro speaks?"

Rufius led the medicus through the house to the cubiculum where Lucia rested. She was still asleep, and now Rufius was deeply concerned. To his way of thinking, she had slept far too long. He informed Salonius she was roughed up by the Watch, elaborating no further, leaving the man to examine his charge. Flavia hovered close by in case the medicus needed anything, or on the off-chance Lucia woke and panicked.

Rufius had not made it to the end of the courtyard when he was halted by a stunned exclamation. Hurrying back to the cubiculum, he asked what was wrong.

"This is Lucia! How did this happen? She looks as though she was run over by a siege engine."

Rufius took a breath and confessed to the medicus all he knew, which wasn't actually very much at all. Salonius was another whose home sported Lucia's wares. His wife loved the brightly coloured shawls and mats Lucia wove, and he was astonished to discover she was the victim of such violence.

"She has several lacerations which have begun to fester. Most likely from being dragged through the dirt or when they tied her to the stake. Those poles are filthy, covered in blood and goodness knows what else from previous executions. At least you had the sense to clean her wounds yesterday."

Rufius asked whether Salonius required anything fetching.

"A bowl of water, preferably warm, and a few clean cloths if you have them. I must dig out any infection, and if I add vinegar and salt to the water it will help kill any poison hidden within the wounds."

Lucia was muttering unintelligibly now, her cheeks were flaring an unhealthy red, and her skin had taken on a clammy sheen.

"Quickly, man! You should have called me last evening," he concluded grumpily. Rufius nodded to Flavia, who rushed to do the medicus' bidding.

"She was not unwell last evening. This has only manifested since I checked on her around the fourth hour," Rufius countered, unwilling to admit to spending the night with Lucia wrapped in his arms. "She was beset by nightmares, but that is only to be expected after so traumatic an experience. She showed no other symptoms of sickness."

Salonius nodded absently, becoming engrossed in his task. Flavia reappeared with a large bowl of warm water and a pile of freshly laundered cloths. Salonius emptied a small bottle of vinegar to the water, and dropped in a handful of salt, swirling the liquid gently until he was sure all had dissolved. For good measure he added a healthy splash of frankincense, the exotic fragrance drifting through the room.

Taking a cloth, Salonius wrapped it around a dowel and began prodding at the first laceration. He worked solidly for several minutes, and to Rufius' eyes it looked painful, but Lucia never flinched, nor did she wake, although her muttering continued. He could not understand what she was saying and surmised it must be in the local dialect.

"She complains about the bloody Romans," translated Salonius, without breaking his ministrations. "Seems they appeared out of nowhere, on horses. The rest I cannot make out, something about animals, but it seems absurd."

"She quieted the wild animals in the arena yesterday and kept them tranquil until I freed her," clarified Rufius. Salonius paused and twisted his body to study Rufius.

"I beg your pardon, Gaius Rufius. Are you saying she controlled the beasts?"

Rufius nodded, telling the medicus what happened in the amphitheatre. "I admit my mind could not accept it, but whatever she did saved her life, so who am I to question it? Perhaps she will tell us more when she wakes." He shrugged, at a loss not only with her actions but how protective she made him feel.

"Why did you want to rescue her my friend?" queried Salonius. "She is no one important and nothing to you."

"She is a person, someone who creates beauty out of the ordinary and who, as far as I know, has never done anything to flout our laws. I could not let them kill her if there was a way to stop it. I have no idea why the Watch gathered her up along with the other offenders, but to allow her to be ripped apart by those animals was more heinous than any of the crimes committed by her fellow victims. It is beneath us."

Salonius inclined his head. "Sadly, this is becoming a habit with some of the Watch, they are corralling anyone they presume to be a threat, and either killing them immediately or handing them over to be used as sport in the arena. Often without trial."

"This was my question to Marcellus yesterday. None had faced a court, they were just thrown in the arena because it was convenient." Rufius shuddered; the image of Lucia slumped against the stake filling his mind.

Salonius studied the ex-soldier speculatively, but refrained from commenting, making a mental note to tell his wife of his budding theory, knowing she would appreciate his perception. "Go, let me finish up here. I will call you when I am done. I intend on making sure Lucia wakes before I leave. Trust me, Rufius," as the younger man made a reflexive movement, "she will come to no harm from me, and I will be as gentle as possible."

Acquiescing, Rufius made himself go to his own cubiculum where he washed, changing into a fresh tunic and pulled on a light cloak. Slipping his feet back into his sandals, he headed out to the workshops one street over, to check on his men.

Most were out on their respective jobs but three were poring over some plans. They greeted Rufius, and the four fell to discussing the rather knotty problem they were dealing with. An hour or so later, problem solved, and men dispatched, Rufius made sure no one else needed his assistance or supervision and returned home.

He walked into the atrium to see Salonius coming towards him through the courtyard, chatting with Flavia, who was chattering back and gesticulating wildly. Amusing as this was to watch, Rufius needed to know about Lucia's condition.

"Salonius, what can you tell me?"

"Ah, Rufius. She has woken, and I explained what I have done. She confesses to feeling hungry, so Flavia here is about to fetch her a fresh platter of food and some of Ana's famous sweet juice. It might be a good idea to ask Ana to add some sage to any dishes she concocts for Lucia, it is efficacious for reducing fever. That should do the trick.

"She is still fatigued, and it would not surprise me if she falls asleep again before Flavia persuades her to partake of any sustenance, but we can only hope. I recommend she rest for a couple of days, but she seems quite resilient and, being young, will doubtless bounce back to full health quickly. Her nightmares... hmmm... they are a whole other matter and not so easy to heal. Just be aware her sleep might be disturbed for some time." He paused. "Now, did you mention fish?"

Rufius chuckled and led his friend through to the triclinium, where they whiled away a pleasant hour or so over a tasty meal and an interesting discussion about the town's current affairs.

CHAPTER FOUR

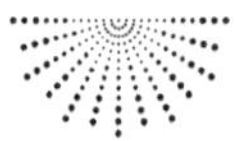

Salonius left — perhaps a little less than sober, but with a full stomach and an interesting snippet to share with his wife, hoping he wasn't called to any serious cases for the rest of the afternoon. Rufius grinned as he watched his friend roll down the busy street, his heavy gait reminiscent of a bear. Shaking his head, he instructed his household on his requirements for the rest of the day before going to see how Lucia fared.

Flavia was sitting with his guest who, as Salonius supposed, was fast asleep again. Flavia informed her master Lucia had managed to swallow a little food, but in her opinion, not nearly enough.

"Give her time, Flavia, infection often confuses us. Lucia is probably hungry, but she may not realise it, because the thought of food makes her nauseous."

Flavia tutted her way along the colonnaded walkway, and Rufius grinned at her frustrated expression. There was nothing he could do for Lucia at the moment, so after asking Tullia to call him when she awoke, strolled around the courtyard to the tablinum and buried himself in reports and other miscellaneous paperwork for the hour or so that remained of his working day.

❀

Night had fallen before Lucia came back to full wakefulness. Prying open her eyes, she became aware of an inexplicable light-headedness, a raging thirst, and her body ached all over, but the reason why would not come to her. She blinked, uncertain of her surroundings, still half-lost in a most perplexing dream, one in which a burly soldier was holding her. He seemed vaguely familiar, and although she could not place him, he made her feel so safe.

The curious thing about it was, she hated Roman soldiers. Well, no, that wasn't quite true, she hated the Watch. The Watch continued to hound the Vettones, even those who, for the most part, conformed to Roman rule. Everyone Lucia knew just wanted the opportunity to make enough coin to buy food, to stay out of trouble, and enjoy a quiet life, and all worked hard to attain it. Instead of nurturing the fragile peace, the Watch seemed determined to stir up unrest.

There had been enough conflict, not only with the Romans but also amongst the other tribes. Recently, however, it seemed some of the latter preferred working together to torment their conquerors, rather than trying to negotiate a mutually advantageous peace. To Lucia's mind they were behaving like pampered children. Yes, the Romans forced them off their traditional lands — not the best way to maintain an accord with those you are subjugating — but Lucia believed the benefits of their presence far outweighed the cost.

The Romans had brought better modes of transport and communication, constantly improving and expanding the old trade networks. They had created a safer environment in which to live and work — present situation aside — and the availability of all manner of goods, many never before seen in this rather primitive hinterland of Lusitania, had increased a hundredfold. Moreover, the Romans had been here for decades, most Vettones becoming integrated — her own mother married a Roman soldier. Wasn't it time to stop all this aggression?

While mulling this over, Lucia tried to work out where she was. She felt as though she should know, struggling to drag the information from her groggy head — a conversation about the arena and being under someone's protection? Who was that with? It was no use, her brain refused to cooperate.

Instead of trying to pin it down, she took a moment to look around. Besides the bed, she spied two carved wooden chairs, a large wooden chest, several baskets, and a low table on which stood a bowl, a pitcher and a cup. Her fingers stroked over the bed covers. They were made of rich cloth and very comfortable. In fact, this was quite the most beautiful room she had ever been in.

Even in the meagre glow from the oil lamp, she could make out frescos on the walls. Blocks of colour each one framed within painted columns, accented with exquisite designs — delicately etched, ornate motifs and elaborate swirls. They captivated Lucia, and the artist in her itched to trace the shapes, already wondering whether she possessed the skill to replicate such designs into her weaving.

She sighed in appreciation, and, ignoring the spasms of pain lancing through her body, flung back the covers, determined to investigate the images further. Just as her feet touched the cold stone of the floor, she heard footsteps approaching.

. . .

A man poked his head around the doorframe and peered into the gloom.

Lucia scrambled back into bed, a whimper of pain hissing over her lips, hectic colour washing up her face. Not only did she feel as though she had been caught breaking some unknown rule by wanting to get up without permission, but also this was the man from her dream. She stared when he entered the room, his bulk filling the narrow doorway, his features in shadow.

"Good evening, Lucia." She detected a hint of humour threading through his tones as he came to sit in the chair by her bed, doubtless he had seen her scuttling back into bed. He was so tall, Lucia feared the chair would shatter under him, but although it creaked ominously, it held. "How do you feel?"

She wobbled her hand. "A little better," Lucia's cracked voice belied her words, "but, throat sore… so thirsty."

Rufius poured something from the pitcher into the cup and passed it to her.

"Drink this, but do not gulp it, let it slide over your throat," he advised. "Ana makes it, with honey added, which she assures me is good for healing."

"It is," rasped Lucia, the cool liquid easing the ache at the same time as the sweet honey coated her inflamed throat. She sipped carefully, draining the cup.

"More?" he asked. She nodded again, holding the cup steady while Rufius refilled it. "Lucia, can you remember what happened to you?"

She frowned and shook her head, her expression troubled. "Only bits. Confused in my head. Hard to think." Her sentences, of necessity, short.

"Then do not try for now. Rest your throat and let me talk. My name is Gaius Rufius Atellus, and this is your second night in my home. I did explain what happened, but it was a lot to take in and you have been quite unwell." Rufius repeated what he had told her the previous evening, watching her carefully to see whether his words were helping her recall. He would have preferred not to make her re-live the trauma, but believed it was better she face it now than bury it, where it would fester like the poison in her wounds.

Fractured images began to flicker through Lucia's mind, making her shudder involuntarily. Soldiers, horses, the arena, wolves, bears, and — again — being held in this man's arms, along with that overwhelming feeling he was her sanctuary.

"You saved me?" she asked, when he came to the end of a tale she could scarcely believe involved her. He nodded, holding her gaze. "Thank you."

Lucia reached out and touched his arm, cool fingers eliciting an unusual response — his skin tingled.

Tired, she was about to snuggle back under the covers, when something he said gave her pause. "Wait… people, the crowd saw me calm the beasts?" *Oh no, no, no! This was bad; this was very, very bad.* She had tried to conceal her gift, knowing to admit to it left her vulnerable to the superstitious, not to mention open to ridicule.

Her mother always impressed on her the importance of keeping her ability secret. Even when called upon to heal an animal, Lucia made it seem as though the creature had been saved because of her knowledge of herbs. That she somehow understood what ailed them was never disclosed.

"They did, but I expect most thought it part of the entertainment. Deliberately planned so one of the 'condemned' could escape at the last minute. I cannot imagine any of them actually believed you calmed wild beasts," he said placatingly.

"What do I do now?" Lucia asked, a little self-consciously,

her head still trying to come to terms with what Rufius had told her.

"Well, first you need to rest and heal. Then we will go out to where you used to live to see whether we can find any of your possessions. After that we will decide the next step. You are under my protection now Lucia, and you are safe. Everything else we can worry about once you are well. Now," he instilled a practical note into his voice, "are you hungry?"

Lucia was about to say no, when her stomach grumbled. "Oh, I do beg your pardon, sir." She blushed, pressing her hands to her hot face.

Rufius chuckled. "No matter, I will be but a moment." He disappeared, leaving Lucia more confused than before he came in.

Memories were beginning to solidify, the events of two days ago becoming less obscure. That she had been tied to a stake sent chills up and down her spine. If he hadn't been there, if she hadn't been able to settle the animals, if, if, if…" her chaotic thoughts spiralled out as she realised how close to death she had come.

Catching sight of her wrists, Lucia noticed, for the first time, they were wrapped in strips of clean, soft cloth. Rubbing her fingers over them she winced, the abrasions were still tender. Unwilling to check them in such dim light, she presumed someone rinsed out any dirt and grime before covering them. She would have to ask… what did he say his name was? Gaius Rufius? That sounded right.

Lucia was not sure she could stay awake until the food arrived. Her eyelids were drooping, and she could not fight the waves of exhaustion washing over her. Her body seemed to float off the bed and before she could question it, she was asleep.

Rufius came back, carrying a platter of food. Lucia was hunched over, having dozed off where she sat. Placing the platter on the little side table, he moved her, gently, until her head was resting on the pillow, arranging her body into a far more comfortable position. As he drew up the covers, she murmured his name. He paused, wondering whether he had woken her, but although her eyelids fluttered, they didn't open.

What was *it about this woman?* The question kept circling his brain, but the answer continued to elude him, and it was doubtful he would come up with anything satisfactory this night. The hour was late; he should get to his own bed. Sighing, he brushed his hand over her forehead, tucking riotous curls off her wan face.

Unconsciously, Lucia pressed her cheek against his palm, and that same peculiar frisson ran up his arm. Inexplicably unwilling to break the contact, Rufius left his hand there, her face pillowed on it, and despite his position in the creaky chair being rather awkward, almost immediately joined her in slumber.

The next few days unfolded in a pattern. Lucia slept more than she was awake, and night terrors continued to torment her, but Salonius was correct, her injuries began to heal, and the bruises to fade. Regular meals, and a proper bed in which to rest, worked wonders, and within ten days Lucia was spending several hours relaxing in the little courtyard, or in the triclinium, the room where the meals were served.

The medicus checked on her every day for the first three days, and then judged the infection to be clearing, continuing to pop in sporadically just to be sure. Thrown together frequently, a cordiality developed between the two. Lucia, as well as being grateful for the medicus' ministrations, took the opportunity to ply him with questions about treatments and remedies, always eager to increase her own knowledge.

Rufius delivered a verbal report to the *legatus*, the commander, at the garrison, Sextus Julius Gordianus, a friend for almost the whole of his career despite their diverse postings, and to whom he remained very loosely accountable. Other than suggesting he not be so foolhardy, Julius barely commented. Rufius was a trusted veteran; he would not attempt such an act of lunacy without being certain it was the right decision.

The anticipated interview with the procurator took rather longer. It was a genial meeting, the two already being close acquaintances. Quintus Antonius Valerius was a reserved man, his position in Emerita respected, owing to his reasonable attitude, and reputation for tolerance and restraint.

In the main, he was responsible for fiscal and economic matters, and here in Emerita, his jurisdiction extended to the monitoring of the small garrison. His authority to dispense justice and his administrative powers, while not all-encompassing, were relatively wide-ranging.

Rufius furnished the procurator with what scant information he had, regarding the raid and its aftermath, but until Lucia threw off her fever, and they investigated further, there was little he could add. Quintus Antonius cautioned Rufius to be discreet.

There was already long-standing animosity between some of the soldiers in the garrison and the native tribes people — especially those living on the periphery of the town. To imply the former deliberately baited the latter in order to make them scapegoats would reignite insubordinate tendencies, quashed by the recent executions. Until they acquired proof, it would be judicious to make it appear as though the matter was closed.

The procurator agreed Lucia was an innocent victim, praising Rufius for his bravery and affirming she would not face any charges. He did remark on the woman's apparent ability to commune with animals, but Rufius managed to divert his attention to another matter and for the time being it was forgotten.

CHAPTER FIVE

Once she began to recover, Lucia's naturally robust constitution took over and she was beset by the fidgets, chafing at the restrictions Salonius imposed. Used to long days of hard work, to sit idle was rare, and she found herself asking Flavia whether she might help around the domus. Flavia gave her a few light tasks, but not enough to keep her occupied.

When she asked, Rufius had no objection to her borrowing an old reed pen and some ink, he even unearthed some spare scrolls of papyrus for her to use, which offered a temporary distraction. The problem was her fingers itched to weave, and here in this elegant home there were so many sources of inspiration, not least the frescoes in her cubiculum.

One morning, while they broke their fast, Lucia broached a question she had wanted to ask for days. "Gaius Rufius. Might it be possible for me to go home?"

"This is your home now, Lucia, and please, how many times must I request you call me Rufius?" Amused at her continued formality.

"It is not proper. You are my protector and a soldier, my status—"

"Your status is the same as mine. Under my protection you may be, but you are a free woman Lucia. You are not a slave or a prisoner. You are not a guest in my home; you are part of my household. Please..." Rufius held her gaze until she nodded her head. "I do agree however, we should check your shelter. I promised to take you back to see whether any of your possessions were left undamaged. I will not renege on it"

"I daresay everything will be smashed or stolen now, many days have passed," she muttered, sorrow coursing through her. Her beautiful loom, and all her threads; her coin, and her few articles of clothing as well as the one item more precious than the rest put together. Given to Lucia by her mother, no one else knew of it, but it was the only thing left to remind her of the love her parents' shared.

"I have call on my time today, but we shall go tomorrow, and retrieve what we can. Do not fret, Lucia, I am sure whatever is missing can be replaced." He smiled gently, wishing she would respond in kind.

Lucia rarely smiled; she remained withdrawn, and utterly composed. Other than during her nightmares, from which she still suffered, she never referred to the day in the arena, or the reason she ended up there in the first place. It was more than two weeks since, and Rufius was concerned Lucia was bottling everything in, for fear of what, he did not know. Surely, she realised she was safe in his home?

"Lucia, maybe you should talk about your ordeal, it may help you come to terms with it."

Lucia lifted her head to study him. *Talk* about it, what was there to talk about? She had been tied to a stake to be shredded by animals for no reason at all. There was nothing to discuss.

"Talking about it cannot change it. It happened, you rescued me, what else is there to say?" Her tones were emotionless, yet Rufius perceived a lurking apprehension. He let it go for now, understanding she would not be drawn, but determined to get to the bottom of it sooner or later.

Lifting his palms in a gesture of appeasement, Rufius conceded. "No matter. I will be back by the tenth hour. Enjoy your day." He rose from the couch.

"May I take a walk, beyond these walls?" Lucia entreated. Rufius frowned, considering the likelihood she would flee into the forest, but it seemed Lucia anticipated his qualms. "I give you my word I will not run. Once in the arena is enough for me," she assured him, wryly.

"You are not my prisoner, Lucia, I just do not want you to run foul of the Watch or any who may have unscrupulous intent. You may go where you please, my only proviso is that you do not go alone. Scaro or Marius must go with you." The latter being his steward, in charge of all domestic staff and the day-to-day running of the household. Marius had been with Rufius for years; a slave assigned to him when in the army, and a man Rufius trusted with his life.

"Thank you Gai— Rufius" Lucia offered a hint of a smile. "I will be careful. I shall see you this evening." Standing also, she bowed her head and hurried from the room.

Rufius watched her go, once again wondering what on earth it was about this petite young woman that turned his normally coherent brain into mush.

Excited at the prospect of leaving the confines of the villa, Lucia tidied her bedroom and herself before rushing to the domestic quarters, looking for either Scaro or Marius. Sacro was nowhere to be found, but at the rear entrance to the domus, she came upon Marius who was taking a delivery of fish. The steward gladly agreed to accompany Lucia on a walk.

"Might you be able to wait until the fourth hour?" he asked "I must complete my chores before the day gets away from me."

"Any time you are free will be suitable," Lucia replied. "I do appreciate you have a busy day, just half of one hour would be sufficient. I should like to go to the market if possible." Marius nodded, and was about to say something else when another tradesman knocked. He grinned and said he would find her later. "I will be in the garden," Lucia supplied and left him to it.

An hour or so slid by, and then Marius sought out Lucia, finding her absorbed in drawing something on a sheet of papyrus. He stood for a moment, watching her progress. The image looked complicated at first until he realised it was one of the architectural motifs from the atrium.

Using a fine reed pen, dipping it into a tiny metal inkwell, Lucia created her pattern. At the centre, four matching images, which were repeated outwards in a circular design. It was extraordinarily detailed and delicate.

Marius was astounded. He had heard Lucia was talented, that she wove all manner of things, but he had no idea how talented.

His shadow fell across Lucia, who glanced up. "Marius, I do apologise. Have you been waiting long? I become so engrossed in my work I do not hear what is happening right next to me." She paused. *Was that how the soldiers came upon her unawares*? It was certainly possible.

"I have been here scarce minutes, mistress. I did not wish to disturb you and found myself fascinated by your skill. You have a rare gift." She did smile then, her first real smile since that awful day, and Marius sucked in a breath. Her face glowed as though lit from within.

"Why thank you, Marius, that is kind of you and please call me Lucia. I am no one's mistress." He dipped his head, and confirmed he was ready whenever she was. "I just need to put on my sandals," she said, and hurried to do just that.

Moments later they stepped into the street. The day was bright and sunny, and the town milled with people going about their daily business. The two headed towards the market. Lucia wanted to see whether her friends had managed to keep her stall for her, or whether another trader had already commandeered her patch. She hoped not, she had paid a month in advance, as was her habit, you never knew what might come up, and that way she always had her stall. Did they even know of her... misfortune?

It did not take them long to reach her destination. As ever, the market bustled, it was noisy and dusty but to Lucia, dearly familiar. For the last ten years this was more a home than the shelter in the woods. She saw the same people every day and had a steady stream of regular customers. She halted in her tracks and breathed deeply. She had missed this.

"Lucia!" a voice hailed her, and she turned to see a plump, motherly woman shuffling towards her.

"Sabina. Greetings, my friend..." anything else Lucia said was muffled when the woman, who Marius presumed to be Sabina, enfolded her tiny friend into a motherly embrace.

"Lucia. Where have you been? We heard there was trouble, and no one has seen you for days." Sabina held Lucia at arm's length, raking astute eyes over her. "Lucia...?" the question hanging. Lucia flushed, shifting awkwardly from foot to foot. She preferred not to share her woes with all and sundry, but Sabina looked out for her. Ensured she had food if she had not made enough coin selling her wares.

"There was some trouble," Lucia conceded hesitantly,

glancing at Marius, aware whatever she said would be reported to Rufius. The steward inclined his head slightly, granting her tacit permission to say what she would. Heaving a huge sigh, Lucia capitulated to the inevitable and explained her absence. By the end of her tale she was surrounded by those market traders with whom she was acquainted, their horrified exclamations ringing around the stalls.

"The only problem is, I do not know whether I will be permitted to sell my goods anymore. I am under the guardianship of Gaius Rufius, and although it seems I am free, he may not approve of me spending my days so far from his protection." She heard a rumble to her left. Marius stood impassively, arms folded, ever watchful, but his jaw worked, as though trying to stop himself from speaking. "Marius is something wrong?"

"Mistr— Lucia…" at her frown, "…I imagine the dominus cares only for your safety. He will not wish to prevent you from carrying on your life as normally as possible. Under the circumstances, however, it might be sensible to consider other options for distribution of your wares."

Lucia narrowed her gaze. "Where else am I supposed to sell things? There is only this market." Waving her hands around. "I cannot afford to rent a taberna, and I know of no one prepared to grant me a corner of theirs. I must be able to pay my dues. It is not fair to expect the dominus to cover the cost of an extra person in his household. He has enough expense."

Marius bit down on a bark of laughter. Lucia clearly had no idea Gaius Rufius was not short of a denarius or two. Her streak of independence was laudable though, and he stored it away to tell his master later.

For now, all he said was, "Lucia, let us just enjoy the after-noon. Until we find your loom, this discussion is moot. You have no goods to sell." Gently.

"Yes, but I have a stall," she flung her arm towards a little table, several feet away, over which hung a brightly painted awning.

"I am afraid you do not, my lovely," interposed Sabina, quietly. "The superintendent determined that since you were not here for five days in a row, you no longer required it. A cheese merchant has assumed responsibility for the plot."

Lucia froze, spun on her heel and stalked over to the spot she used to inhabit. His back to her, a portly gentleman was sorting out large blocks of smelly cheese.

"Vibius Porcius Blaesus." She enunciated the words slowly and clearly, her tones full of contempt. "I should have guessed it would be you. I would not put it past you to call the patrol down on me, just so you could steal my table. You underhanded rat. Are you so cheap you need to lurk on the fringes, waiting to pounce when some poor unsuspecting vendor ends up tied to a stake in the arena?"

Incensed, her voice rose, everything she worked for, wasted, lost in the blink of an eye. *Where were all her painstakingly woven pieces? Where were her drawings? Had someone else sold them and pocketed the proceeds, or had they just been thrown away?* In the midst of her fury, Lucia felt betrayed and bereft.

What was the point?

She had nothing.

She did not even possess the wherewithal to start again.

Her thoughts darted back to that afternoon in the arena… *had stopping the animals been worth it…?*

Not far away a tall, veteran soldier, on his way to check on some repairs to one of the roads, heard a commotion, and followed it to its source. To his amazement, although perhaps not his complete surprise, it was Lucia.

Hands on hips, hair crackling around her head, her foot tapping in her fury, berating a red-faced gentleman standing behind a table, who seemed to be doing his utmost to become one with the impossibly large, and definitely unstable, pile of cheese.

Striding into the midst of the melee, he barked an order, and the crowd fell back at the appearance of a soldier, even one retired. Many recognised Rufius, who was well respected among the stallholders because of his measured and calm approach to any disputes. Plus, he was always stopping to buy this and that, a subtle way to cultivate a cordial relationship with the locals.

"What is the meaning of this racket?" his voice boomed, and to his consternation he saw Lucia flinch, then straighten her shoulders. She spun slowly around to face him, her lips clamped shut, and her eyes flashing grey fire. *By all the Gods she was magnificent.* Rufius shoved aside an unexpected urge to kiss her into insensibility and concentrated on the matter at hand. Porcius launched into a diatribe about stupid little girls who thought they could keep a stall they were not paying for.

When he paused for breath, Lucia, ignoring Rufius, pounced.

"How do you know whether I had paid? I pay a month in advance. This site is paid until the day after tomorrow. How dare you? Your behaviour is tantamount to theft." A disagreeable suspicion formed, and Lucia's anger chilled from blazing to freezing. To Rufius, the mercurial hue of her eyes was reminiscent of the *mare nostrum* — the sea surrounding Italia — in that moment after a storm when the sun kisses its turquoise depths. She was utterly mesmerising.

Unaware of the effect she was having on Rufius, Lucia folded her arms and regarded Vibius Porcius with distaste. "Are you in league with the superintendent? Does he inform you when rent is due? Do you offer him bribes for the chance to grab a stall, should a payment be delayed, or worse missed? If I discover you are behind the attack on the encampment, you will rue the day you were born." Her deadly tones, while quiet, reached everyone in the widening circle, and the onlookers relished the quarrel.

Most knew of the underhand dealings the superintendent, a veteran by the name of Hostus Ovidius Caecus, engaged in, but Lucia did not trust rumours. She preferred to make her own judgement of those she did business with and, despite what she had heard, the man seemed considerate enough.

Unbidden, an unsettling incident popped into her head. About three months ago, Ovidius had invited her to his home for a meal. He was much older than she and, as far as she knew, was also married. Uncomfortable with the idea of spending any time with him, Lucia politely declined. Now, running her mind back over the last few weeks, she realised there had been a change in his manner, his attitude becoming surly.

Was the raid by the Watch coincidence or by design? Unable to comprehend someone could act thus over so minor a matter, Lucia discarded it, but it continued to pester at the edge of her consciousness, refusing to be quieted.

CHAPTER SIX

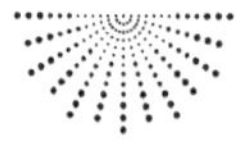

R ufius questioned Porcius, who denied any knowledge of corruption either in his own business or the management of the market as a whole. Rufius was not gullible enough to take the merchant at his word, reminded that Porcius' cheese was usually mouldy, probably a good indicator of the man's principles.

Without taking sides, Rufius managed to extract the full story from those involved, a few other stallholders also offering their perspective. He found it difficult to believe Porcius or Ovidius would be so cruel as to call the Watch, but neither did he rule it out.

Rufius was well acquainted with Ovidius. They had served in the same legion, and Ovidius' reputation was that of a vengeful soldier, notorious for a complete lack of mercy or empathy to conquered armies or peoples. It would seem his years of retirement had not softened him. Rufius made a mental note to ask around about the superintendent, maybe he could discover whether he was targeting Lucia specifically or the Vettones in general, and if so, why.

· · ·

Lucia, reluctantly accepting the stall was no longer hers, walked away to be halted in her tracks when Porcius threw a spiteful remark over his shoulder. All Lucia heard was mother and Vettone whore, but it was enough to spark her smouldering anger into a burning rage.

Spinning around, she spat a few choice insults of her own, and stalked towards her quarry with the same lethal purpose as a hawk on the hunt for its prey. Marius tried to halt her, but she dodged him easily. Not so Rufius, who simply grabbed her around the waist, lifting her bodily out of the fray.

"Do not listen to him," he muttered in her ear. "He baits you deliberately. A wise man, woman," he amended quickly, "pays no attention, appears oblivious to those seeking to undermine her confidence, rendering the abuse meaningless."

Lucia struggled in his grip, but he held her tightly, until without warning the fight went out of her.

"Please take me home," she whispered. Rufius heard her voice shudder as she swallowed a sob.

"It would be my pleasure. Marius?" Calling for his steward. "Please check with Sabina here. I would appreciate a report on anything untoward." While not in Rufius' purview to police the market, his instinct told him something was amiss, and he wanted to investigate further. If corruption was rife, it needed to be stopped before it infiltrated other pockets of business. It would not take too much to undermine the trust so painstakingly achieved between Roman and local.

Marius nodded, and Sabina, saying goodbye to Lucia, went off with the tall steward.

Rufius stood Lucia on her feet, noting her lowering expression and pale face. It was not much more than two weeks since that day in the arena. Her sleep continued to be disturbed and her appetite was lacking despite Ana's tasty dishes.

"Come, let us call in at the bakery for a honey roll. I smelt them cooking when I walked passed earlier. A treat of sorts."

"I am not a child to be diverted by sweet morsels," Lucia huffed, "although I do love honey rolls," she added ingenuously.

"I have no mind to divert you, Lucia. I too like honey rolls. It is after the sixth hour and I have a hankering for one. I simply thought you might like to join me." Mildly spoken.

Lucia flushed. "I apologise, that was churlish of me." She peered up at him while they walked. He towered over her, and she was almost running to keep up with his long stride. "Rufius, please slow down I cannot match your pace."

Rufius chuckled, and shortened his step, the two continuing at a more leisurely stroll. The bakery still had honey rolls, and they munched one each while making their way back to the domus.

Once inside, Lucia thanked Rufius before slipping away to her cubiculum. Sitting on the edge of the bed, she mused over the morning. As far as she was aware, she had never done anything to upset anyone, until declining an invitation from Ovidius. It seemed trivial, but perhaps the superintendent felt slighted, and to give away her stall was by way of revenge.

Frowning, Lucia ran her mind back over the last several months. Nothing else stood out as being questionable, so had Ovidius been the one to alert the Watch or was it coincidence? Maybe she ought to discuss it with Rufius — so far he had been nothing but genial, and without knowing why, Lucia trusted him.

Decision made, she freshened up using the water in the bowl on the table in her room, then made her way along the colonnaded walkway. The afternoon was warm, the smell of herbs and blossoms drifted in from the courtyard garden. Birds twittered, the lazy hum of insects was soporific, making Lucia feel drowsy. Determined to have her discussion with Rufius, she shook her head and walked purposefully to the tablinum. Knocking on the wooden doorjamb she waited, not very patiently, until she heard his quiet invitation to enter.

Glancing up absently, Rufius was surprised to see Lucia advancing in to the room.

"Is something wrong?" he enquired.

"I am not certain. My instinct tells me there is, but I have no way to prove it. It is barely even a feeling." She shifted from foot to foot, clearly uncomfortable.

"Sit down, Lucia, and start at the beginning."

Lucia did as he asked and began to speak. The telling took some time, because Lucia was unable to recollect many details of the days leading up to Watch raiding the camp, so she kept second-guessing herself. In the end Rufius asked her to recount what she could, and they would find a way to uncover the remainder.

"Please do not misunderstand me," she concluded, "I am not suggesting the patrol targeted me, that smacks of arrogance, but I am unable to dismiss the notion that the timing of their attack was no coincidence. I am rarely at the shelter during the day. I went to..." she paused, frowning "... because..." she stood and began to pace, unconsciously picking up items scattered about the room and putting them down again, scarcely aware of her actions. "Why can I not remember the reason I was there? Was it a message, a warning, what?"

Waving her hands around wildly, Lucia was becoming

agitated. This awful hole in her memory might be hiding something of real importance. "It is a blank, like a thick white cloud, nothing of any substance. What if..." she sank back into the chair opposite Rufius. "What if it was no coincidence?"

Rufius saw panic swirling in the misty greyness of her eyes, and wished he could reassure her, but she was correct, there was a chance, slim though he believed it to be, she was the reason for the raid. Hence, those who were caught along with her were sacrificed for no other reason than they were in the wrong place at the wrong time.

Lucia came to the same conclusion, and the same horror she experienced in the arena slammed into her. "By all the Gods, no, they could not, they would n—" rising from the chair, she staggered out of the room, bouncing off walls as the magnitude of possibilities crashed through her mind.

Her stomach rebelled, and she vomited into a convenient plant pot. Images reared up in her mind, animals tearing people apart, blood everywhere, and the deafening roar of a crowd. The world began to spin, everything receded, and the last thing she heard was the sound of her own screams.

Rufius cursed — not for encouraging Lucia to unlock her memories but for what came with them. He did not for one moment think it was her fault others died that day. Most were criminals, who had long been tabled for execution.

Concerned the Watch were exceeding their mandate, Rufius had made his business to discover what he could about those brought in with Lucia. Except for the most recent member of his household, all had radical tendencies, and at least three were involved in a string of brutal attacks on the garrison. They did not deserve to be ripped to pieces, but they were not innocents. Lucia on the other hand, seemed to live an exemplary existence, staying out of trouble and never coming to the attention of the authorities.

He shot out of his chair, when Lucia lurched from the tablinum, incomprehensible babble spilling over her lips. Before he reached her, she was violently sick, reeling away, seemingly blind to anything in her path, and careening off walls, as though drunk.

Her babble became haunted screams and she bent double, arms going around her waist as though in acute agony. Her reaction reminded Rufius of men whose battlefield experience was so horrific their mind seemed detached from their body. Afraid Lucia was losing herself in a similar madness, Rufius knew he needed to break through what was plaguing her.

Just then Lucia collapsed, crumpling to the cold stones, the sudden silence as penetrating as her shrieks. His staff appeared from every direction, mouths agape, all except Marius, who at that moment returned from the market. Rufius glanced at his steward, who inclined his head, an indication they should talk. Nodding his understanding, Rufius scooped Lucia into his arms and carried her to her cubiculum.

Once again, he was baffled by the gamut of emotions this tiny virago educed in him. One moment she was quiet and reserved, the next fighting for her rights in the middle of the marketplace, the next subsumed by a terror he might recognise yet could scarcely comprehend. He tried to lay her on the covers, but even in her insensibility, she clung to him.

As he did the night he rescued her, he kicked off his sandals, lowered himself carefully onto the bed, and held her close. Intermittently, talking to her, and stroking her hair, he tried to call her back from the darkness into which she had descended.

Marius poked his head around the door. "Dominus, the

woman Sabina, informed me Ovidius has not asked about Lucia, not once. He has made no enquiry as to her whereabouts since the morning of her capture. Whether he already knew of the arena, and that you rescued her, she cannot say. I asked around the market, Ovidius is only tolerated because they have no choice.

"One of the other stallholders did mention he, Ovidius I mean, gathered together all Lucia's items, and tossed them in the fire at the back of the market, before anyone could stop him. Many suspect he wants to bed Lucia, and either she refused him outright or was not aware of his intent and spurned him unintentionally."

Marius suppressed a shudder. "The man is married, must be forty years her senior and has three adopted children, all of whom are older than Lucia. I…" spreading his palms in an 'I give up' gesture, drawing a light chuckle from Rufius.

"It is not unheard of, Marius. Maybe his wife is no longer interested in satisfying his baser urges, and then a seemingly sweet, nubile young woman, whom he expects to be compliant, crosses his path." He sighed. "Poor Lucia. Not only has she lost her stall and her work, but also she now believes Ovidius set her up to be caught, and that she bears the responsibility for the deaths of those with her in the arena. I need her to wake in order to convince her this is not the case."

Marius tutted. "Sabina also told me Lucia has been on her own for about ten years. Her mother died during a bad winter, fever apparently. Her father was killed in a skirmish with one of the tribes when Lucia was still a child. Being half-Roman, she is vulnerable, so Sabina and some of the others keep an eye on her. She took pains to tell me Lucia is fiercely independent and does not trust easily." He looked down at the tear-stained face of the unconscious woman, his impervious heart softening. "That said, she seems to have a way of getting under your skin," he observed quietly.

Rufius looked down at Lucia. "She certainly does," and without thinking kissed the top of her head.

The day's events caught up with Rufius and it was not long before he fell asleep, cradling Lucia in his arms. Afternoon faded into evening. The household carried on with its regular routine, not all of which was conducive to anyone trying to rest, yet the two in the small cubiculum remained undisturbed.

Her dreams were convoluted. Wolves and bears tangled up with horses and people running. Men in armour shouting, metal clashing, and the screams — always the screams. Lucia bolted upright, sweat pouring off her, the nightmare clawing at her consciousness. Gasping for air, the room was too warm, the blanket too heavy. She tried to push it off, only to realise what she thought was a blanket, was a body.

Stifling a yell, Lucia twisted on the bed to see Rufius snoring gently beside her. Brow creased, she fought to recall why he was in bed with her, a quick check confirming both were fully clothed. The day's events filtered into her mind. The argument at the market, and the dawning awareness she might well be the one for whom the soldiers were searching in the woods. After that, everything was muddled, but her throat was scratchy as though she had been the one screaming. *It would not be the first time*, she mused ruefully.

Shuffling carefully, so as not to wake him she raised herself up onto one elbow to study Rufius in the dim glow from the oil lamp burning on the table. Dark, slightly shaggy, brown hair — longer than military regulations permitted, but he *was* retired. Weathered complexion, tanned from years spent under the glaring sun, rather angular, with tiny creases at the corners of his eyes and mouth; her mother called them laughter lines. Thick black eyelashes fanned out over the rise of his cheekbones, a hint of stubble shadowing his jaw. This man, who did not know her from a criminal in the cells, who without a second's thought had rescued her and then provided her a home — a home of unimaginable comfort.

Even when her mother was alive, their existence was frugal; no luxuries, sometimes not even food. As a Vettone who dared to consort with the hated enemy, her mother was an outcast, Lucia also. Her father remained a vague figure; so distant in her memory she sometimes wondered whether she'd conjured him up to legitimise her existence. The only evidence he ever walked the earth, was the treasure she hoped remained concealed in the woods.

Bringing her wayward thoughts back to the present, she contemplated Rufius. His smile melted her insides; his touch sent delicious tingles right through her, all the way to her toes. She found the hours he was out on business dragged, yet when he returned their time together was not long enough. The urge to have him kiss her — and she had never been kissed — was both irrational and undeniable.

What was it about this man?

Lucia continued her scrutiny, enjoying being able to do so covertly. Leaning away, she raked her eyes down his powerful frame. His tunic, now askew, revealed an expanse of thigh, and the sight of corded muscles flexing as he breathed, triggered a corresponding tremor in the centre of her being. Her hand fluttered closer, the temptation to stroke his flesh almost uncontrollable. Pausing, she peered at his face. *Was he asleep or was he feigning?*

Minutes ticked by. Rufius did not stir, his chest rising and falling in a steady rhythm. Emboldened, Lucia traced his shape. Light fingers memorising every facet, every curve, and every hollow, his physique becoming as familiar as a pattern on her loom. She felt him quiver when her hand drifted over his hips, but she did not, could not, stop her exploration.

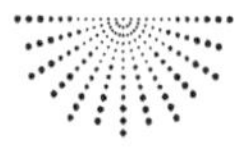

CHAPTER SEVEN

Rufius was dreaming. It was a warm summer's day, and he was half-reclining on a colourfully woven mat, by the river, just outside Emerita. At his feet — a basket overflowing with food, alongside him — a beautiful woman dozed. Hair, the colour of aged wine, tumbled in riotous abandon around slim shoulders, her clothing was mussed, and her face flushed.

He knew without a doubt they had been kissing, he could taste her on his lips and hers were swollen. His heart thudded and, wholly unable to help himself, leaned close to kiss her again. Her eyes fluttered open, glorious grey-green, framed by sooty lashes, she stared at him until he questioned whether he was falling into her gaze.

"Rufius…" his name slipped out on a sigh, and she lifted herself up on one elbow, hair streaming behind her in chestnut rivulets. Pressing her lips to his, she stroked one hand across his chest, over his waist, and on down, coming to rest on his thigh. *Surely she must feel his need for her?* Inquisitive fingers crept under his tunic, gliding over his skin, her touch a brand. He shuddered when she circled his rigid manhood, at the same time as she brought her gaze back to his face, eyes glinting wickedly in the sunlight.

"Make love to me, Rufius," she purred.

"Lucia…" her name a guttural groan, as he felt cool fingers cupping his cheek. He jolted awake, momentarily disoriented by his surroundings, the gloom of the cubiculum replacing a sunny riverbank. His body resisted, the dream was too close, and he wanted nothing more than to sink back into it.

"Rufius?" Her gentle voice caressed him, and he became aware that the hand on his cheek was not his imagination. Waiting until his eyes adjusted to the lack of light, Rufius tried to calm the chaos in his head. *What was she doing? Did she not know what her touch did to him?* He knew his body was reacting, heat pulsed through his veins, and it would not take much to lose control.

"L-Lucia…" he rasped. "Have a care. Your touch is torment."

She snatched her hand away and, despite the dimness of the room he saw the red stain flare up her face.

"I-I am s-sorry. P-please forgive me. I meant no harm. I j-just… your face… needed t-to…" Mortified, and with traitorous sobs building, Lucia turned away. Flinging back the covers, she made to get up, uncaring it was the middle of the night and Rufius was in her bed. *What a fool, no man as worldly as Rufius would ever care for her, a half-breed with nothing to offer. Why had she been so brazen? She had ruined everything.*

She had not even placed her feet on the cool floor when an arm snaked around her waist.

. . .

"Where do you think you are going?" a voice growled in her ear.

"Let me go, Rufius," she implored, her voice full of tears. "Please, I should not have touched you… only… never mind. I was mistaken, it no longer matters."

"What makes you think I do not want you to touch me?" He spun her to face him, tucking a wayward lock of hair off her face.

"You said it was torment. Do not worry," when he tried to interrupt, "I understand. I forgot my place and behaved inappropriately to the one person who risked so much to save me. Please, just let me go," she repeated her plea, wriggling in an attempt to extract herself from his hold.

"Lucia, will you let me speak?" Tilting her chin until their eyes met. Rufius took a breath. Lucia was like a skittish lamb, one wrong word and she would vanish like the dawn's mist, and that he could not countenance. Whatever was growing between them, he wanted the chance to see where it might lead. "When I said your touch tormented me, I did not mean it was painful."

She stilled, and leaned back, frowning. "Then what *did* you mean?" Scarcely even a murmur, but he discerned a hint of hope warming her tones. He sucked in another steadying breath, deciding at this point, he had absolutely nothing to lose.

"I was dreaming, dreaming we were together by the river. It was a warm day and you were asleep next to me on a rug. It was clear we had been kissing, a lot, and were about to… errr… repeat the experience, when I awoke. Lucia, when you touch me, something deep within me responds, it is almost primal, instinctual, and it takes everything I have not to make love to you."

Rufius stopped and dragged a hand through his hair,

suddenly apprehensive. Likely his admission would not be welcome. He was much older than she, and it was doubtful Lucia considered anything more than friendship might grow between them. About to retract his words, Lucia spoke.

"You *liked* it?" Wonder in her voice. He nodded, his own cheeks colouring. Men did not talk this way, yet with Lucia, it seemed… felicitous. "You wish to make love to me? *To me?*" She squeaked this last, "…but… I am nothing… have nothing… to offer one such as you."

Rufius tutted in exasperation. "Lucia, I know not how you come by your nonsensical notions. You are a desirable woman. That said, you are also years younger than me, not much more than a child, and under my protection. I cannot abuse my position or your trust."

"How old do you think I am?" she asked curiously, cocking her head, yearning to smooth away the crease marring his forehead.

"Maybe ten and seven or eight years."

Lucia laughed then, the first time Rufius had heard her mirth and it was *the* most appealing sound.

"Truth be told, I do not know my exact age, but my mother told me I had seen seven summers when father died. She died five or six summers after that, which was perhaps ten summers ago. I am not so young, Rufius. I have seen at least twenty and two summers. Moreover, since mother died, I have looked after myself," shrugging, "I believe I have a greater maturity than my years might suggest, and you are not old."

"I am thirty and six, a veteran who was wounded out of the army. I have a comfortable life, a job I enjoy, and am now responsible for an enchanting minx who turns my head to pulp." He grinned at Lucia's stunned expression, suddenly light of heart.

Lucia turned this over in her mind. Did he harbour an affection for her or was it just sex? If it was the latter, she had no opinion either way. Sex was just sex and as far as she could tell, people seemed to take pleasure in it whether they cared for each other or not; like an itch you needed to scratch. At least she assumed it was, never having indulged in that particular pastime, but she knew sex and affection did not necessarily go hand in hand. Oddly, she did not want it to be *just* sex with Rufius.

Contemplating his words, Lucia realised she wanted more, she wanted everything. She wanted him to make love to her every day until they were too old or infirm to know what attracted them in the first place, but glad anyway. She wanted to be part of his life, not as his mistress — although if that was all he could offer she would take it — but as his wife. He was retired, and free to marry whomsoever he chose, but did *he* want that? It was too soon to tell him any of this, but tonight was for them, whatever happened moving forward, she would always have this night.

"Lucia…?"

Hesitantly, daringly, she slid one hand along his jaw, her thumb just brushing his bottom lip and felt a tremor run through him.

"Rufius…"

It was that same sigh, the one from his dream.

"May I kiss you?" he entreated, cupping the back of her head, entangling his fingers through her hair.

"Please…"

His lips grazed hers.

It was Lucia's first kiss.

She had no clue what to do, and determined not to make a complete idiot of herself, remained immobile.

Amused at her reticence, Rufius was astute enough to realise that making light of her diffidence, right at this moment, was probably not the best way to encourage her to kiss him back, and instead sought to ease her mind. "Relax, Lucia," he spoke against her mouth, the stubble on his chin tickling her soft skin. "Do not try to overthink this, just let go."

Lucia swallowed, her heart rate increasing as his fingers trailed up and down her spine. "I do not know what to do," she muttered, self-consciously. "You must think me ignorant."

"I think you are the most beautiful woman I have ever laid eyes on, and innocent you may be, ignorant you are most definitely not. Now hush while I kiss you again." Recapturing her lips, Rufius moved his mouth over hers, tenderly and leisurely. His fingers continued their dance, his touch whipping up the most incredible sensations. Lucia could not prevent a throaty moan, as intuition led her fingers to tug on his clothing, needing to feel his skin under hers.

"Rufius, would it be acceptable for me to remove your tunic?"

The naivety of her plea was almost his undoing. Unfolding his large frame from the bed, Rufius stood, and shrugged out of his clothing.

Lucia's mouth fell open. *By all the Gods, he was stupendous.* "Ohhhhhhhh…" she husked, kneeling on the covers and reaching out her hand to take his, drawing her back to him. "Rufius, your body …" her fingers flew over him, tracing his shape, gliding across the hard planes of his chest and abdomen. "I want to draw you." Her artistic brain revelled in his honed physique. "Are all soldiers so… firm?" Raising an eyebrow.

Rufius stifled a bark of laughter. "Most, I expect. Do you really want to talk about that now?" His lips blazing a scorching path over her shoulder and across her throat. "In my humble opinion, you are also wearing rather too many clothes. Perhaps you would grant me the privilege of removing them?"

Shyly, Lucia nodded, forgetting she was still wearing her daily attire.

Untying the belt at her waist, he dropped it on the floor. Her ankle-length dress followed, coming over her head like the brush of a bird's wing, the quiet swish of the material when it landed next to the belt, one of the most sensual sounds Lucia had ever heard. He removed her simple under-garments, almost without her being aware, and then took her hands. His eyes tracked over her diminutive frame, causing a hot flush, only partly to do with being naked in front of a man who only days ago was a virtual stranger.

"You are... sublime." The reverence in his tones and the intensity of his expression made her blush even more, but under his heated gaze, she was also shivering in anticipation.

"Please, kiss me again?" she begged.

Rufius needed no second invitation, crushing his lips to hers. Sparking a fire, which ebbed and flowed as his skilful fingers described a tortuous path over her body, followed by his lips, leaving no part of her untouched. Lucia writhed underneath him, desperate for what, she did not know. Then, just when she suspected she might burst into flames, he paused, and lifted his head.

Gasping for breath and puzzled at the interruption of what she swore was sorcery, for how else was it possible to experience this exhilaration, she waited.

"Lucia, from your words, I suspect you have not lain with a man before. I am honoured to think I might be your first, but I do not wish you to do this because you are grateful, or believe you owe me a debt." His words came in short bursts, his control hanging by the narrowest of threads, but he absolutely would not take her unless she wanted it too.

"Does it hurt?" she asked, her fingers almost absently

stroking the muscle throbbing against her hip, unaware her tentative ministrations were sending his heart rate through the roof, and blood rushing to his loins. Rufius stayed her hand, the better to speak with a modicum of coherence.

"I cannot lie, there will be momentary pain, but I understand it is fleeting, the pleasure eradicating any memory of discomfort." His words were ragged.

Lucia was already lost, her body was screaming for his, her instinct telling her, the only way her need would be slaked, was if he continued.

"Make love to me, Rufius…" unknowingly echoing her entreaty of his dream. Lifting her head, she kissed him, her tongue slipping into his mouth, tasting him, and wrenching a groan from Rufius.

He resumed his journey; hands, mouth, and tongue, drawing Lucia higher and higher until he felt her convulse around him, his name torn from her lips as he tipped her off the precipice.

Lucia was spinning like a leaf in a whirlwind, the most extraordinary sensation rippling through her. No one could survive this rapture, but as she floated down from the heavens, she was astonished to note she was still very much alive, and Rufius was still kissing her.

"Rufius, where on *earth* did you learn to do that?"

Rufius chuckled, kissing her damp brow. "It comes with age." Was all he said.

"Is there a way for me to reciprocate?" she asked, eyes holding his.

Rufius' breathing stuttered. "I have not yet finished pleasuring you."

"You mean it gets better?" Her eyes were wide with amazement. He grinned, nodding. "So, what you just did, that wondrous feeling, was not all of it?"

He shook his head, laughter building. She was adorable.

"Tell me how to give you the same joy."

"Lucia, I…"

"Rufius, please, just tell me."

"Women are not usually enamoured of it." He tried to dissuade her, but she was having none of it. Capitulating he, slightly red-faced, and in as few words as possible, explained.

Lucia listened, and to his continued amusement asked several questions. This woman never ceased to astound him.

"Right, now let me see whether I am any good at this." Pushing him back against the pillows she proceeded to carry out his explanation to the letter and then some.

Good at it? Rufius lost the ability to think entirely, questioning whether his body was splintering into several pieces, as Lucia wove her own brand of seduction around him.

"My turn," before he completely lost control, he grabbed her wandering hands, and rolled her underneath him. Resting on one arm, and rising over her, Rufius nudged her legs apart, fingers drawing her back to the brink. The moment Lucia believed she might die of ecstasy; he slid into her, as gradually as he was able, letting her body adjust. The pain he warned her about was sharp but immediately forgotten when he began to move, the steady rhythm sending thousands of tiny shockwaves through her.

Involuntarily, her legs hooked around his hips, and her back arched, taking him in further, the peak she was seeking, tantalisingly close. Staring down at her, Rufius recalled his dream, tousled hair, swollen lips, and eyes heavy with arousal. Lucia held his gaze as he sank into her and, their tempo increasing, they surged towards the crest. He felt her muscles contracting around him, and knew they were both close. Moments later, the world erupted, and he heard Lucia scream his name as he shuddered in release. Panting hard, bodies slick with sweat they rode the vortex down, clinging to each other.

Rufius was murmuring endearments, and to Lucia they were the most beautiful words she had ever heard.

Struggling to make her brain behave rationally, she blurted out what she believed in her heart.

"I love you."

"I love you." Rufius spoke at the same time.

CHAPTER EIGHT

They stared at each other, and Lucia was unable to prevent a broad grin curving her lips.

"I know it is too soon, we met less than a month past, but despite our brief acquaintance, I know it is the truth." Rufius did not want her to feel beholden to him, to say what she thought he expected to hear. As he would, time and again, Rufius underestimated her.

"Hush my rescuer, my soldier, my solace. Do not diminish your declaration. I think I fell in love with you when I awoke in this room, with no recollection of how I came to be here, and you were holding my hand.

"Of course, I am grateful to you, and appreciate all you do for me, but the feelings I harbour are not gratitude or obligation. They are part of my sentiment, but only a minuscule part. I miss you when you leave to attend your business. My heart beats too fast when you return, when you smile, when you listen to me as though my words are important. I burn with the desire to touch you, and I dream about you every night." Lucia was trembling with her admission. *Did she dare say it all?*

"Rufius, you are a man of standing, and I would not have your reputation discredited because of an association with me. I will take what ever you offer within these walls, and to the outside world, remain as nothing more than your ward."

By the time she finished speaking, Rufius was gaping at her. "So, to clarify. You would share my bed, yet expect nothing from me?" He quizzed. Biting her lip hard to stop it from quivering, Lucia nodded.

Rufius ran a thumb over the bruised skin, following it with a kiss. "Lucia, I want you as my wife. To be by my side every day until I draw my last breath. Before you blew into my life, I never thought to wed. As a serving soldier it is not recognised, and now retired, I believed myself too old and set in my ways, but if I try to picture my world without you in it, it is naught but an arid landscape, barren and desolate."

He ran a hand through his dark locks, dubious as to whether he was forming a persuasive argument. Apparently, he was doing better than he realised, because without warning, Lucia began kissing him all over, and between each kiss she whispered yes against his skin. Her mouth sent Rufius into a paroxysm of passion, inspiring him to spend the next little while sealing their fate.

The following morning, Rufius awoke later than was his custom, to find Lucia snuggled into his chest. It was reminiscent of that first morning after he brought her home, when they woke in much the same fashion, and he felt a smile forming. *She loved him. What more could a man ask?* Unwilling to disturb her, he tried to disentangle himself, only to feel her stretch sinuously against him.

"Good morning," Lucia greeted him, her cheeks a little pink.

"Good morning, my love." He kissed her nose.

"Must you get up?" she wriggled, the movement doing deliciously wicked things to his body.

"I really must. I have a meeting this morning, and this afternoon we are going to your shelter. Did you forget?" Grabbing her hands, which were beginning to seduce him all over again. "Woman, you will be the death of me," he muttered, dipping his head to plant a searing kiss on her lips.

Lucia giggled. "Maybe so, but you would die with a smile on your face."

"Why you…" Gathering her to him, Rufius conceded defeat and it was another hour or so before he finally strolled to the adjoining cubiculum to prepare for the day.

Lucia took her time dressing, indulging in a thorough wash and a fresh tunic; yesterday's now in a rumpled bundle on the floor. Fiddling with the garment, wishing she had her own clothes, making a mental note to make some new dresses — these Roman-style tunics were so annoying — Lucia realised she felt shy after their avowals during the night. She knew Rufius to be an honourable man, but were his words spoken in the heat, the breathtakingly incandescent heat, of the moment?

She mulled over them while she dressed, spending longer than usual tidying her chamber, coming to the conclusion Gaius Rufius never said or did anything he did not mean. His actions, his decisions, were always properly considered. Therefore, she would presume, unless his behaviour indicated otherwise, his words were the truth. Hugging herself with joy, Lucia, made her way to the triclinium, where a meal was waiting.

· · ·

Rufius was already there, tucking into a platter of food. He paused when she entered, waiting for her to take the couch to his left before continuing with his meal. Lucia found eating in the reclining position typical of Romans, most uncomfortable, preferring to sit upright, the platter on her knee, to everyone's amusement. The two ate in quiet contentment, at ease in each other's company.

Placing his empty platter on the table, Rufius wiped his mouth on a piece of cloth and confirmed he would return by the sixth hour.

"We will ride out to the forest, it will take too long if we walk," he elaborated. Lucia nodded, standing also. "I have horses, stabled at the rear of the domus. Do you ride?"

"Not often, but I daresay I will manage." Smiling up at him. Horse riding was not something people of her status could afford, but she was loath to admit it, hoping, if nothing else she would be able to calm the creature if it was restive.

"I will see you soon." He took three strides, then spun on his heel and, retracing his steps, lifted her bodily off the floor, kissing her most satisfactorily. "That is a habit I will enjoy getting used to." He grinned and disappeared, calling to Marius that he hoped to be back before *prandium*, the light meal usually served around midday.

Left to her own devices, Lucia carried the food and bowls back to the kitchen, helping Tullia to wash and stack them. Then she swept the triclinium, leaving it ready for the next meal. Going to her cubiculum, she dug out her pen and ink, and the scroll of papyrus she had been using the previous day.

Was it only yesterday she visited the market? It seemed a whole lifetime had passed since then. Sitting in the sheltered exedra, she worked on her design until she was happy with the result. Adding a few words in the corner to denote the different thread colours, she turned the sheet, musing for a few moments before beginning another picture.

❧

Rufius returned, but Lucia was so engrossed, she did not hear his approach along the colonnaded walkway or the slap of his sandal on the mosaic floor of the exedra. She heard nothing until he crouched down beside her and cleared his throat.

"*Salve*, Lucia," he murmured, leaning in to kiss her ear, his breath tickling her neck.

"*Salve, mi dilecte*," she whispered her reply, tilting her neck to give him better access. He scattered kisses along her throat, feeling the quiver of her erratic pulse under his lips.

"We have much to do," he groaned, "or I would continue this to its delectable conclusion. Come, Flavia has prepared prandium." He took her hand and pulled her up from the seat. Her papyrus, forgotten, fluttered to the ground.

Spotting it, Rufius bent to pick up the sheet, the intricate design mesmerising him. "This is your work?" he asked as they walked along to the triclinium. Lucia nodded. "It is exquisite. You wish to translate this into a piece?"

"I think it would make a lovely floor covering, or maybe a wall hanging. That is, if my loom is not broken. Your home offers many different sources of inspiration," she said, shyly.

Rufius turned the sheet, the sketch thereon halting him in his tracks.

"Lucia." His stunned tone brought her up sharply.

She swung around, one eyebrow raised. "Yes?"

He waved the sheet. "Why… when… why…?" Words failed him. Lucia's clever hand had reproduced his image on the papyrus. It was like gazing into a polished circle of metal or seeing his reflection in the river. The likeness, astonishing.

Lucia shrugged nonchalantly. "I wanted something by which to remember you."

"I am not going anywhere, my love, I thought you understood that after last night." Puzzled.

"Life is ephemeral, Rufius. What seems perpetual one moment might vanish in the blink of an eye. You of all people must accept this. To have you committed to papyrus keeps you with me, if ever the worst should happen." Lucia's fatalistic perspective sounded bleak, but Rufius, reminded of the injury, which nearly took his life, acknowledged her foresight.

"It is a shame I cannot have one of you then," he countered.

"You would wish to have a keepsake?" They were now sitting in the triclinium, enjoying a tasty repast.

"Of course… although your face never leaves my mind even when we are apart. I do not think I could ever forget you." Rufius held her gaze while he spoke. Lucia gripped the edge of the couch, the desire to rip off his tunic and make love to him right there, almost irresistible. She gulped with the shameless nature of her thoughts, unaware Rufius was attuned to her every emotion.

"Perhaps a less fraught topic of conversation might lower the temperature of the room." He chuckled, watching her face bloom with colour, and then applied himself to the remainder of the meal with gusto.

Shortly thereafter, Rufius led Lucia along the narrow passageway to the rear of the building where the horses were stabled. They seemed enormous to the petite woman, but she made no comment other than to question how on earth she was expected to mount such a creature.

"Like this…" Rufius lifted her straight up onto the horse

nearest to her, a mare whose pale creamy-golden coat and almost white mane and tail shone in the sunlight. Lucia squawked in shock at the sudden change in height, shuffling on the thick rug covering the wooden frame, which was cushioned and strapped on the mare's back.

Leaning forward, she stroked the horse's neck, murmuring softly, thanking the creature for allowing her to ride, the mare nickering back. To Rufius' interested gaze, it was as though they were having a conversation, and the scene in the amphitheatre came into his mind.

"What is her name?" she asked.

"Eos." He grinned at Lucia, who crinkled her nose at the peculiar word. "She was the Goddess of the Dawn in Greek myth…" Rufius felt compelled to elaborate. "…and this fine gentleman is Ares." Patting the flank of the huge black stallion currently stamping with impatience and tossing his head — aptly named for the god of war — before gathering the reins in his hand and mounting with practised ease.

Lucia did not have any time to admire his prowess, because at that moment, Rufius clicked the horses and they moved forward. Clinging onto the reins for dear life, Lucia listened to Rufius' instructions on how to ride. After several minutes, she became more comfortable, and it wasn't long before they were able to increase their pace from a walk to a reasonably brisk trot.

The route out to the encampment took them along the *cardo maximus* — the main street running north-south through Emerita — and across the river Albarregas. This was the road leading north to Asturica. Vast swathes of forest, dark and forbidding, loomed ahead of them in the near distance. They rode alongside pasture where livestock grazed, then on past fields of olive trees. It was a glorious day, the sun was shining, the sky a cloudless blue, birdsong and the hum of insects almost the only sound once away from the town.

While they rode, Rufius broached the subject of the raid, explaining to Lucia that even had it been orchestrated to target her, those others rounded up were not innocent bystanders. So perhaps she was mistaken, she was just in the wrong place at the wrong time. He could see she was not convinced, but did not press the issue, leaving her to process it the best way she could.

Lucia listened as Rufius endeavoured to relieve her mind about those who died in the arena that fateful afternoon. The foreboding lurking at the fringe of her consciousness did not diminish with his disclosure, but if he had taken the time to investigate the matter, she trusted his words to be the truth.

Soon they left the warmth of the sunlight. The horses slowed to a walk, picking their way along the well-worn track through the green coolness of the forest. Rufius and Lucia fell silent as they approached the glade where once an encampment bustled.

Today it was abandoned, the detritus of humanity all that remained. Pots and pans were scattered across the ground; ragged pieces of clothing, or shoes, left behind in the rush to flee. Small indentations, the only evidence of what had been fire pits, were now covered with mud and branches, the earth reclaiming its own. Large squares of weatherproof cloth that once acted as shelters from the elements were shredded — reduced to scraps of material fluttering in the breeze like standards.

The air around the clearing vibrated with fear, even weeks since the raid. Lucia reined in Eos, the horse stamping one of her feet, sensing the turmoil. Lucia soothed her, talking quietly, letting their minds touch, until Eos dipped her head and blew a soft snort, becoming passive.

Sliding off the mare's back, Lucia paused, getting used to

being on the ground, her legs aching from the unaccustomed position on horseback. Rufius joined her, tying the reins together, and hitching them to a nearby low-hanging branch; the two horses content to nibble the lush grass under the sprawling shade of the tree.

Breathing in, Lucia remained motionless, letting the atmosphere flow around her, memories of the raid filtering through. Closing her eyes, she shut her mind off to everything except that afternoon.

Rufius leaned against the trunk of a tree, watching her. Lucia seemed to withdraw, turn inwards and after several minutes began to speak. Her voice was monotone, but her words no less dramatic.

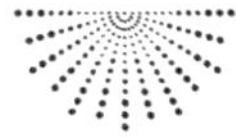

CHAPTER NINE

"It was a day like any other. I rose with the dawn, washed in the river," flinging her arm towards the babbling brook at the far side of the glade, "and took my wares to the market. I was there maybe an hour, when I received a message. A customer, whose piece I was working on wanted to check on my progress. This is not unusual, especially if I am creating something larger than normal. I do not bring unfinished items to market; they might get dusty or damaged.

"Sabina offered to watch my stall, and I trust her. I hurried back, wondering why they could not wait until the following morning. It took me nearly an hour, to get here. I keep," she glanced around, "kept, my things in a wooden chest, tucked away in the branches above my shelter. High enough to be out of reach of any forest creature who dared to venture into the encampment, protected from the weather and the occasional thief."

She was unable to prevent a whimper, as images congregated, flooding into her mind almost too fast to interpret.

"I was unpacking my box, lifting out the rug, when there

was pandemonium. The Watch simply rampaged through the camp, with no care for anything in their path — people, animals, or things. Shelters were dismantled, equipment destroyed, everything slashed, stomped on, or shattered. Patrols often come through here, but until that day were generally polite and respectful.

"This time it was different. The carnage was appalling; horses just mowed people down. I do not know whether any were killed in the skirmish, or who survived, who was taken to the arena, and who fled. The reason behind the raid continues to confound me."

Lucia wandered through the clearing, picking up this and that, turning them over, trying to determine what they might have been, searching for anything of hers.

"Did they think we harboured criminals? That this camp was a centre of subversive activity? I never saw or heard a single thing leading me to believe that was the case. The people who lived here were artisans and craftsmen. They create beauty, not extinguish it."

With a low cry, Lucia fell to her knees, scrabbling in the undergrowth. "Look what they did?" she pulled out a pile of smashed pieces of wood, multi-coloured threads hanging off some of the bigger shards. "This was my loom." She raised her eyes to his. "For what purpose? This is…" her voice trailed off, her eye catching an upturned box, lodged against the trunk.

Scrambling over, with little regard for her attire, Lucia held her breath, lips moving in a silent petition that something had been saved. Fingers, suddenly stiff, were unable to undo the catch, so she rattled it — nothing happened. She could feel frustration, almost akin to panic, mounting. Then Rufius was beside her. His strong hand placed the box upright on the ground before opening the lid. Inside threads and material were all tossed together. They looked a bit mangled but remarkably intact.

Lucia sat back on her heels, turning the pieces of cloth over and over, inspecting her wares, oddly heartened when she saw her few dresses, tossed between the other pieces. At the bottom of the trunk lay several scrolls of papyrus, some burnt splints of wood, and a roll of leather in which she stored her brushes and pens. Heaving a huge sigh of relief, Lucia lifted out each item, checking them for damage.

"They are not broken. The gods must be smiling on me. Might we take these back to your domus?" she ventured.

"Of course, and when will you accept it is *our* domus? You were already a member of my household, last night merely corroborated what I already knew." He crouched down next to her, helping to put everything back neatly, sneaking a kiss on her cheek as he did so.

"Gaius Rufius Atellus, you are insatiable." She giggled, swatting at him.

"Do I detect a complaint?" Unrepentantly.

"Hmmm…" she was not allowed to finish her sentence, Rufius caught her by the shoulders and spun her to face him, stealing her mouth in a heart stopping kiss.

"Errr… no… no complaint," she gasped when he relinquished her lips sometime later.

A cloud passed in front of the sun, throwing the glade into shadow, and in that instant, it did not feel so welcoming. "I need to get out of here," she muttered. "This place is no longer agreeable." She stood, and was about to pick up the chest, when Rufius intervened. He lifted it and, going over to Ares, tied it by the handles onto his saddle.

"It will be better there, I am used to awkward objects when I ride. You, I assume, are not." Winking at her. Lucia grinned and thanked him.

"Wait, I must find it."

"Find what?"

"My most precious treasure." Lucia sank to her knees, at the base of a tree, close to where she found the wooden box. Carefully, she pushed her hand under a thick and gnarly root, withdrawing a leather pouch.

With the same reverence Rufius had seen devoted to religious rituals, Lucia loosened the drawstring and removed an object, rolling it her hands. He could see a glint of red, and when she opened her fist, what rested on her palm took his breath away.

It was a ruby.

"Lucia...?" Rufius gaped at her, while she stared into the stone, mesmerised by the sparkles of light bouncing off the facets.

"Yes," she murmured, absently.

"May I be so bold as to ask how you come to be in possession of that?" He had never seen a gem like it. It was not quite an oval, not quite a teardrop, something in between, and as Lucia held it between her fingers, it seemed to glow and pulse in the sunlight.

Unbidden, Lucia found herself lost in memories. Bringing to mind conversations of so many years ago rendered her tone contemplative, and added a mysterious, faraway note, to her voice.

"My mother gave it to me. She received it from my father on the day they married, and said it represented their love, strong enough to withstand the forces trying to tear them apart. I have no idea how he came by it; it could have been part of a bounty from a war for all I know. Mother said it was a token of gratitude, gifted to him from someone whose life he saved. It was quite a tale. Almost mythical if I am honest, and I used to worry he told her that because the truth was harder to comprehend. What if in reality it was plundered, or acquired as tribute? What if it was imbued with bad luck?"

Lucia shrugged, "My parents were deliriously happy together though. I know I was young when my father died, but that is a clear memory. Maybe by loving her so deeply, he cancelled out any misfortune attached to it."

"It is certainly a unique stone. Does anyone know of it?"

Lucia mused over his question. "Unless someone who knew my parents is aware of it, I doubt it, for I keep it hidden. It is not something I talk about or put on display. To be irresponsible enough to lose it, or have it stolen would seem as though I had no regard for them, almost a betrayal."

Rufius understood her sentiment. Superstition was rife in this part of the world, and despite a healthy scepticism for all things pertaining to be controlled by gods — Roman ones included — he was not about to undermine anyone's beliefs.

"Shall I put it in your box?" he asked. Lucia hesitated, but there was nowhere else to keep it while they were riding. She nodded, and replaced it inside the pouch, reluctantly handing it over. Rufius unlatched the box, found a soft piece of cloth and bundled the pouch up into it, then secured the lid tightly. "It cannot come to any harm in there, and we can store it in a safe place in my tablinum when we get home…" he paused, "…are you done, Lucia?" he asked, solicitously.

"Yes, I am, there is nothing for me here. I am not sure there ever was but it was a place to lay my head for a time." Her expression a little sad but resigned.

"Why did you not find a room in one of the insulae? It could not be comfortable living here, especially in the winter." At her incredulous look, Rufius realised he might have struck a nerve. Before he could apologise, Lucia told him exactly why, clearly piqued.

"So speaks someone who has never had to worry about

where his next meal will come from." She expostulated, waving her hands about in emphasis. "Have you any idea how much it costs to rent somewhere in this town? I never had enough coin, and my friends were here. We looked out for each other. It is hard being half-Vettone, half-Roman. I do not belong with either. The Vettone considered my mother a traitor for marrying a Roman, and the Romans shunned my father for loving a Vettone. When they met, people were far less tolerant of the two cultures mixing than they are now, and some remain thus. It is becoming easier, but my parents faced a lot of prejudice.

"After mother died, the landlord gave me a day to get out of the home we lived in, and I had nowhere else to go. Sabina knew my mother, and upon hearing of her death, persuaded me to join the community out here. It is an uncompromising lifestyle, but what choice did I have? I lived here for over ten years, and until a few weeks ago, we enjoyed a relatively untroubled existence, nobody interfered." Her voice had risen in her need to make him understand that, for her, there was no alternative.

Muffling an oath, Rufius drew Lucia against him and kissed the top of her head. "I beg your pardon, my love, I did not mean to sound insensitive. You are correct, I do not know what it is to be without coin, but I do appreciate what it is to be cold and hungry. Not every battle was fought in comfort, you know." His tones were rueful as he tilted her chin with one finger, and smiled down at her cross face, relieved to see her expression soften.

"You are safe now," he reiterated. "You have a roof over your head and a dry bed. I know of someone who can make you a new loom, and you will be able to resume your weaving within days. I am sorry this was destroyed. As far as I can determine, the attack was wholly unwarranted, although I think we should be vigilant, on the slim chance you were their quarry." With that, and another quick kiss, he gripped Lucia around her slim waist and swung her up onto Eos, before unhooking the reins from the branch, and remounting Ares.

One last look at the place she had considered home for a decade, then Lucia turned Eos around, and trotted out of the forest and into her future.

The ride back to Emerita seemed to pass much more quickly than their outward journey. The sun was beginning its slow descent towards the horizon; the balmy haze of the late afternoon was still full of insects, their wings iridescent in the golden light, their buzz soporific. Rufius and Lucia fell into easy conversation about nothing in particular, just enjoying each other's company.

Rufius watched Lucia while she talked, enchanted by her exuberance, her animated gesticulations, the way her hair floated around her head, and the sparkle in her eyes. To a soldier, wearied and somewhat jaded from long years of war, not to mention dealing with the harsh realities of a land where conflict simmered just under the surface, it was as though he was reborn. His world was brighter, the colours sharper, even the air smelt fresher. He knew, in reality, this was pure fancy, but Lucia revived something he presumed long since dead.

His zest for life.

For the first time in more years than he cared to count, Rufius felt inspired, and motivated. He wanted to travel, to explore this world, to experience new and exciting things. He wanted to laugh, to make love, to learn, most of all he wanted to live, really live, and he wanted to do them all with her.

· · ·

Had Rufius but known it, the subject of his desires, felt much the same. Lucia did not expect to find someone with whom she wanted to share her life. Someone who would challenge, but not rule her, someone who would treat her as an equal yet still cosset and cherish her.

Then she met Rufius. A man who snuck under her shield, a man who represented everything she abhorred. A man who did the unthinkable in a world where the sanctity of life was not the same for everyone, where people could be thrown away without a second thought, risking his own life to save her, a woman he barely knew, and giving her a second chance. Lucia would ensure Rufius never regretted his decision.

They arrived home, leaving the horses in the capable hands of the stable boy, before making their way into the cool of the domus. The fountain in the centre of the garden burbled a welcome, and the delicious aroma of cooking drifted through the atrium. Lucia sighed with happiness.

"Thank you, Rufius," she said as they strolled along the walkway.

"What for?" he queried, puzzled.

"Everything." She stopped, lifted onto the tips of her toes, and stretching up, brushed her lips to his cheek. "You will never know how much, what you have done, means to me."

Rufius grinned, and leaning down returned her kiss, before they continued along to her cubiculum.

"Where would you like to store this?" Indicating the wooden chest he was carrying.

"Maybe on the top of the other chest, it will seem part of the furniture, and will be easy to access." She waited until Rufius placed her capacious box onto the even larger one on the floor opposite the bed, and then opened it to withdraw the cloth wrapped around the pouch containing the ruby.

"Please put this somewhere safe," she begged. "It is better that way." She did not elaborate, but Rufius saw the sense in it being secured, away from her belongings. Nodding, he took the pouch from the cloth and said he would see her in the triclinium shortly.

Lucia stood for a moment after he left the room, pondering on the day. The loss of what she considered a safe haven, made bearable by the stalwart presence of Rufius. His calm acceptance of what could not be altered, soothed her sorrow, and as her gaze drifted around the room, she conceded his domus was like an emperor's palace in comparison.

All she needed was a loom and she could begin to contribute to the household. Freshening up and changing into a clean outfit, Lucia meandered slowly along to the triclinium, pausing along the way to breathe in the heady fragrances of the blossoms and herbs in the neat garden.

It felt like home.

CHAPTER TEN

T he evening passed quietly, Lucia excused herself earlier than usual. She was tired. An emotionally wrought day, following a night of passion was not conducive to staying awake long into the evening. She was also unsure of Rufius' expectations with regard to their sleeping arrangements.

Last night he said he wanted her as his wife, and once again she wondered whether that was uttered in the throes of passion? She did not think so. Rufius had never given any indication he was a man who said things he did not mean, but maybe he wanted to wait until they knew each other better before making their relationship more… official.

If this was the case, did he want to share her bed? If so, how often? She wanted to sleep with him every night, to wake up beside him every morning, whether they made love or not, whether they were husband and wife or not. Rufius might prefer to maintain separate rooms. Inordinately shy of broaching the topic, Lucia decided it was easier to go to her own chamber, he knew where to find her.

Her ablutions complete, Lucia was folding back the

blanket about to slip between cool sheets, when her sharp ears caught a familiar footfall. Presuming Rufius was going to his own room, she did not turn, only to be surprised when an arm curved around her, drawing her against a firm body. A pair of lips seared a line from her shoulder to the sensitive skin behind her ear.

"R-Rufius…" she stammered, immediately losing the ability to think straight. *How was he able to reduce her to a quivering heap, with barely a touch? It was mystifying.*

"Sleep with me?" It was a request not an order, the deep timbre of his voice sent shivers of delight up Lucia's spine, and made her legs tremble.

"I-I was not… did not… whether you… mmmm…" when his lips continued their slow seduction. Inhaling sharply, she tried again. "Are you sure? I thought perhaps you might like your space, and just… come to my bed, when you… errr… need me."

Lucia did not know how relationships worked. The only one she was witness to, had been all-consuming. Her parents loved each other deeply and passionately, it was though each needed the other to breathe, for their hearts to beat, and she had not seen another, which came close to replicating it. Lucia wanted that same commitment, even as she acknowledged it was an implausible aspiration. In her admittedly limited experience, it seemed most couples barely tolerated their spouse.

"What on earth gave you that idea?" He sounded genuinely astonished.

"I… well…" she spread her palms. "It is not my place to assume, Rufius."

"Lucia, I am going to say this once and once only. My home is your home. I love you, I want you to be involved in, be part of, every aspect of my life. I want to share my days with you, listen to you talk, watch you weave or draw, and I most definitely want to share my nights with you. Yes, maybe we only met a handspan of time ago, but I know my heart, I know my mind, and both of them desire you more than anything I have ever wanted in my life."

He cupped her face, his eyes on hers, nut-brown on moss-green. "Lucia, I asked you to be my wife. I have never asked this of another woman, nor did I ever expect to make such an offer, but as I attested last night, when first I proposed, if I try to picture my life without you, there is only darkness."

He paused, searching her face, reassured when the turmoil clouding the laurel green depths of her eyes cleared, revealing a glimmer of something, which set his heart racing.

"Truth be told, I share your sentiments. This," she flicked her hand between them, "crept up on me, surprising me with its tenacity. I do not trust easily, but from your first words, I knew you to be sincere and a man of principle. I never believed people could fall in love from a single glance, but the moment I saw you, my heart recognised the other half of my soul, even as my head denied it was possible. Our lives converged at the most improbable moment, prompting me to wonder whether it was pre-destined, and we would be churlish to ignore Fate's decree." Lucia smiled, a rare gesture, but all the more eloquent for it.

"I love you, Rufius. It is neither explicable nor definable, but I do. I will love you until I draw my last breath and, as I affirmed several times last night..." making him grin, "...I would be honoured to be your wife."

Rufius drew Lucia close kissing her into a dizzy spiral, before swinging her into his arms and striding into the room adjoining hers. Giving her no time to admire its understated refinement, he distracted her most effectively until exhausted, they fell asleep, wrapped together, their lives as entwined as their limbs.

As good as his word, Rufius returned one evening, maybe a week later, two men following behind carrying an unwieldy item. Quietly, he opened the door, letting his eyes adjust to the gloom of the atrium. Thanking his subordinates, and handing over a generous amount of coin, Rufius closed the door and stood a moment.

Over the last several days, Lucia had begun working on some new designs, which she hoped to translate onto cloth. The frescoes in his, now their, cubiculum, the motifs scattered throughout the domus, and the statues gracing the garden, all acted as inspiration, and Rufius was mesmerised by Lucia's dedication to her art.

Tracking down a merchant, whom he had been assured was the expert in all things weaving, Rufius engaged the trader in a long discourse regarding essential requirements in setting up a loom. If the merchant was astounded Rufius' household did not already own one, he forbore to comment.

After virtually depleting the man's stock of weights, and the different types of thread — the technical terms defeated him — Rufius secreted them away in his tablinum until the frame was finished. Thankfully, the merchant had labelled one box *stamen* and the other *trama*, differentiating between the stiffer, stronger cords, which hung vertically, and those softer, more malleable threads woven horizontally, together creating the whole, saving Rufius the confusion of remembering.

Armed with detailed instructions, Rufius commissioned one of his carpenters to fabricate a sturdy loom, not too big — Lucia was a petite woman — but considerably larger than her previous one. The replacement model would give her more scope to produce pieces of varying sizes, even something as substantial as a toga or a cloak, if she chose.

Now, all was ready. Going along to the kitchen, he summoned Scaro, to help him carry the loom into one of the spare rooms at the opposite side of the house to the triclinium. It was currently standing empty, its large doorway, and long narrow window high in one wall, let in plenty of light.

If Lucia preferred to work in natural light, the loom could be moved into the courtyard with comparative ease. This room, however, was a good place to work in inclement weather, and was somewhere to store it and all its accoutrements, along with the rest of her art supplies.

Taking a good look around, Rufius was satisfied. Grinning, he strode along to the exedra where Lucia was engaged in an animated conversation with Flavia about something or other. Rufius waited less than patiently until the two women finished gossiping, then took Lucia's hand.

"I have something to show you," he said, leading the way along the covered walkway.

"A surprise? Rufius, how exciting." Lucia gripped his hand and tried to keep up, his long legs easily outpacing her. "Slow down, my love, I cannot match your stride." Giggling at his expression. "What is so important I—" her question died on her lips when he drew her into the room.

Oil lamps trimmed and lit shed soft light over the loom. Lucia gulped, turned to Rufius, turned back and tried to speak. Nothing came out, she just gaped, stunned.

She summoned up a croak. "Rufius, how did you… what did you… when did you…?" Hands lifting, fighting the impulse to rush across and stroke her fingers over the smooth wood.

"I found a merchant, he told me what I needed. One of my carpenters made the loom, and I organised the rest of the necessary materials."

Lucia noticed the boxes lined up atop a low wooden table, each one neatly labelled. Threads, weights, papyrus, brushes, pens, ink — so many supplies. Unable to get her head around what she was seeing, Lucia remained as though frozen.

"Do you think this is something you might use?" Rufius' nervous tones broke the spell, and she spun to face him.

"Rufius, never in my life have I received so thoughtful a gift. This is…" she paused, searching for a suitable way to express her delight, "… absolutely perfect."

Rufius leaned against the doorframe in studied nonchalance, but Lucia detected a smug gleam in his eye. Closing the gap between him, she stood on her tiptoes to kiss him. Rufius enclosed her in his arms, returning her kiss with passionate interest.

"You are a remarkable man, Gaius Rufius Atellus. Thank you from the bottom of my heart," she gasped, when he let her take a breath. "Oh, I cannot wait to begin." Her fingers fairly itching to weave something, anything – it had been so long.

"Maybe tomorrow, when the light is better. On dry days you will be able to work in the garden or the exedra, but at least having this room set aside for the purpose, gives you somewhere to work all year around."

Lucia sighed with pure happiness, torn between staying put, snuggled into Rufius' embrace and inspecting his gift. "I am stunned at the lengths you have gone to, *mi dilecte*. You are beyond measure."

"I am glad I was able to replace what you have lost. I know this is rather bigger than the one which was broken, but it gives you more options." He kissed her silky hair. "Now, I believe it is time for the meal, this will still be here later."

"Later, I will be showing you just how happy I am," she growled close to his ear, prompting Rufius to consider forgoing the meal completely. Feeling his breathing quicken, Lucia ran her hand down his body, inquisitive fingers seeking under his tunic to encircle him. He inhaled sharply, and Lucia released him, deliberately trailing her nails over straining flesh. Grinning at his pained expression, she added. "Let us eat, you are going to require all your strength tonight."

Rufius swallowed a strangled grunt. "You are a temptress and no mistake. How is a man supposed to concentrate on food after that?"

Pressing a fervent kiss to his wry smile, Lucia tugged on his hand. "The quicker we eat, the quicker we can… test your stamina." Gurgling with laughter, when Rufius all but hauled her bodily across to the triclinium.

Summer moved on, the blistering heat tempered each evening by the mild breeze rolling in over the gently undulating countryside. The cool of the domus was a haven, and Lucia rarely stepped outside during the day, it was too hot. By the time the light began to fade, however, she needed to stretch her muscles, tired after long hours at the loom, or hunched over a design.

Before their meal, a pleasant habit developed, the couple taking long walks around the neighbourhood. It was a time when they chatted about their respective days, shared any news or just enjoyed the sights and sounds of Emerita during the evening. Passing bustling *thermopolia* — delicious aromas enticing the hungry businessman, or the noisy *popinae* — where patrons could eat, drink, gamble, and be merry long into the night.

Lucia loved to observe anything and everything, her artist's brain always on the watch for inspiration. It could be as simple as the way someone walked, the sway of their body, a gesture, the way a lady's hair was styled, the way a lamp threw shadows on a wall, light flickering through leaves, glimmer of moonlight on dark streets.

To Lucia, everything had its own beauty and the more time they spent together, the more Rufius began to appreciate his surroundings. He had lived in Emerita for over two years, after being granted his discharge and offered his current position, but rarely took the time to actually admire it.

Emerita was the antithesis of the rural community on the lower slopes of the Apennines in Italia, where Rufius grew up, but no less spectacular. Moreover, the climate here was more tolerable, especially the winters. A veteran of many wars, and therefore used to life on the move — temporary marching camps or forts the norm — Rufius settled in Emerita surprisingly quickly.

He owned a comfortable and permanent home, relished the challenges presented by his job, and enjoyed an enviable lifestyle, but until Lucia he never really *looked* around him, he just took it for granted, and through her eyes, realised how fortunate they were.

CHAPTER ELEVEN

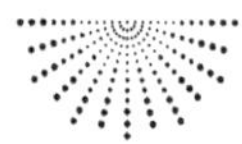

About a month later, a loud rapping on the front door disturbed Lucia. In the middle of painting an image on a large tile, she dipped her brush into the jar of water, rinsed it and dried it on a piece of old cloth. Patting her hair, catching a few stray wisps and tucking them away neatly, she headed for the atrium, unaware her face was smudged with powdered pigment, and forgetting her hands were similarly stained.

Marius was speaking to a burly gentleman with greying hair, someone Lucia did not recognise. Hearing her light tread, Marius turned and smiled.

"Ah, just the person. Lucia, this is Marcellus Aculeo, lanista at the Gladiators' School."

Lucia had started forward a bright smile on her face, which immediately faded upon this introduction. Her footsteps faltered, and her face paled to white. It was the man who had ordered her tied to a stake. *Had he come to take her away, to finish what he started?*

Noting her expression, Marcellus hastened to allay her

fears. Lifting his palms in a conciliatory gesture, he said quietly.

"Lucia… may I call you Lucia?" Waiting until he saw her brief nod. "I come to ask a favour."

Her eyes widened.

The lanista offered a tentative smile, which softened his grizzled features and, unexpectedly, Lucia's panic began to subside. "One of the creatures in my care is wounded, but my handlers are unable to check the injury, she will not let them anywhere near. I was reminded of the way you calmed the animals… errr… that day… and hoped you might be amenable to repeating… errr… it." Unsure quite how to phrase what he thought Lucia had done.

Lucia gaped. "You wish me to treat a wounded beast?"

"No, just to settle her enough that my handlers can clean and bind the injury… well unless you are able…" peering at her optimistically. "Lucia, while you may not agree or approve of what we use the wild beasts for, they are as costly a commodity as my gladiators. I provide food, water, and a place for them to sleep. Regardless of what happens in the arena, I cannot leave a wounded animal untended, it is inhuman."

Frowning at the irony of his statement, and while discerning the lanista himself did not realise what he had said, Lucia pondered his request. She had no mind to let an animal suffer either, even one who not so long ago was prepared to tear her limb from limb.

"How do I know this is not some cruel trick? You persuade me to accompany you of my own free will, but when I get to the enclosures, you lock me up with the criminals in preparation for my execution at the next games?" she demanded bluntly.

"I will come with you, Lucia," interposed Marius. "Dominus prefers you do not go anywhere without Scaro or myself." He noticed Marcellus arch a questioning eyebrow. "Gaius Rufius is of the opinion, as am I," he added, elaborating, "that Lucia's presence at the encampment the day of the raid was deliberately orchestrated, to ensure she was picked up by the Watch. The reason eludes us, perhaps in revenge for a perceived slight. Gaius Rufius continues to investigate."

Lucia and Marcellus stared at him, their mirrored expressions, stupefied.

Marcellus' mouth fell open in shock. "You cannot mean this?" he spluttered. "Why would anyone do such a thing? I agree the executions are supposed to be a deterrent to others of a criminal persuasion, but to send an innocent to her, or his, death simply because they may or may not have caused affront is heinous." Ostensibly oblivious to the fact he had been prepared to exactly that in Lucia's case.

"Rufius is still investigating?" Lucia murmured. They last discussed the possibility weeks ago, neither mentioning it since, but as she ruminated on Marius' words, Lucia realised she was never alone except within the safety of the domus. Warmth suffused her at Rufius' gallantry.

Dragging her mind back to the discussion at hand, she said. "If you think my presence beneficial, I am glad to assist, but you must agree to Marius being with me at all times." Shrewd eyes cooling to the colour of lead, pinned the lanista and he nodded.

"I give you my word, Lucia."

Lucia slid her gaze to Marius who inclined his head and smiled, encouragingly.

"In that case, shall we go now? I imagine the sooner the better," Lucia relaxed, pent up tension rolling out of her. "Give me a few moments." She shot off to tidy her workroom, and then washed her hands and face, not quite removing every streak of paint, before getting changed into an old dress she discovered at the bottom of her wooden chest. Well worn, it would not matter if it got covered in mud or straw. Satisfied, she slung a wrap around her shoulders and retraced her steps to the atrium.

"Lead on, sir," she said to the lanista, who grinned and begged her to call him Marcellus.

"I have an inkling we might see each other frequently over the next few days, and formality will just get in the way, please, my name is Marcellus."

Lucia blushed and agreed, waiting until Marius closed the front door, then the three set off towards the amphitheatre.

The *scholae bestiarum*, the place where the *bestiarii* — the men who both trained and fought wild animals — as well as the animals they hunted, was situated alongside the amphitheatre; the two buildings connected by a tunnel. As they approached, the sounds of men practising filled the air.

Marcellus ushered them in, through the entrance to the Gladiators' School, leading them along a cool, colonnaded walkway, surrounding a dusty training ground. Lucia paused, admiring the skill of the men practising, some against each other, some against wooden posts or stuffed bags of canvas, presumably representing an opponent. Then she saw the shackles, remembering many within these walls were prisoners. A wave of melancholy swept over her. What crime resulted in their lives being forfeit for the entertainment of others?

Seeing the direction of her gaze, Marcellus sought to explain. "Yes, those men are criminals, sentenced to spend the rest of their lives here. Most at the school are prisoners of war, and a few chose this life." At Lucia's cynical look, he continued. "On discharge, many soldiers are at a loss, unable to settle into civilian life, and find being a gladiator suits them. Unlike prisoners and criminals, they can come and go as they please.

"A skilled fighter quickly becomes a celebrity, with all the glory that goes with such status, so there is healthy competition. All under my care are clothed, well fed, and have decent accommodation. Yes, even those who are not free men. Gladiators of every status are an asset, and to ignore their needs would be a costly error."

Marcellus pointed out the *spoliarium* — where dead and dying gladiators were taken; the *saniarium* — the treatment rooms for wounded gladiators, and the *armamentarium* — where the weapons used in combat were locked away. There were also workshops, and of course the gladiators' accommodation. The complex was vast, and kept many gainfully employed.

By this time they had reached the section where the animals were housed, the *scholae bestiarum* or as Marcellus simply described it — the *bestiariorum*. The smell was overpowering, and Lucia crinkled her nose, hesitating momentarily as her senses adjusted.

"Are you sure you are comfortable doing this," Marius asked, for her ears only.

She nodded. "Just stay close," she muttered, wishing Rufius was there so she could draw comfort from the touch of his hand.

"I am here," the genial steward assured her. Straightening her shoulders, Lucia followed the lanista into the realm of the beasts.

The building was huge. There were numerous enclosures of differing sizes, separated by wide passageways. Each enclosure comprised a double entrance — a small internal cage so the animals had no opportunity to escape, when the main gate was opened — and a run leading to the *fossa bestiaria*, currently barred.

The lower portion of the structure was constructed of stone, the upper half of wood. Long, narrow openings where the walls joined the roof, allowed in light, and any breeze to filter through, pushing out the stale air. At regular intervals along the roof itself, openings — crude *compluviums*, through which the rain fell into rectangular pools below, draining into a series of gullies feeding a water trough in each enclosure.

The high walls of the pens ensured, with the exception of the bears — who could peer over the top if they raised themselves up on their hind legs — the diverse mix of animals could smell each other, providing the familiarity of scent, but had no visual contact. The ingenious design meant that until in the arena they never crossed paths.

In spite of her trepidation, Lucia was impressed. As they passed the gates she peeked into each enclosure, spying clean straw, full water bowls and vestiges of food — although she preferred not to look too closely at the latter, it resembled something you might see hanging in the *laniena* — the butcher's shop. The animals appeared docile, but a full belly might explain their quiescence.

"Which animal is injured?" she quizzed, realising it might have been pertinent to check this before agreeing to help.

"One of the wolves. The alpha female."

Lucia gulped, the ululating howl, a haunting echo in her mind, predatory amber eyes imprinted in her brain. She could do this; she had quieted more than twenty in the arena.

"Just here…" Marcellus stopped in front of the penultimate enclosure, which turned out to be two pens joined together, large enough to accommodate the entire wolf pack.

In an effort to replicate their natural habitat, a few large rocks and gnarled branches were scattered about.

Opposite the entryway, a makeshift cave — fashioned using a thin layer of concrete shaped like a dome, stones and more branches placed at random around the base — hugged the corner. Most of the pack was stretched out, enjoying a post-prandial doze, but Lucia discerned a low growl emanating from the darkness of the shelter.

"That's her," Marcellus confirmed, before Lucia had a chance to say anything.

"How am I... are you... the handlers, supposed to treat her if she hides in the cave?" Lucia asked; her head telling her this was a mistake. A cornered, injured wolf was dangerous, and to approach was foolhardy in the extreme.

"We can lift the cave," Marcellus said, indicating the pulley system above the enclosure. "We regularly move the animals around, and so particular elements must be portable."

"What of the other wolves? I cannot control the whole pack if one is injured."

"We can slide a dividing fence between them and her."

Lucia noticed the pack was gathered at one end of the pen, where remnants of their meal lay. Deliberately separating them from their alpha. "Clever," she commented, tapping her chin. "We should proceed, while they rest, where are your handlers?"

Marcellus barked an order, and four men appeared through a door in the side of the building.

"This woman is here to calm Feronia, you will treat her with the utmost respect. Your lives depend upon her."

"You named the she-wolf?" Marius interjected in astonishment.

Marcellus replied, somewhat diffidently. "According to

myth, Feronia is the goddess of wild things, and patroness of freedmen. The name seemed… fitting."

Lucia and Marius stared, stunned into silence by the lanista's macabre wit. Shaking her head to rid it of the image his words evoked, Lucia readied herself, watching the handlers slide the dividing fence into place, effectively cutting off the pack from their leader. The low rumbling from the cave was ceaseless. Lucia could feel the animal's pain — it swirled around the edge of her consciousness.

"I must enter the pen. I need to get as close as possible without spooking her. She knows my voice, she will recognise my mind." Hearing her own words, Lucia pondered whether she had fallen asleep over her loom and this was, in fact, a twisted dream. Marius tried to dissuade her, it was too hazardous a task. "Marius, have a little faith in my ability. I would not risk it, if I did not think I had a chance. I will reach out to her before I enter, but she needs to trust me, to trust we are not going to kill her. A wounded wolf is no use to the pack. In the wild, she would be abandoned, maybe even killed. Here in the confines of the enclosure her position as alpha will be challenged by a subordinate wolf, and death of one or the other is the only outcome."

Marcellus affirmed this was the case. "Strength reigns supreme, it is ever thus." Giving a fatalistic shrug. "My handlers will ensure Lucia's safety at all times."

Lucia raised an eyebrow but said nothing. The four men would run as though Pluto himself was after them, if Feronia so much as looked in their direction. Taking a steadying breath, she followed the handlers into the small cage, watching as they secured the outer door. *There was no escape now*. Opening the inner door, all five moved cautiously forwards.

Feronia's rumble became a snarl, and Lucia sensed, even in her agony the alpha was preparing to pounce.

"Please stop and remain still. Give me a moment to see whether I can soothe her fear."

Letting all around her fade into the background, Lucia concentrated on Feronia. Reaching out with her mind, she crooned softly, persuasively, calling silently to the alpha, explaining, in what was rather like a sequence of pictures, what they wanted to do. She felt their spirits connect.

Feronia lifted her head, amber eyes dull with pain, her thoughts a jumble of confusion, but she granted Lucia access. Cautiously, the human female traced the source of the pain to a gash in the wolf's left hindquarter, and a torn pad in the paw of the same leg.

"She was challenged," Lucia murmured, just loudly enough for Marcellus to hear. "Her rear left paw and thigh need cleaning and dressing. She should be separated from her pack for a week granting her the chance to recover without further confrontation. If this is not done, they will kill her."

While Lucia spoke, her mind continued crooning to the wolf, whose snarl subsided to a grumble and whose demeanour became passive. Without thinking, Lucia moved closer, crouching to enter the cave. Marcellus, barely stopping himself from yelling a warning, nodded to the mechanics who manned the pulley. They lifted it slowly, very slowly, allowing both inside to adjust to the changing environment almost without awareness.

Lucia bowed, her face expressionless, her eyes unfocussed, her mind completely entwined with that of the massive creature a hair's breadth in front of her.

You are in pain my beauty? Would you permit me to clean your wounds? I promise to be gentle. If you trust me, I will tell the keepers to stay where they are.

Feronia emitted a long low growl and dipped her head, resting it between her front paws.

CHAPTER TWELVE

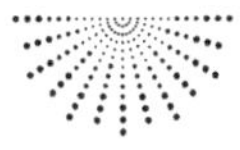

Huffing a relieved sigh, Lucia stepped back to collect a basket laden with all manner of ointments, a bowl, a flagon of water and cloths from the handlers, quietly informing them she would assume responsibility for the wolf and her wounds.

"She seems to trust me, there is no point everyone getting involved. The more people crowding her, the more alarmed she will become. Please wait here," she instructed in undertones. Easily persuaded, they lingered close to the escape cage.

Scanning through the contents, Lucia spied vinegar, salt, and frankincense, and smiled grimly. They were well prepared. Maintaining the connection, she returned to Feronia's side, and if ever a wolf could look dejected the alpha managed it. Her mournful expression tugged at Lucia's heart, as she placed the basket on the warm straw and began lifting out what she needed.

Half filling the bowl with water, Lucia added the three ingredients she knew were good for cleaning and would promote healing. Soaking one of the soft cloths, she explained to Feronia what she was about to do, again using pictures, but this time she also spoke out loud, modulating her voice to a low singsong.

She let the wolf sniff the cloth before she applied it to the gash, feeling the creature flinch when cool water came into contact with abraded flesh. With her free hand she stroked the wolf's head, scratching her behind the ears, talking all the while. It took some time, but eventually Lucia was satisfied all the filth accumulated therein was removed.

Might you consent to me checking for poison? Lucia asked through their silent bond. Feronia made a sort of snuffling sound and mewled, which Lucia took to be her assent, and as gently as possible prised open the sides of the wound to check for indications of infection. Nothing, and although this did not rule out the chance it was festering deep within the alpha's body, as yet there was no manifestation. Bearing in mind the wound was not fresh, this was a good sign.

Next, she examined Feronia's paw. The pad was torn, and Lucia could only imagine the cause, probably teeth. Repeating the ritual of cleaning, rinsing, drying, and then prodding, she was pleased to note the injury seemed free of malignancy.

I must apply balm to your wounds and bind them, Feronia. Do you agree? Lucia felt the alpha's acceptance, through her mind, along with an awareness the discomfort was diminishing. The effort to bank down her own fear that the wolf would turn on her, as well as sustain their connection, was exhausting Lucia, but she shoved it aside, intent on making sure Feronia was comfortable.

Digging about in the basket she found a creamy-looking ointment, which smelt like honey and calendula with a hint of myrrh and more frankincense. Scooping a sizeable dollop on her finger, Lucia pressed it into the wound on Feronia's thigh.

The alpha rumbled and shifted. Lucia paused, momentarily uncertain, but did not break their thread, crooning softly, almost a lullaby. Feronia settled back in tacit permission for Lucia to proceed. Taking a steadying breath, Lucia finished smoothing the balm over the gash and, after placing a wad of cloth over the wound, bound it securely in place. Then she did the same with the paw, sensing the wolf beginning to relax.

Wiping her hands on a fresh piece of cloth, Lucia sent images of her returning to check the bindings every day, until it was healed.

Stroking the wolf, she murmured aloud. "Thank you, great Alpha, for heeding my call in the arena, I owe you a debt. Maybe by helping you, I have begun to repay it." Without thinking she dropped her forehead onto Feronia's — their eyes meeting, sage-green on burnt amber — and kissed the furry nose.

Feronia lifted her muzzle and howled, the unearthly sound sending prickles over Lucia's skin. Lowering her head to rest it once more between her paws, the wolf closed her eyes, effectively dismissing the small human.

Quietly collecting everything together, and stacking them in the basket, Lucia stood, her legs trembling from being tucked underneath her for so long. Wobbling a little, she backed out of the pen. As soon as she was inside the little cage Lucia started to sever their connection, slowly withdrawing her mind, until she was no longer aware of the alpha.

By the time she was in the passageway, everything was returning to normal, except Lucia was unutterably weary. She had been in with Feronia for over an hour, it was the longest she had stayed connected with an animal. All she wanted to do was sleep.

Forcing herself to concentrate, she explained to Marcellus what she had done, and that she would come back every day to examine the wounds.

"It is easier for me to do it than have your men worry about the possibility of an attack. She is in pain and is weaker than normal, and so her instinct is to strike. At least I can calm her, and she seems to trust me. Feronia is a beautiful soul, very old, and has been alpha for many years. I am surprised at her longevity."

"She was prepared to rip you apart not so long ago," Marcellus remarked, quite reasonably he supposed.

"Of course she was. To deliberately starve wild beasts, and then turn them loose amongst a group of terrified prisoners, dirty, beaten, and bloodied, fear roiling off them would smell like a sumptuous feast. Animals do not distinguish, prey is prey, and I know but for Rufius, you, and the procurator, I would be dead. That does not lessen my awe of Feronia."

Aware she sounded as though she was lecturing the lanista, Lucia shut up, and handed the basket to a willing slave. Her whole body ached, and her head felt too heavy for her shoulders. "I shall see you tomorrow, Marcellus Aculeo. Now, I must rest."

Lucia managed four steps before fatigue overtook her, and she folded gently onto the stone flags in, what looked to those with her, like a dead faint.

"Rufius will have my hide for this," muttered Marius. He

scooped up the petite woman, aware her head was lolling against his shoulder, as he followed Marcellus out of the building.

"You cannot take the blame. Lucia knew what she was doing. See her breathing is steady, I believe she is simply asleep, rather than unconscious."

"Yes but it is not many weeks since..." the steward stopped, unwilling to cause offence but not knowing how to put his frustration into words without sounding as though he was chastising the lanista, who had seniority of status.

Marcellus was not to know how protective those in the Atellus household were with regard to Lucia, and how worried they would be if they knew she was placing herself in a dangerous situation.

Since her recovery, Lucia had worked hard every day; she helped around the domus, and spent long hours weaving or drawing, amassing a collection of wares to sell. She had become part of their lives so seamlessly, the staff struggled to recall a time when she hadn't lived there, and despite Rufius informing them her status was that of mistress, Lucia treated everyone as equals.

That is not to say she was biddable or submissive, Lucia was stubborn and opinionated, and owned a fiery temper, which could flare without warning, but died just as quickly, and if she misconstrued something, apologised immediately and unreservedly.

She was a fine match for Rufius, who after years of being in charge, giving orders, and expecting them to be carried out with alacrity, had met someone who did as he asked, *if* he asked politely, but took her own sweet time about it. Marius grinned in recollection of some of their spats, while at the same time, trying to find a way to explain all this to the lanista.

. . .

Marcellus showed no resentment, reiterating he would accompany Marius. The two hurried through the late afternoon sunshine, their long strides taking them to the domus quickly. Marius, shouldering his way through the door, called for Flavia to help.

"You need to undress and possibly bathe her. She has been in with a wild beast, and the pen is not the cleanest place," Marius instructed.

To her credit, Flavia did not question his words, merely scurried after him through the house to the bedroom, muttering that Lucia being carried in unconscious, with filthy clothes was becoming a habit.

Marius chuckled. "She was incredible Flavia, she treated a wounded wolf. Can you imagine that?"

Flavia's mouth fell open. She had heard rumours regarding Lucia's alleged ability, but presumed them to be just that — rumours. "She can really talk to animals?"

Marius shrugged, as he laid Lucia on the bed. "I do not know whether she talks to them, but she seems to understand what ails them, maybe she possesses a heightened awareness. Whatever it is, she was able to find where the wolf was wounded and treat her. If I had not watched the whole thing, I would not have believed it."

"Well, I am astounded." Flavia replied, hands on hips. "Maybe she *is* favoured by the Gods."

"Stranger things, Flavia, stranger things." Marius left Flavia to it, strolling back along the covered walkway to find Marcellus deep in conversation with an irate Rufius.

"You are telling me, after everything she suffered in that damned arena, she went with you willingly, to treat the wolf that would have eaten her?" Rufius' disbelieving tones echoed around the atrium.

"He speaks the truth, dominus, I saw the whole thing. She fell asleep as she exited the enclosure. Flavia is with her now," Marius intervened.

Rufius dragged his fingers through his hair. This woman would be the death of him, yet her response to Marcellus' request was — as he was coming to recognise — typical. If she thought she could help, she would, regardless of the consequences.

"She might have been killed," he growled. "What were the pair of you thinking? If indeed you *were* thinking."

"She was never alone, the handlers were within a stride of where she was working," Marcellus appeased.

"You know as well as I do, a wolf moves with greater speed than any of your handlers." Rufius glared at Marcellus.

"Gaius Rufius, before you take umbrage, talk to Lucia. She was stupendous, and I would like to discuss the possibility of her being on call should any of my animals require medical treatment."

"She will do no such thing."

"Who will do no such thing, and what is the thing?" a tired voice demanded from the far side of the atrium. Lucia — barefoot, dressed in only her night attire, a wrap around her shoulders — stood with her arms folded, brows lowering. In three paces, Rufius was at her side, taking her hand.

"I do not want you going back to the bestiariorum, it is too dangerous."

"I believe that is my choice, my love," she countered acerbically. "I told Feronia I would return daily until she is healed. You do not expect me to renege on a promise, do you? That would be most impolite. I think she and I have reached an understanding, she will not hurt me."

Rufius gawked; she referred to the wolf as though she was human, not animal.

Lucia yawned prodigiously. "Please do not be angry with

these two. I was not coerced, and I am simply exhausted. A good night's sleep and I will be my normal scrappy self." She swayed on her feet. "Goodnight, gentlemen." Waving a hand airily, she turned, staggering a little. Rufius caught her against him, lifting her into his arms.

"I can walk." Muffled against his chest.

"I know, but this way I get to carry you."

He heard a smothered laugh.

"Fine. I meant it, Rufius, do not take out your frustration with me on Marius and Marcellus." Her words were slurring. "If you must berate someone, berate me, but you will have to wa—" and she was asleep.

Rufius chuckled. She drove him to distraction, but he wouldn't have it any other way. Laying her on their bed and covering her in warm blankets, he brushed his lips to hers.

"Rest, my Lucia, I will join you later." Turning to leave, he was halted when she grasped his hand.

"I love you, Rufius."

"I love you too, now go back to sleep."

"Yes commander." A wicked smile curving her lips.

Returning to the atrium, Rufius called for some food, inviting both men — who were waiting, not sure whether he had finished chastising them — to join him in the triclinium.

"It seems my beloved has made up her mind, and I shall not oppose her. I would, however, appreciate a complete report of what transpired, and more details about your expectations." This last to Marcellus.

The two men provided a succinct account of the afternoon, from the moment Marcellus arrived at Rufius' house to their return. The meal was served, and still they talked. Rufius shared his concerns about Lucia being a target, expressing his unease that her attendance at the Gladiators' School left her vulnerable.

"If she is there on a regular basis, anyone observing will be able to track her routine, becoming familiar with any moments when her guard is down." He raised his hands, "I know I sound overprotective and somewhat paranoid, she is a grown woman and used to fending for herself, but I cannot shake the impression she is in someone's sights. They have been thwarted once, I doubt they will make the same mistake a second time."

"Have you discussed this with the legatus?"

"Yes, he is as flummoxed as I. They were apprised of a plot to attack the garrison, and as there have been several over the past few months, it was neither untoward nor unexpected. The difference being, the informant insisted the group was hiding at the encampment, and he would ensure the only people there at the time of the raid were those agitators who were planning the violent assault. Julius had to follow it up, to ignore a threat, even one gauged as less than credible, is unpardonable. If an attack happened, and they had not investigated every warning sign, the repercussions would be dire."

The other two nodded their agreement.

Rufius continued. "Quintus Antonius Valerius bid me maintain my vigilance. He concurs with my supposition. An unknown trouble lurks, and regardless of whether it involves Lucia, it needs uncovering. It could be widespread, placing Emerita itself in danger. We have worked too long and too hard to allow a few malcontents to destroy this peace. I just hope the recent executions acted as a suitable deterrent."

Back and forth went their discussions, long into the night and it was hours later before they went their separate ways, but they believed they had reached an accord. Marcellus would speak to his trusted guards at the Gladiators' School.

Marius, in the guise of gossip, would introduce the idea someone was using the Watch to intimidate or exact revenge, among reliable friends and acquaintances within the extensive network of domestic staff. This oft invisible tier of the population was privy to all manner of information — hopefully someone would slip up.

That was all they could do, to pursue the issue with vigour would alert whoever was behind the plot and they could not risk it. Lucia would not be free until they got to the bottom of it; hopefully she was simply a casualty of circumstance not design.

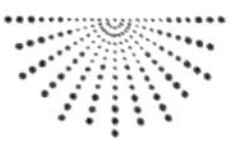

CHAPTER THIRTEEN

Lucia slept solidly, and strangely enough, given the events of the day, without dreams. Coming awake just as the dawn bathed the world in its pearlescence, she lay for a moment admiring the dust motes dancing in the soft pink light, and the intricate shadow play on the walls of their cubiculum.

Rufius was fast asleep, snoring gently, his arm draped over her stomach, her back against his chest. Lucia never took this for granted, endlessly amazed he cared so deeply for her, loving his claim that his slumber was more peaceful when holding her close.

Wonderful though it would be to luxuriate in his embrace a while longer, Lucia was wide-awake and impatient to get back to her loom. A new and rather intricate design had begun to pester at her subconsciousness and she was eager to see how it would unfold.

Cautiously, she began to extricate her entangled limbs, and was almost free when Rufius stirred. She froze; he was tired, and she hoped not to disturb him. It was a vain hope.

His lips grazed the back of her neck, sending a delicious frisson down her spine.

"Where are you going?" he murmured drowsily.

"To work on my weaving. Go back to sleep, Rufius, it is still early." Twisting around, she pressed cool lips to each of his eyelids, one finger stroking along the stubble on his jawline.

"If it is still early, the weaving can wait." He pulled her on top of him, ignoring her squeak of surprise, and divesting her of her shift, proceeded to banish any thought of looms, or patterns or anything at all.

By mid-morning the domus was quiet, expect for the regular swishing clack of the loom. Lucia, rather later than she planned, was wholly absorbed in her work. Beautiful, fine cloth, taking shape from a multitude of threads.

The piece was edged by an intricate double twist, in soft natural hues reminiscent of autumn. For the centre, Lucia planned a stylised circular floral motif in the same colours as the border; both themes were tricky and involved absolute concentration.

She was unaware of anything going on around her, in fact a herd of wild horses could have stampeded through the domus and she would be none the wiser.

When Flavia came to tell her prandium was served, it took Lucia several minutes to refocus, during which time she recalled that she needed to check on Feronia. Munching through her meal, Lucia let her thoughts wander back to her weaving, her brain sorting and planning which threads would need to be introduced at what stage, making notes on the tablet she carried at all times when immersed in a project.

Marius stuck his head around the doorway of the triclinium shortly thereafter, asking whether she was ready.

"Might you give me a half of one hour?" she queried, an abstracted expression on her face. "I have something I would like to do first."

Accustomed to her preoccupation when working, Marius nodded saying he would come and find her at the appointed time. Lucia smiled, and hurried back to her workshop, immediately forgetting what they had agreed.

True to his word Marius found her, once more engrossed, and it took him three attempts to get her attention.

"Oh, Marius, my apologies. Goodness me, I was miles away."

Marius merely chuckled, suggesting after noticing her bare feet that she might like to consider footwear before they stepped out. Lucia hurried away to prepare for the afternoon. Soon the two were strolling along the warm pathways, chattering about this and that. Before long, they were being greeted by Marcellus and escorted along the cool passageways of the bestiariorum. The snuffling grunts, and the sweet fragrance of fresh hay, mixed with the smell of warm animals, were comforting, although Lucia could not explain why.

Approaching the enclosure wherein Feronia lay, Lucia slowed her steps. One did not rush these things. Collecting the basket from one of the handlers, she stood to one side, until the same man unlocked the outer door. Stepping inside, she waited patiently while he locked the outer door before unlatching the inner one.

"Stay here," she instructed, walking into the pen. She stopped and loosened her mind, letting her senses flow out, seeking Feronia.

I am returned, Alpha. How do you feel today? The wolf's reply came back in a series of images — the creature was uncomfortable but the pain was not debilitating. *Might you let me check your bindings?* A rustling within the cave and Feronia's head poked out, her eyes boring into Lucia's, and the latter swore the wolf nodded.

Cautiously, Lucia traversed the pen, her movements unhurried. Placing the basket on the floor, she knelt next to Feronia. The alpha sank onto the straw, her hind quarters closest to Lucia. Filling the bowl with water, Lucia washed her hands, before carefully peeling away the bindings. Once the balm was rinsed away, she spent some time inspecting the damage, which looked less raw and angry than it had the previous day.

Cleaning any residual ointment from within the gash, Lucia applied a fresh dollop and massaged it in gently; conscious Feronia found the action soothing. Then she bound both wounds firmly.

All the while she crooned to Feronia, with her mind and her voice. As she completed her ministrations the massive beast stood, her lithe frame dwarfing Lucia who experienced a moment of alarm. Then, to her astonishment, Feronia turned and nuzzled her snout against Lucia's neck, inhaling her scent, a long rumble resounding through her chest. Lucia forced herself to relax, and unconsciously leaned against the animal's bulk.

Their connection, now established, was indelible. Feronia would protect Lucia — with her life if necessary, and Lucia would do the same. In much the same way as Lucia was inextricably bound to Rufius, she was also bound to Feronia. Her gift, both a blessing and a curse.

Pleased with the healing process, Lucia thanked the she-wolf, and confirmed she would return the next day. Marius was waiting for her, tension rolling off him in waves.

"I fear I cannot breathe while you are in there," he grumbled when she finally reached the safety of the passageway.

"She will not harm me, Marius. You need to have a little faith." Her voice lacked its usual strength.

"Dominus was correct, this was a mistake. You are wearied again."

"I am young and healthy, it will be but a few more days and Feronia will be fit enough to rejoin the pack. Do not fret. See, I have managed ten steps and am still upright." An impish grin forming.

Marius huffed his indignation. "Lucia…"

"Lucia nothing. Come, let us hasten home, I would like to take a bath before Rufius returns from his business." By now they were at the exit of the Gladiators' School, and once in the street, Lucia quickly diverted Marius' concerns by asking him a question about what they were having for the evening meal.

The afternoon was balmy, people milled about, the atmosphere almost festive. Marius and Lucia were laughing at the antics of some children, when a large rock sailed toward them, missing Lucia's head by a handspan. It crashed into the wall, shards of stone exploding around them.

Instinctively, everyone in the vicinity ducked, which was a good thing because another rock followed seconds later. People screamed, children cried, the two who appeared to be at the centre of it all, crouched together in shocked silence.

"Lucia, are you hurt?" Marius bit out after gathering his wits. He stood and took her arm helping her upright.

Lucia shook her head slowly, "Thank you, Marius, and no, I am not hurt," she assured him. Now standing, she scanned the area while distractedly brushing dirt off her tunica. "Were you hit?" she asked, running her eye over him, checking for blood. He was as dusty as she, but seemingly unscathed.

Bystanders came up asking questions but were unable to answer Marius' in return — no one saw who threw the rocks.

It was a mystery.

Shaken, Lucia was quiet for the rest of their walk home. So far, she had tucked any possible threat to the far reaches of her mind, certain her being corralled by the Watch was merely a ghastly mistake. This changed everything. One stone might, conceivably, have been an accident, two, most definitely not, and fear began raising its ugly head.

When they arrived at the domus, she thanked Marius and scuttled off to her original cubiculum, needing the privacy and time alone to process the incident. It was unlikely Rufius was home at this time of day anyway, but just in case.

Unbeknownst to Lucia, once she was safely inside, Marius instructed Scaro to be on guard, and he hurried back out into the waning afternoon to find his master. Tracking Rufius down to his workshops, Marius waited until he was free, and gave him a report.

"My humble apologies, dominus. I did not foresee such an attack on the streets in broad daylight, surrounded by our neighbours."

"No need to apologise, Marius, this was not your doing. Be thankful you were with her, who knows what might have happened had she been alone." Rufius frowned, rubbing his chin in thought. "Despite the perceived threat, I believe we should pursue our daily routine, without changing our habits. I cannot imagine Lucia would take kindly to being restricted to the domus. Moreover, if someone is determined to reach her they will do so by whatever means they feel necessary. Vigilance remains the key, Marius, and I shall endeavour to dig deeper into those whose lives have touched Lucia's. Especially Hostus Ovidius. I know him, and I know his tactics, although if he indeed is taking revenge for being slighted, his mind has clearly become even more twisted than when he was in my centuria."

"In all seriousness, do you consider Lucia's life to be in danger?"

"I wish I was able to say no, but Ovidius does not think rationally. He would take Lucia's rejection of his invitation as a snub. Instead of forgetting it and moving on, he will let it simmer and become warped out of all proportion." Rufius sighed, tidying his desk while he pondered the situation.

"We served together in Sirmium... Pannonia..." seeing Marius' blank expression, Rufius clarified, "...where I was posted before you and I met at Oescus... and the proximity of barbarian tribes meant there were regular skirmishes. There is a difference however in quashing rebellious natives, and gratuitous slaughter. Regrettably, Ovidius could not or saw no reason to distinguish. He dispensed the harshest of retribution, even for minor infractions, and was brought up on charges of insubordination several times.

"Finally, I handed him over to the legatus. Ovidius was discharged dishonourably before his term of service was completed, and as such was not granted his termination payout, neither is he entitled to his army pension. He has never forgiven me for depriving him of the income he believed was his due, regardless of his behaviour. In his opinion, any rebellion should be annihilated…"

Rufius paused. *Was this what he was doing? To have the Watch round up possible agitators and have them dispatched without trial. His way of ridding the world of those he suspected were a threat to the peace of Emerita? If so, the man was deranged.*

He voiced this to Marius who considered the possibility, agreeing Rufius' theory was eminently plausible.

"By extension, therefore we might acknowledge Lucia was not the main target after all, but because she thwarted him, it was a way of exacting revenge without appearing to do so."

"It seems an extreme punishment. Even if Lucia did rebuff him, her intent would not be to hurt him or his pride," Marius ventured.

"Everything Ovidius does is extreme, good or bad, although I am unsure he has ever done anything good," Rufius replied contemplatively.

"Surely he must care for his wife and children?"

"His wife is a widow, and I am given to understand he adopted her children upon their marriage. The few times I have seen them together as a family, he seems to tolerate them, but other than that I cannot comment. We live in the same town, he was superintendent of the market before I was transferred here, maybe he thinks his status is higher owing to that."

"You are responsible for the infrastructure of the town, dominus. There are few civilians who rank higher than you." Marius' tone was respectful without being obsequious; he was simply stating a fact.

"Maybe to anyone with a rational mind, Marius, but Ovidius' perception is likely skewed." By now, Rufius was satisfied his office was in order and all tasks completed for the day. He said goodbye to the two veterans still engrossed in their work, and followed Marius out of the door.

Absorbed in conversation, neither man noticed the golden haze and lengthening shadows as the sun descended towards the horizon, nor were they aware of a furtive figure who, after following them discreetly for some of the way, veered off along a side street, pleased with what he had overheard.

Before long Rufius and Marius were indoors, the smell of hot food welcoming them home.

Lucia, weary from the day's activities had fallen asleep in her room. Rufius, after greeting his household, went in search of her, perplexed when she was not where he expected her to be. Several minutes elapsed, and he was starting to think she must have left the house when he thought to check her old cubiculum; somewhere she seldom went any more.

Peering through the door, he saw Lucia curled up in the middle of the bed, fully clothed and deep in slumber. Her hair spilled around her, dusty remnants from the shattering rock turning it slightly grey. Rufius stood for long moments, his tender gaze perusing her tired features; her lashes — dark smudges fanning across wan cheeks, her mouth, slightly curved, her head pillowed on her hand.

Even in her current state of exhausted dishevelment, to Rufius, Lucia was breathtakingly beautiful. He wanted to kiss her awake at the same time as he wanted to watch her sleep — peaceful and safe.

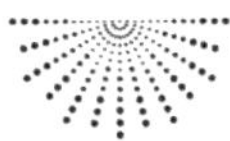

CHAPTER FOURTEEN

Leaving her to her rest, Rufius walked soundlessly along to the tablinum, taking the time to address any matters arising throughout the day, and settle any accounts due. It grew dark, the lamps were lit, and Rufius ate a meal in solitary silence. Lucia slept on.

It was almost midnight and he was leaning against a pillar, thinking it was time he retired to bed, whilst admiring the moonlit garden, when a cool hand slipped into his.

Glancing down, he saw Lucia gazing up at him, her elfin face composed.

"Why did you not wake me?" she reproached gently, "I have slept the evening away."

"You were fatigued, my love. I felt it better to leave you."

"But now we have wasted hours." She could not prevent a yawn and swayed into him. Rufius caught her against the warmth of his body and dropped a light kiss on her hair.

"We have a whole lifetime of evenings ahead of us, one missed is of little consequence."

Lucia wound her arms around his waist, resting her head on his chest. "I suppose Marius told you?" Her quiet question dragged his thoughts back from the provocative to the prosaic.

"He did, and we will discuss it tomorrow. Are you hungry? You slept through dinner." He felt Lucia nod, and taking her hand led her along to the triclinium, calling for Flavia on the way. A platter was brought in piled with tasty morsels, causing Lucia's stomach to rumble in response — to Rufius' well-concealed mirth.

They chatted while Lucia ate; Rufius elaborating on what, or who, he believed was behind the rock throwing incident.

"Hostus Ovidius?" Lucia's mouth fell open in surprise. "I knew he was vexed I declined his invitation, but surely he would not..." she trailed off, studying Rufius' expression. "Was it not enough I ended up in the arena, witness to a horror I will never be rid of? Did he orchestrate it?"

"No, the more I investigate the matter, the more it seems likely you were an unfortunate casualty of a misguided or overzealous patrol. I have no doubt the Watch were sent to corral those who until then had evaded capture. That you were caught up in it might have been deliberate, but I cannot think he intended you to be killed, probably injured in some minor way. Not that it makes his actions any less heinous. I am simply giving him the benefit of the doubt. To accept the alternative, suggests he has murderous intentions, the consequences of which... well you know what they are..." He let that hang between them.

Lucia leaned back against the plush material of the couch, her head resting on the ornate frame. "But you believe him responsible for this afternoon's incident? Why would he continue to attack me? He has taken my stall, and almost had me killed. Would that not be revenge enough?"

"Regrettably, I fear you may be targeted because of me."

Flummoxed, Lucia stared at Rufius. "Wait, let me get this straight. Initially, he wanted to hurt me for rejecting his overtures, but since you rescued me, he's going to take his annoyance out on you? That does not make any sense."

Rufius went on to explain about his prior connection to Ovidius and his unceremonious ejection from the army.

"Yes, but you were discharged too?"

"I was discharged because of injury and was granted everything due to me. Because Ovidius was dishonourably discharged he was not accorded the same benefits."

Diverted momentarily, Lucia said. "You were injured, where, when, how?" Her brow creased in worry.

"A little over three years ago, I was wounded in a rebel attack on the fortress at Oescus, which is in Moesia… beyond Italia," spotting Lucia's baffled expression. "It is strategically important, as a trade route and a frontier, and because of this we were always on high alert. The ambush, however, came one winter's night, and although not wholly unexpected, we were not prepared for it in such inclement conditions. We repelled their attack, but there were numerous deaths and injuries on both sides. I was unlucky." Rufius shrugged. It was three years ago; he had survived, albeit against the odds.

Lucia was quiet for long moments. "Is that why you have a slight limp?" Rufius nodded. "Might you be so kind as to give me a little more detail? I imagine in certain weathers, your leg pains you and I may know a way to alleviate the ache when it strikes."

Rufius pondered her question, he disliked revisiting the day of the ambush, he lost many friends and the aftermath was traumatic. Then he realised this was something else which connected them. He expected her to talk about the day in the arena; she deserved no less from him.

"It was dark, and cold, snow lay thick on the ground. Just to train in such conditions is arduous; to fight an enemy in them increases the risks tenfold. They had the advantage from the start, because we did not expect them to attack. They breached the outer defences, but thankfully our efforts prevented them gaining access to the fortress itself. They came upon us during the changeover of the Watch.

"It was chaos, and it took longer than it should have done for us to form a cohesive stance. Many soldiers were injured or slain in those lost minutes. My centuria engaged a group near the outer palisade. We managed to repel them, but as we were dispatching the last of them, one of their number, wielding an axe, cut me down. On its own, that was bad enough, but as I fell, I was trampled by a horse, breaking my leg in several places."

Lucia moved to sit alongside him, taking his hand and gripping it tightly, stroking her thumb up and down his in a gesture of comfort.

Rufius smiled, squeezing her hand gently. "I was fortunate. Our medicus was highly skilled, and familiar with such injuries. I lost a lot of blood and my life hung in the balance for days, but he was tireless in his efforts, and thankfully my life was spared. The wound in my side did not damage any internal organs, but my leg remains a little twisted and I am unable to stand for any length of time."

He paused in recollection of those days when he could not walk, thought he would never walk again. "I expected to be assigned an administrative position within the army, but my superiors decided to retire me. They did, however, offer to transfer me here to Emerita. I love my work, and it led me to you, so perhaps Fate was smiling on me after all."

Rufius became aware that a weight, a burden he did not even realise he carried, was rolling off him. This was the first time he had discussed the attack and its consequences with anyone. They were dark days, the unrelenting pain, the nightmares, the hours and hours of rehabilitation, all hung like a millstone around him. His limp, a constant reminder of what he lost — a career brutally curtailed.

He kissed the top of Lucia's head, feeling her settle against his shoulder. Their fingers were now entwined, Lucia continuing to rub his thumb, her touch soothing.

"Thank you for telling me, Rufius, it cannot be easy to recall such a time. Maybe one day I can share what happened to me. I confess it is too raw, and I fear if I talk about it the nightmares will return." She shook her head. "The blood, there is always so much blood. I cannot…" she pressed her lips together, images rearing in her mind. "I promise to tell you when I can do so without wanting to scream." Her voice dropped to a whisper.

"It has taken me three years to talk about the ambush. I can wait until you are ready, my love. In this I shall not push you."

"Might you be able to accompany me tomorrow when I check on Feronia? I would like you to meet her," Lucia asked, her thoughts going off at a tangent.

Used to her, Rufius did not question the rather random request, but did shift his position on the couch until they faced each other, his expression puzzled. *She wanted him to meet a wolf?* "If I have no other call on my time, I would be glad to, for no other reason than to ensure you are safe, but for what purpose?"

"I believe it is imperative she recognise your scent. The scent of the man who rescued me. The scent of the man who has become the most important person in my life. I cannot explain why, I just know it is so." Leaning close to graze her lips against his. "You will come then?"

"Of course," Rufius agreed, smiling at her eager face. "That is for tomorrow, tonight is for us. Talking about scent…" Entangling his fingers through her hair, Rufius inhaled the subtle fragrance that was essentially Lucia, an evocative combination of almond blossom and cherry with the faintest hint of citrus. Bringing her mouth back to his, he forgot everything else except the sensations simply kissing Lucia aroused. It was not too long before they sought their cubiculum.

Immediately after prandium the following day, Lucia and Rufius made their way to the bestiariorum. In truth, Lucia was excited to have Rufius and Feronia meet. An indefinable instinct had prompted her question the previous evening, and Lucia rarely ignored her intuition, it had served her well on many occasions.

Upon arriving, they were escorted through to the enclosures by one of the handlers, whose name Lucia recalled was Gallio.

"She seems less grumpy today," he offered, while they walked between the cages.

"That is good news, Gallio. Hopefully the infection is diminishing," Lucia replied, smiling at the handler, who grinned back in unabashed admiration. The young man had never seen anything like what this tiny woman did, and he continued to be in awe of her skill. He handed her the basket — the bowls and stoppered jug of water tucked in neatly among the bandages and ointments.

The sharp stench of animal urine and faeces wafted along the passageways, as the veritable army of handlers cleared out the enclosures, replacing the dirty and wet straw with fresh. The sounds of the men chatting as they completed their chores, the occasional growl or whine from the creatures scuffling around in their pens had become familiar to Lucia and were oddly benign.

They passed through the two gates. Rufius was nervous.

An unwilling spectator to the devastation these creatures had no hesitation in inflicting on each other, not to mention condemned humans, he found being so close to the one who apparently reigned supreme, daunting.

"Trust me," Lucia murmured quietly, attuned to his anxiety. "Feronia will sense your alarm. Ensure any move you make is smooth, not jerky or sharp. Do not raise your voice and remain calm. That is all I ask. Stay here. If Feronia wishes to scent you, I will call you over." Lucia held his eyes until, unwillingly, he acquiesced. "This is my third visit, Rufius, the only danger here today, is you. Do not react to anything you hear or see."

With that she knelt on the straw. Closing off her mind to everything around her, Lucia let her thoughts merge with those of the great wolf.

Greetings, my Alpha. I understand the pain has abated a little. I hope this is true. I am here to check your wounds and redress them. Do you consent? Motionless, Lucia waited. The she-wolf's answer came on a weary sigh and faded images. The pain had indeed lessened, but she was so tired.

Lucia sought to encourage. *Once your foot is healed you will be strong again, ready to rule your pack.* The images swirling around Lucia's head indicated Feronia was vacillating about remaining the alpha. She wanted to be freed. To feel the grass under her feet, to smell the rain when it chased down the hills. To run unencumbered for just a little while.

Lucia felt tears building. She knew Feronia to be a fearsome beast, but her sadness was palpable. *Give me some time. I might persuade the lanista to grant you your liberty. You deserve to be released, you have served him well.*

Feronia made an odd grunting sound, which Lucia took to be consent. Cautiously, she approached. Feronia lay on her uninjured side and allowed the human female to tend her wounds.

Lucia removed the bandages, cleaned out the residual balm, and rinsed the lacerations thoroughly. Using a dowel wrapped in a piece of cloth, she prodded at the damage, but there continued to be no sign of poison. Leaning close, she sniffed, pleased to note no noxious aroma emanated from either injury.

Satisfied the wounds were healing as they should, Lucia applied more of the soothing ointment and made sure the dressings were securely affixed. Then she introduced the subject of Rufius.

My mate is with me this day. I humbly beg permission to bring him closer. I would like you to scent him. He is the man who cut my bonds in the arena. I believe our fate is now entwined with yours. My heart tells me we three will have need of each other before the year is out.

Lucia waited, head bowed, until Feronia flooded her mind with pictures. Lucia was seeing the day in the arena through the wolf's eyes, becoming aware she approved of the man who dared rescue the innocent. Feronia inched forward, her posture relaxed, her massive head resting on her front paws, but her amber eyes remained watchful.

Straightening her back, Lucia twisted to face Rufius. "Rufius, please come forward, slowly and steadily. Kneel in front of Feronia."

Rufius gaped at her. *Kneel in front of a huge wolf? Was she mad?*

Lucia bit down on a giggle at his appalled expression. "I said trust me. Come." She held out her hand. He took two steps and their fingers brushed when his hand slid along hers, engulfing it. He felt a gentle pressure, as she drew him forward. He took two more steps and dropped to his knees in trepidation; he was submitting to a wolf. From this vantage point, Feronia could rip out his throat in the blink of an eye, yet she remained placid. Her ancient eyes scrutinised him, and they seemed to see right inside his soul.

Rufius swallowed and, without pausing to consider his actions, bowed.

"Thank you for agreeing to… err… meet me, great Alpha." He heard a low rumble and steadied his breathing, willing himself not to panic.

Feronia sniffed, the low rumbling continued. She stretched her neck, her long snout snuffling at his clothes, over his skin, and up to his face. Determined not to voice his underlying terror in an unmanly yell, Rufius remained as though carved from stone, letting the wolf imprint him on her consciousness. At one point their eyes met, rich brown on fiery amber. Feronia did not blink and Rufius was disinclined to, seconds ticked by, then the creature dropped her head back onto her paws.

She gave her blessing.

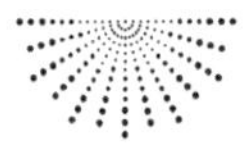

CHAPTER FIFTEEN

Rufius forgot to breathe, the experience in this confined pen, a cell by any other name, challenged everything he thought he knew. Yes, he witnessed Lucia pacifying the beasts, and accepted it without really considering its import.

Today, with Feronia, there was no mistaking the affinity Lucia shared with a wild creature. Yet his beloved seemed wholly unaware of the enormous potential her gift afforded, the potency of being able to commune with animals. She was more concerned with the well-being of the she-wolf than trying to control her.

His thoughts were arrested by her soft voice.

"Rufius, it is time we took our leave. Feronia is weary, and I need to rest. To maintain our connection, while remarkable, is also arduous."

Rufius studied her face, which was pale and etched with fatigue, her eyes shadowed. "How does our retreat work?" he asked in calm undertones.

"Just step backwards until you are close to the gate, and then turn. I will follow."

Rufius did as Lucia bid, but was unable to relax until she joined him in the passageway.

Handing the basket to Gallio, Lucia thanked him, and confirmed she would return the next day at the same time. "She is healing well, but it may be necessary to find her a separate enclosure. I believe she is ready to relinquish her position as alpha."

Gallio gawked at her, his expression a mixture of incredulity and confusion.

Lucia smiled slightly. "Do not try to wrap your mind around it, Gallio, and do not worry. Just accept it is so. Maybe I should discuss this with Marcellus tomorrow."

"I will mention it, domina, but you might need to elaborate. Telling him this is the wolf's decision might not be enough." He grinned wryly, never imagining in his wildest dreams he would be discussing the long-term habitation of a wolf with a woman who apparently shared deep and meaningful conversations with said wolf.

Lucia returned the young man's smile, and then Rufius tucked her arm through his, the couple heading slowly home.

Rufius barely spoke, his thoughts crowded with the extraordinary scenes from the afternoon. When they reached his house, he pushed open the door, standing to one side to allow Lucia to pass through ahead of him. She paused on the threshold.

"Is something amiss, Rufius?" Her question was laden with weariness, and hinted at something else – was it resignation?

He stared down at her, reading apprehension in her eloquent eyes, and sought to reassure. "Nothing is amiss, my love. I am simply rendered speechless by your gift. I suppose, despite having observed your skill, before today I did not comprehend its magnitude. I was more interested in getting you out of the arena that first time than assimilating the significance. Might I ask how you… do it?"

"Let us retire to the triclinium. I need to sit down, to hold the mind of a creature as powerful as Feronia is enervating. Smaller, weaker animals are easier." They strolled through to the welcoming ambience of the dining room, and Lucia sank onto one of the couches.

Rufius called for refreshments, neither speaking until they had eaten their fill of the tasty morsels Flavia brought in, and were sipping *mulsum*, the honeyed wine popular at this time of year.

After a time, Lucia began to talk, explaining how she connected with the mind or soul of an animal.

"I know it sounds preposterous, but to me it is as natural as breathing. I have always been able to do it. As a child I knew when animals were injured or sick or dying. It is as though I can sense what ails them, but you must understand, this happens only when I am nearby." She leaned over to press his hand, knowing how outlandish it sounded.

"I do not feel it all the time, you know, when a bird flies overhead or, like the other day when we passed that herd of cattle in the field. I am glad of this for I think it would drive me to insanity. I can become aware of a problem when in proximity, and once I merge my mind with an animal, if it grants me permission, I can usually determine its cause. I have to be touching it or be very close. I presumed everyone had the same ability, until the day I upbraided a soldier for ignoring the violent toothache from which his horse was suffering, appalled he could be so callous."

Lucia smiled ruefully. "He denied the animal was in pain, affronted that I had the audacity to question his animal husbandry and told me I should mind my own business. Three days later I saw him at the market and he apologised for his rudeness. Apparently, he asked the ostler at the garrison to check the horse, and I was correct. I think, although it made him wary of me, any whisper of… unusual traits in a person provokes suspicion; he also seemed to respect me. He was never anything other than polite on the few occasions we met. I believe he must have recommended me to one or two of his comrades, because for a little while I received requests to visit a number of animals who appeared unwell."

Lucia closed her eyes; dark lashes sweeping over cheeks beginning to look less pallid. She sipped her drink, lost in the memories of those days. Bringing her mind back to the conversation at hand, she continued.

"I do not speak with the animals, well, yes I suppose I do in a way, but silently." She cocked her head trying to come up with a simple way of illustrating her point. "It is like a piece of very fine thread stretching out, linking up with the mind of the animal. They respond in what I can only describe as a series of images, which together form a pattern, like the cloth on my loom. The longer we are connected, the more cohesive the picture, until it is as clear to me as though they are actually speaking." She shrugged diffidently. "Does that make any sense… at all?"

Rufius ruminated over her words, asking questions, which Lucia answered as best she could. It was not easy for her. To define her gift was like trying to account for why and how a person dreams. It was an innate part of her, like thinking or walking. Moreover, this was the first time she had ever discussed it and knew her revelations were probably disconcerting.

Unexpectedly, Rufius discovered Lucia's interpretation *did* make sense. He already knew she did not fit into a typical feminine mould, at least for Roman women. She was too unconventional, more than a little idiosyncratic, capricious, and maybe even eccentric, but he would not change her for the world. Her secret enhanced rather than detracted from his attraction to her. It was also an oblique affirmation of how much she trusted him.

Rufius felt wary eyes boring into him, and Lucia repeated her question. He hastened to reassure her. "Yes, it does. Thank you for telling me. While I cannot say I comprehend your gift, I appreciate and am in awe of it."

"You are a rare and enlightened man indeed, Gaius Rufius. Many remain superstitious of anything they are unable to validate, hence my reluctance to have what is private, made public. After helping Feronia, I realise my skill may be broadcast by those who enjoy gossiping, but if we can keep it to a minimum I would be grateful. I do not relish a queue of people knocking on your door demanding I heal their sick goat or teach their bird to sing."

A wry smile tugged at the corners of her mouth, as she attempted to lighten the atmosphere in the room with a little humour.

"I, we, will do what we can to quash any rumours. Do you wish me to accompany you again tomorrow?"

"Would you?" There was no disguising the yearning voice.

"Of course. I shall come with you each day unless my other obligations prevent me." He sensed, rather than heard, Lucia's relieved sigh and she nestled against him, their fingers entwined across his stomach.

The silence settling around them was comfortable and relaxed, they chatted for a while then, as evening became night and the oil lamps began to dim, Rufius realised Lucia no longer answered him.

Shifting slightly, he noticed she was fast asleep. Smiling good-humouredly, unperturbed that his insightful, and witty banter was not scintillating enough to keep Lucia awake,

Rufius placed his goblet on the table, and lifted her into his arms.

Carrying her along to their cubiculum, he laid her on the bed and removed her clothes. Stripping out of his own garments, which he tossed aside with little care, he slid under the covers drawing her against him, her back to his chest. With her head tucked under his chin, Rufius fell asleep, immediately, and deeply.

The subsequent days seemed to be, to a greater or lesser extent, a repeat of the one before. Lucia worked at home in the morning, Rufius attended to his regular tasks, returning home at midday. After prandium they went to the bestiariorum.

The ritual greeting never changed, Rufius continued to join Lucia in the enclosure, and Feronia's wounds healed well. She would retain a weakness in her hip, but for now she was regaining some of her former strength.

Lucia had discussed the possibility of the alpha wolf being freed, but to date Marcellus had denied her plea.

"She is integral to the pack, and they are pining for her. Feronia will resume her position as leader until I deem it pertinent to relieve her of it."

"By relieve you mean kill, don't you?" Lucia inquired, a tad belligerently.

"Not necessarily, but I cannot just retire a wolf, or any of the animals within these walls, on a whim. They are not a hobby, a novelty easily replaced. I know you believe they are exploited for entertainment but each one is a valuable asset to the school, their worth, inestimable. No, Lucia, while I sympathise with your request, I cannot agree."

Lucia informed Feronia of the result of her negotiations

with the lanista, the wolf's response — a disgruntled, but resigned, humph.

*

Time passed, busy summer days melding into one another and, one morning while fiddling with a tricky pattern, Lucia was surprised to realise it was nearly four months since her close encounter in the arena. She remained tight-lipped about that day, unwilling to let it intrude on her happiness. What happened could not be changed.

She believed it was better to put the whole sorry incident behind her and move on. That her trauma was not entirely forgotten was evidenced in her nightmares, which although sporadic were acute.

Interestingly, violent as they were, Rufius was always able to soothe her terror; his voice seemed to reach through her torment, his touch a balm. In turn, if he was fatigued after a hard day's work, or frustrated over a problem that absolutely refused to be solved, Lucia's probing questions, her slender fingers massaging his aching shoulders, and the press of her lips to his cheek, released any inner tension.

This is not to say their relationship was smooth. Both were spirited individuals used to being in control. Neither gave the other quarter if riled up, and their quarrels were as fierce as they were brief.

To be fair, Rufius was known to provoke Lucia simply because he loved to watch her in a temper; dark hair crackling about her head, eyes — the colour of storm clouds — flashing a warning, hands gesticulating wildly in agitation.

Since the day at the market, Rufius delighted in goading her, just as much as he relished interrupting her tirade with a sizzling kiss. His Lucia was certainly a virago, and he could never complain that life with her would be dull.

. . .

Not long after their discussion about Ovidius, Rufius presented Lucia with a dagger, a *pugio*, asking her to carry it with her if ever she left the house without an escort. Lucia hated weapons of any kind and was uncomfortable but saw how important it was to Rufius. Rather than abide by his wishes, she hid it in a box in her original cubiculum, and all but forgot about it.

The two were now wholly relaxed and comfortable together, their lives completely entwined. Rufius already knew how talented Lucia was and, in her turn, she begged to see the work Rufius was engaged in. She was fascinated by the ingenuity of the Roman engineers and builders, her interest in the many projects large or small being undertaken, by no means feigned.

Away from business, they also enjoyed the variety of leisure activities Emerita offered, most especially the theatre; something Lucia had never had an opportunity to attend until she met Rufius. The productions ranged from comedies, to acrobatic displays, to festival performances, and she was endlessly thrilled at the prospect of an evening's entertainment.

A requirement of his position, Rufius was among the contingent of soldiers and veterans who monitored the crowds during the gladiatorial games. He would not dream of asking Lucia to accompany him, and the days he was on duty, simply said he would be late. Lucia was grateful for his sensitivity, although she tended to be restless until he was safely home. Under normal circumstances, his role should not bring him close to danger, but riots were not uncommon, and it was the soldiers' responsibility to control any disorder.

Despite the lingering anxiety Rufius might get hurt, Lucia was a sensible soul and pushed this to the back of her mind. Weaving and painting took much of her time, more so since Rufius had negotiated the use of a corner of one of the tabernae located at the front of a neighbouring domus.

Selling an eclectic mix of jewellery and footwear — mainly lady's sandals — Lucia's scarves, throws and wraps, added extra interest, and she had already received commissions for cushions and decorative tablemats. Relatively small orders they may be, but Lucia hoped, if her customers were pleased with the result, their recommendations would build her reputation and more requests would follow.

She continued to visit Feronia, who was now reunited with her pack. The elderly she-wolf had not been challenged, but Lucia perceived it was only a matter of time. The youngsters were prowling both figuratively and literally, and every challenge would weaken the alpha's status and her health. Lucia kept pleading with Marcellus to free her. But the lanista remained adamant.

Not yet.

Little did Lucia realise how thankful she would be for his determination.

CHAPTER SIXTEEN

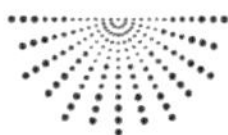

September waned, the days became shorter, a cool edge to both dawn and dusk hinted at the change of season. The light mellowed, gentle hues replacing the vivid blue of the long summer. Refreshing rains swept the landscape, briefly reviving tired fauna — arid browns becoming lush greens, before the countryside around Emerita was swathed in the rich tones of autumn, purple, red, and bronze.

It was stunningly beautiful. Some townsfolk travelled to villas on the coast of the mare nostrum, it being milder during the chill winter months, but most remained.

There were no more unnerving incidents, and although there was an odd occasion when the back of her neck prickled as though in warning, Lucia never actually saw anyone following or watching her. She presumed it was her overactive imagination and banished the perceived threat to the outer reaches of her mind.

Other things took precedent, most notably when Rufius, in front of his household — neither he nor Lucia having any family in Emerita — presented her with a betrothal ring. Despite living together and sharing a bed, Rufius was determined they be married. Lucia, who wanted this more than anything, never discussed the possibility. Since his affirmation of intent, the evening of their visit to the encampment all those months ago, the topic had not been raised again, and Lucia was not confident enough to remind him.

Rufius had not forgotten, he was simply biding his time, making sure he was not pressuring Lucia into a commitment she was not absolutely certain of, or entered into out of a misguided sense of gratitude. One night she unwittingly gave him the sign he was waiting for.

It was a cool, autumn day, a stiff breeze rattled shutters and swirled piles of fallen leaves along dusty streets. It was unpleasant to be outside, but Lucia wanted to check on Feronia. She spent longer than usual in the bestiariorum, for as she exited the alpha's enclosure, Marcellus asked whether she might observe one of the bears who seemed, for want of a better description, melancholy.

Lucia agreed, but communing with the depressed creature took time, he being somewhat recalcitrant and very surly. Eventually, he was persuaded to accept Lucia's overtures, at which point she discovered his angst was simply a lover's tiff. She gave him short shrift, instructed him on the finer points of keeping a female happy, and left him to it.

Unfortunately, it wearied her. All was fine until the middle of the night when her exhausted mind relaxed its vigil, and long suppressed fears manifested themselves in her dreams.

She was in the arena. She could smell blood. What? Not possible, not again. How could it happen to her twice? Marcellus promised she was safe, that no one would hunt her down. This time she was on her back, spread-eagled on a rock, her ankles and wrists manacled.

Heavy chains, presumably attached to unseen hooks, effectively immobilised her, their weight preventing all except the slightest movement of her head. Not that this stopped her wrenching on them in a futile attempt to break free.

The sun beat down, and to her everlasting shame Lucia realised she was naked. A face swam into her line of vision, it was Ovidius. She frowned in confusion. Why was he here? She heard an ugly laugh.

"Time to enjoy a little retribution." His sneering tones sent shivers across her overheated flesh, and she tried to lift her head.

"What did I ever do to you?"

He scorned her plea. "It is not you, my sweet, but Rufius who is paying the price. You are merely a tool with which to inflict the pain."

"I do not understand." There was silence. "Are you still there?"

"Of course, I would not miss this for the world. Rufius cannot save you this time, and your death will be his downfall."

"Why..." her voice was thready, her mouth dry as a desert. She licked her lips, desperate to get some moisture on them, twisting her body, yanking against the chains, as though the rusting metal would simply drop away. Not quite comprehending her fate.

"He ruined my life, and now I will ruin his. The Gods favour my revenge. Rufius has been sent to deal with a minor infraction. His return will be perfectly timed to witness the beasts shred you limb from limb, and this time he has no chance of stopping it."

Unadulterated terror ripped through her and, ignoring the minuscule portion of her brain telling her to do so would give Ovidius the ultimate satisfaction, Lucia began to scream for help. She screamed until she was sure her throat was ruptured.

No one came.

Ovidius just laughed, and kept laughing, the discordant sounds blending with her shrieks to create a macabre harmony.

In the midst of the cacophony, she heard a voice. "Lucia, Lucia, sweetheart, wake up, you are safe."

A hand stroked up and down her arm. A soothing gesture but a wasted one if she was going to die.

Cool fingers cupped her cheek. A thumb gently traced her bottom lip.

Again, she heard the voice, its rich timbre breaking through the horror. "I am here Lucia, I shall never willingly let any harm come to you. Trust me, my love."

Her eyes fluttered open, colliding with an anxious brown gaze, dark pools searching panicked grey-green.

"Hey there, you frightened me. It is an age since such nightmares beset you." He brushed her lips with his. Lucia remained silent, her breath coming in shuddering gasps, her mind half-trapped in the dream. She reached out and touched his face, the stubble along his jawline grazing her palm.

"Rufius?" Needing affirmation.

"I am here, my love."

Lucia gulped, and before she could stop them, a torrent of sobs wracked her slender frame. She tried to tell him, but her words were garbled, so he just held her close, waiting until the storm abated. Wrung out, Lucia nestled against Rufius' broad chest, hiccuping in the aftermath. Slowly she calmed down, and when she could string a sentence together more or less cohesively, shared the nightmare.

"He was using me to hurt you, he wanted you to see me being killed. Oh Rufius, how could anyone…?" She started crying again, the idea another person could be so cruel beyond her comprehension.

"It was a dream, Lucia, just a dream." Rufius tightened his hold around Lucia, pressing soft kisses on her hair. "Who wanted to hurt me?"

"Ovidius. H-he said you r-ruined his life and n-now he would ruin y-yours. I cannot l-let him h-hurt you. I c-cannot be the cause of your p-pain. M-may be I should l-leave, if I am not h-here, he cannot u-use me." Her words stammered, sobs lurking.

"Oh, my love, first this is only a dream, nay a nightmare, but it is not real. It is simply the fear of possibilities, not actuality. Secondly, you are tired. You were many hours with the beasts this afternoon, which doubtless exhausted you. It may be your mind warning you to have a care, but it is not a premonition of your doom."

"He said my death would be your downfall," she muttered, wretchedly.

"Of course it would. Without you, my life has no meaning."

Lucia leaned back, staring at him in shock. "Would you please repeat that?" she demanded quietly.

He did, brushing her tears away with a gentle finger. "Lucia, you are the reason I breathe, without you there would be little point. I know you love me, but I wanted to give you time. Time to adjust to my proposal, to the upheaval wrought on your life, your world, your expectations."

"Rufius, surely you kn—" Lucia tried to interrupt.

"Please let me finish, let me say this. You suffered a terrible wrong, since when your life has undergone momentous change, and because you appeared to be the focus of another's resentment, I had no mind to muddy the waters. You assured me gratitude played no part in your decision, the night you agreed to become my wife, but you deserved the chance to consider everything at your leisure, and without feeling pressured."

He kissed her, this time on the lips, familiar heat washing through him when she sighed against his mouth.

Lucia decided to be honest. *"Mi dilecte,"* she said, her voice barely above a whisper, "I confess that to be your wife is more than I dared hope. Yes, you proposed marriage, but then, nothing. I feared you concluded I was not suitable and could not find a polite way to withdraw your offer. I am grateful for all you do for me, but that is not why I love you. I love you because you are strong, loyal, and protective, because in a world where slaves are ill considered, you treat your household with dignity and respect. I love you, because you listen when I talk, you value my opinion, and share yours. You care about my day, and I cannot wait to hear about yours. We talk, we laugh, and we enjoy being together. Such contentment, such happiness, is rare and should be savoured."

Lucia paused. Rufius stole her lips again, her brain quickly becoming mush.

She batted at him, a giggle escaping at his mock-offended expression. "Let me finish," she pleaded, echoing his words. "With a single touch, you conjure up a fire I would gladly be consumed by. Your glance sets my heart racing. When you smile, it is as though I have come home. Rufius, since first I accepted your proposal there has never been any question. I may be your reason to breathe, but you are my heart, you are my fate, what has gone before, merely a prelude."

"Lucia, of course you are unsuitable." He kissed away her tears, grinning as she narrowed her eyes, ready to do battle. "You are fiery, intransigent, argumentative, and totally unbiddable. You are rebellious, impulsive, capricious, and headstrong, but you are also kind, generous, patient, and far too willing to help anyone in need, not to mention being the most beautiful woman I have ever laid eyes on. Your smile caresses my heart, your glance warms my soul, and your touch fires a passion only you can douse. It was never my intent to have you doubt my commitment to you. Lucia, with your permission, I shall arrange for us to be wed with all haste…" he hesitated mid-sentence.

A practical man, Rufius struggled to express his innermost emotions, leaving him unsure his words illustrated how deeply he loved her, and why he felt it necessary to wait; for her, not for him.

He was more eloquent than he realised, for Lucia began kissing him with a fervency that left him in no doubt of her answer, the night slipping away on a tidal wave of ardour. As the soft light of dawn dispatched the darkness, what once seemed equivocal became unassailable, and two hearts finally beat as one.

The following morning, Rufius presented Lucia with a betrothal ring. The usual ritual was not possible. Lucia's family was dead and Rufius' parents lived in Italia, necessitating an adjustment to suit their circumstances. Their neighbours, and close-knit group of friends knew of their relationship, and simply living together for the prescribed period of one year would be enough to class them as married.

Rufius, who had absolutely no intention of waiting a whole year, was also determined to follow as many of the customs as possible. Lucia did consider some of them to be somewhat archaic, even superfluous, but she made no comment, secretly pleased Rufius wanted to abide by them.

Rufius knew Lucia's status was uncertain. Her father was a Roman citizen, but was a soldier when he married her mother, and a serving legionary when he was killed. Thus, the marriage was not legal under Roman law, and any offspring not recognised.

The rules regarding citizenship seemed to be in a state of flux, however, and because Emerita was such an important strategic town, many prominent locals were bestowed citizenship, as a way of cementing their loyalty to Rome. Rufius asked for and was granted an interview with the governor who, following a lengthy discussion, sanctioned his union with Lucia, a freeborn woman with Roman heritage.

As Lucia had neither parents nor guardian, the couple declared their intent, and consent to be married by appearing in public holding hands. Rufius consulted the haruspex, to seek the approval of the gods and determine the most favourable day to formalise their union.

In the midst of all this, Lucia felt as though she was standing at the edge of a whirlwind while preparations went on around her at a dizzying pace, and often disappeared to the bestiariorum. She found solace in the, surprisingly — given the reason they were held captive and their inherent natures — restful company of the animals.

By now, Marcellus and his staff were used to her visits and treated her as one of them; her presence always able to soothe even the most unsettled — human and wild beast alike. Rufius, who continued to be concerned about the time she spent there, kept his counsel, although he did remind her to take an escort, something she frequently forgot.

If she was not at home when he returned at the end of the day he strolled along to the Gladiators' School, waiting for her at the rear entrance, for the simple pleasure of being able to walk her home.

CHAPTER SEVENTEEN

Lucia made her own marital dress, sitting up late every night at her loom. As a general rule, she preferred the style of clothing worn by Vettone women, because it was less fussy. For her wedding, however, she wanted to uphold Roman tradition. As was customary, she fashioned a *tunica recta* and a *stola,* both in white but Lucia was determined her outfit would also reflect her personality and so, flaunting convention, took the time to include a delicate pattern on the hem of each garment, replicating one of her favourite motifs from the bedroom she first awoke in.

Flavia often joined Lucia while she worked, relishing the opportunity to share her apparently extensive knowledge of marriage rituals to her somewhat captive audience.

The *flammeum* or veil, which Flavia procured from some-where, although no one was ever sure where, was oblong in shape, made from a gossamer fine material dyed a warm orange-yellow. Flowers, fashioned into a wreath, were used to hold the veil in place and it matched the sandals Lucia would wear on the day.

A woollen belt fastened in the intricate *nodus Herculaneus,* a knot representing virility, cinched the tunica recta at the waist and could only be untied by the *nova nupta's* — the bride's — new husband.

Flavia explained, on the day of the ceremony, the bride would normally process from her home to that of her new husband. Clearly, that was impossible for Lucia, so Flavia suggested she walk around the neighbouring streets, escorted by the requisite number of participants.

The nova nupta was handed over to the man who would become her husband, at which point there was a brief exchange of vows, and an offering made. There were so many facets to memorise, Lucia stopped listening, presuming, correctly, Flavia would ensure she followed the formalities to the letter.

Ordinarily, the bride, with her family, welcomed the groom into her home, whereupon the ritual words were spoken, an animal was sacrificed, its entrails read, and good fortune bestowed upon the happy couple. If there was a contract, it was signed, and witnessed by ten people who attached their seals to it. Much later, after a celebratory feast, a procession walked the couple to the home of the groom. The bride carried out more rituals before being lifted over the threshold. It was at that point they became officially husband and wife.

Unfortunately, Lucia did not have a house, and although she deemed the observance peculiar, was of no mind to upset Rufius by telling him it was not requisite. Luckily, Marcellus came to the rescue, offering one of the rooms at the Gladiators' School for the purpose, then Quintus Antonius, the procurator approached Lucia, offering to stand in place of her father. The ritual would be... unconventional... but Lucia and Rufius appreciated the efforts made by those who cared enough to make their nuptials special.

Rufius and Lucia counted the days until their union was official. Despite eager anticipation, when the day finally arrived, Lucia felt unduly nervous. Waking just as the dawn broke, she slipped out of bed without disturbing Rufius, and crept quietly along to her old cubiculum where their respective wedding finery was laid out.

Brushing suddenly trembling hands over the soft material of the tunica, then tweaking the veil, Lucia's fingers came to rest on the *toga praetexta,* the ceremonial toga Rufius would wear, her artist's eye appreciating the contrast of the dark red band, bordering the stark white of the garment.

Two arms encircled her, and she felt the press of lips against her hair.

"Second thoughts, Lucia?" She could tell he was smiling by the tone of his voice.

She chuckled, and leaned into him, bringing her hands up over his arms, and stroking his fingers. "Of course not, *mi dilecte.* I woke early and could not get back to sleep. I wanted to check that everything is as it should be." She paused, her voice becoming uncharacteristically hesitant. "Maybe I needed to be sure this is not an illusion. That what we share, the love we bear for each other, *will* be officially recognised. Perhaps I fear someone, or something will prevent our union."

"No one and nothing will prevent the ceremony going ahead, my love. Come back to bed, it is barely daylight and I believe I know a way to assuage your concerns." Swinging her into his arms, Rufius strode back to their cubiculum, and proceeded to do just that.

To Lucia's relief, everything went off without a hitch. It was a perfect autumn day. Clear blue sky, bright sunshine, with the merest hint of a breeze. As soon as the first meal was over, Lucia was borne away by Flavia and Tullia to be bathed, dressed, and have her hair styled in the appropriate manner expected of all brides. Then she was escorted to the Gladiators' School, to be met by Antonius, whose placid demeanour calmed her.

At midday, with far more pomp than necessary, and much to his amusement, Rufius was led to the Gladiators' School, whereupon Lucia guided him to the place of ceremony. The couple exchanged their vows, surrounded by their household, friends, neighbours, and those with whom both Lucia and Rufius worked.

A sacrifice, a feast, and much carousing ensued, and it was early evening before the guests accompanied the newlyweds back to Rufius' house. True to Flavia's instructions, Lucia rubbed oil around the doorway, before Marcellus and Marius carried her over the threshold, after which she purified herself by touching fire and water, banishing any bad fortune.

In accordance with Roman law, Rufius and Lucia were now husband and wife.

The festivities continued until after midnight, and eventually, after thanking everyone for their generosity, Rufius managed to usher the merry guests out of the door. Well wishes floated down the street, as people wended their rather inebriated way home. Laughing at their antics, Rufius left Marius to secure the house, and pulling a very sleepy

Lucia up from her seat on a bench in the courtyard, virtually carried her to bed.

While attempting to divest herself of her clothes, not very successfully, Lucia reflected on the day. She could not explain it for, despite living with Rufius for months now, their relationship had undergone an almost indiscernible shift. Pensively, she sank onto the rich covers, pleating her tunic distractedly, while trying to fathom why it should be so. Rufius, attuned to her every emotion, came around to sit next to her.

"What is it, my beautiful wife?" Grasping her fingers.

A shiver ran through her at his claiming. "Naught of concern." Gazing down at her small hand swallowed in his large one. "I have longed for this moment, to be bound to you in the eyes of the law, not just of each other, although that was always enough. Strangely, now it is indelible, a feeling of peace, of contentment, and utter bliss possesses me, one I have never before experienced. I find this strange, for in essence, nothing has changed. Our love remains as profound as it was yesterday. Our lives will not be unduly altered by our new status, yet during the ceremony it was as though something strengthened, became steadfast, that we have truly become one. A union of our hearts and souls, not just of the law, everlasting and indissoluble."

Lucia hesitated, rubbing her nose with her free hand. *Rufius will think you drunk; your words are absurd. On your wedding night too. Honestly, woman, you should be seducing your husband, not waxing poetical.*

"Pay me no mind, Rufius, maybe I drank too much mulsum." Untangling their hands, she attempted to stand up, but her new husband was having none of it. Sliding his arm around her shoulder, he gathered her against him.

"Lucia Atella…"

Hearing him link his name to hers, binding them on yet another level was, to Lucia, like listening to a lullaby.

"…I love the sound of that," she interrupted on a sigh.

"…likewise," he grinned, "now hush and let me speak."

She twisted in his embrace, and tried to look affronted, which he ignored, kissing her into silence.

"I too have longed for this day. My heart has been yours for many moons, but I desired greatly to affirm my devotion in a way no man can now sever. Today was the culmination of that desire. I do not find it easy to lay bare my soul. I am a soldier, we are a pragmatic, plainspoken, and rational bunch, but with you…" he paused, and kissed her again, "…with you, I become irrational, spontaneous, and artless. It is as though we are two halves of a whole, one complementing the other, and while I do not wish to possess you, you are mine. However," his tone becoming one of supplication, "I am also yours, ad infinitum."

His fingers stole around her waist to untie the *nodus Herculaneus.* The very act of removing the elaborate belt, released both the material of Lucia's tunic and any self-consciousness she might have harboured for this special night.

A feeling of liberation swept through Lucia, and before she could curb her wayward tongue the words spilled out. "Gaius Rufius Atellus, I love you beyond explanation and reason. Now I do believe it is also a tradition, on this, the night of our wedding for our bodies to be united, preferably many, many times."

She slipped out of his arms and stood, holding his gaze while she lifted the wreath from her intricately styled hair, placing it on a wooden chest at the foot of the bed. Leisurely, she removed her veil and the simple tunic, her slender body moving sinuously, as she deliberately stretched out to add them to the little pile.

The atmosphere in the room fairly sizzled. Reaching for Rufius' hand, Lucia pulled him up off the bed. Unwrapping his toga, she folded it neatly, and placed it next to her clothes, hearing his sharp intake of breath when she tugged the tunic over his head. The flicker from the oil lamps created wild shadows over their bodies as they stood, hearts thrumming, desire burning, husband and wife together at last.

With a guttural groan, Rufius hauled Lucia against him, his lips and his hands inducing a myriad of sensations – *was she drowning, was she flying?* Unable to tell where one emotion stopped and the next started, she gave up trying, falling into a maelstrom of passion, their ardour so fierce, it was not slaked for the rest of the night.

At the far side of Emerita, someone who did not warrant an invitation to the happy event was nursing a goblet of foul tasting wine, brooding over his next move. His continued surveillance had not presented an opportunity, but he was a patient man… if the result was worth waiting for.

A sneer curved his lips as the most delicious scheme began to take shape in his head. It would take a little planning, but if it worked, it would be sublime.

The year plodded on, autumn became winter and, with it, came the rains. To many, this weather was the bane of their lives, the streets ran with water, the dust becoming mud and it seemed as though everything was always wet.

To Lucia, who had lived the last ten years of her life in a camp, it was wonderful. She moved her loom so she could work facing the garden, in order to watch the rain cascade off the sloping roof. The effect of the droplets splashing into the fountain or onto the ground, offered yet another source of inspiration for her growing portfolio of designs.

Lucia's pieces were selling steadily. As the weather grew colder, her wraps became popular and she was kept busy, leaving little time for leisure. It gave her great pleasure to be able to contribute to the household, ignoring Rufius' assurances that it was not necessary.

During the winter months, no gladiatorial games were held but Lucia continued to visit the school two or three times a week. She enjoyed checking on the animals, and her regular presence ensured even the slightest ailment or injury did not go unnoticed.

Over the course of several weeks, a number of Rufius' colleagues asked to speak with her. Their enquiries related to animal husbandry, most especially horses — although one or two did ask about goats — and Lucia was pleased to offer what assistance she could. It was a refreshing change to discuss remedies and treatments with intelligent people, who although may be a little sceptical about her abilities, were open-minded enough to trust her instincts.

Lucia realised she was becoming an integral part of this community, and not solely because of her relationship with Rufius — in her own right. Not only through her weaving and painting, and her care of the animals at the bestiariorum, but also now, men who trusted Rufius, had begun to have faith in her. The warmth this knowledge gave her was as unexpected as it was welcome.

Rufius was also buried in work. The colder months never failed to bring with them a multitude of complaints from business and homeowners. Infrastructure suffered at this time of year. In addition to ongoing street repairs — pipes burst, road surfaces cracked, walls crumbled, and bridges needed strengthening, as well as occasional restoration work required at the amphitheatre and theatre.

On their own, each were minor, it was the accumulation, which presented a significant drain on Rufius' relatively limited resources. Still, he had a loyal and diligent team of men who strove to maintain the high standards he and the town's other officials expected.

It did seem that the incidents requiring emergency repairs had increased, but Rufius had no idea many were deliberate acts of sabotage, until it was too late.

CHAPTER EIGHTEEN

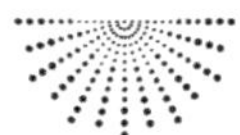

Despite being monopolised by their respective jobs, Rufius and Lucia managed to share quality time with each other, even if that was — as was becoming a habit — nothing more than a brief chat over *ientaculum*, the first meal, or snatched kisses before they fell into an exhausted sleep.

Rufius was determined that one day, or even just an afternoon, each week would be their special time together. Whether that involved a long walk in the wintry countryside, sipping hot *calda* — the spiced wine popular in the cooler months — curled up together in front of a blazing fire while enjoying lively conversation or simply indulging in an afternoon of making love... they were newly-weds after all.

On a miserable day towards the end of the year, Lucia was called to the bestiariorum. One of the she-wolves was in pup and seemed to be struggling. Wrapping up warmly, Lucia told Flavia where she was going, and hurried off into the dank morning, without waiting for an escort.

It had been many weeks since she discerned any threat, and the foreboding brought on by the odd nightmare, notwithstanding, Lucia believed, secure as the wife of a ranking official within Emerita, she was no longer a target.

Hours later, she was making her way home, when an unkempt and weaselly faced man she had never met before begged her to help with his horse. Lucia hesitated. Frigid rain had begun to fall, and she really wanted to get home into the warm.

He pleaded, and against her better judgement, which she should have listened to, Lucia followed him through the mean streets. Huddled into her cloak, she trudged after him, across the bridge towards the meadows just outside the town wall. Plenty of horses grazed in these grassy fields, and Lucia was familiar with some of them.

One or two came over to her as she tried to keep up with this stranger, who had not spoken since his petition. Pausing to give them a quick pat, Lucia reached out with her mind.

Do you know this man? she ventured. The images crowding into her head were a confused greyness, no recognition from any of the three creatures she 'spoke' with. Wary now, Lucia slowed her steps, looking over her shoulder; that curious prickle of premonition beginning to seep down her spine.

"Just here," he called, his voice rough. His features, accent, and demeanour suggested he was Vettone, possibly Turduli. He certainly wasn't Roman, and by the looks of him, probably not from within the city walls of Emerita. Lucia presumed him to be one of the outlying farmers, or perhaps a trader.

He was approaching an old mare, clearly in need of some tender loving care. Even in the waning light, Lucia could tell the creature was malnourished — her ribs were sticking out, and her coat, which should have been soft and thick, felt coarse.

Reaching out to stroke the mare, Lucia whispered loving words, but the minute she touched the horse's nose, she was deluged with a barrage of images, dire warnings about the cruelty of the man casually chewing a stem of grass less than five feet away.

Glad it was raining, and her hood was up, Lucia forced all expression, other than mild interest from her face. She steadied her breathing and crooned silently to the horse, assuring the mare she was in control.

"She requires good food, a wash and a proper groom, and maybe a little medicine to perk her up. Have you been feeding her?" she asked sharply. Pleased to note she sounded vexed rather than scared.

"She's old, I'm not paying out good coin for a nag like her." Brusquely.

"Don't you listen," Lucia murmured, resting her forehead on the mare's nose, feeling a light huff of breath in acknowledgement. "You are worth a hundred of him." Lifting her head, she turned and fixed the man with a fierce glare. "This mare has served you well. She deserves to rest out her days in a modicum of comfort," she paused, thinking quickly. "Would you sell her to me? I can give you a fair price."

The man laughed, an unpleasant sound with no joy in it. "You'd be a fool to buy her, she's only good for eating, and that's probably stretching it." He gave her a calculating look. "What will you offer?"

Lucia pondered that for a moment. "Seventy-five denarii." It was an exorbitant amount to pay for an aged horse, but Lucia couldn't bear the thought this begrimed man would kill the mare as soon as her back was turned.

He cackled with laughter. "We have a deal," he said and put out his hand. Lucia looked down at his hand and back up to his face, her brow creased. "You shake hands to seal the deal." He huffed a long-suffering sigh.

"Oh." Lucia smiled, and mimicked his gesture. He gripped her hand, and instead of shaking it, yanked her closer. Fear coursed through her and she opened her mouth to yell, but nothing came out. Instead, she heard an odd whooshing sound, a split second before her head exploded in white light.

Then nothing.

Two miles away, Rufius was perplexed. He had arrived home much later than usual, as he had been called to deal with yet another complaint. This time, it was a hole that suddenly appeared in the *decumanus maximus*, the main road, which ran east to west through Emerita. It was a major thoroughfare and its repair could not be delayed. By the time Rufius organised a team to fix it, he was well over an hour late.

Expecting to be greeted by his wife, to hear about her day, he was surprised to discover the main part of the house was dark and silent. No lamps had been lit, no Lucia smiling as she walked over for her customary kiss. Where on earth was she? Seeking answers, he went through to the domestic quarters where he found Flavia helping Ana. Flavia had not heard Lucia return, informing him his wife had gone to the bestiariorum hours ago.

"She ought to be home by now, dominus. Are you sure she has not just gone for a rest?" Flavia suggested.

Rufius checked through the house, nothing. He peeked into her workroom. It was in darkness; her loom stood quietly, the familiar and measured sound of the shuttle sliding back and forth, stilled.

An unexpected sense of dread chilled him. There was no reason to feel unnerved at the silence, but he did.

. . .

Shrugging back into his damp cloak, Rufius hurried out into the gloom, his long strides quickly covering the short distance to the Gladiators' School. He found Marcellus enjoying a drink with some of his staff, and all were surprised to see Rufius.

"*Salve*, Rufius, to what do we owe this pleasure?" Marcellus grinned, lifting the jug of wine, tacitly offering his friend a drink.

Rufius shook his head. "No time, Marcellus, have you seen Lucia?"

"She was here until the ninth hour. One of the wolves was birthing and she needed assistance. Why?"

"She is not at home."

Marcellus sat up straight, his relaxed attitude vanishing in an instant. "Did she have call to go elsewhere?"

"Not that I am aware of. Marcellus, I…" unwilling to voice his unease, Rufius bit off his words, but the grizzled lanista was no fool.

"You think something is awry?" he stated quietly.

Rufius started to shake his head then slowly nodded. "Regrettably, I do, although how and from where I cannot say. Where do we even begin to search?"

Marcellus gave Rufius no time to ponder. He stood and barked out a list of instructions to the men in the room with him, concluding with… "then gather up as many staff as you can find without leaving the school unguarded." They shot off to do his bidding.

Rufius caught Marcellus' arm. "My friend, she may just be late."

"Has she ever been late before?"

"No never, but I am loath to drag men out on so wretched

an evening, if she has simply forgotten the time while chatting with friends."

Marcellus looked at Rufius appraisingly. "Is that something she does often? Forgets the time?" Rufius' expression was all the answer he needed. "I did not think so. Lucia is a responsible soul; she would not want you to worry. If she is expected home and is not there, we need to find her, and quickly."

Rufius said he would alert the Watch and also see whether he could persuade any of his subordinates to help in the search. Pulling his hood back over his head, he dashed back out into the rain. Calling at his domus on the way, he informed Marius, who said he would round up some of the neighbours. Lucia was well liked, and they would not wish any harm to come to her.

Within the hour, a number of men, both civilian and soldier were gathered at Rufius' home. He apologised for asking them to leave their warm dry houses, before explaining what he thought might have happened. Careful not to name names, he simply said Lucia had been targeted some months previously, and he was concerned something untoward had befallen her.

All knew of Lucia's close encounter in the arena, her story kept the gossipmongers happy for weeks, but they also respected and liked her. She was unfailingly generous with her time, and always had a kind word — unless you behaved improperly, whereupon you would undoubtedly feel the lash of her tongue. Once upbraided though, she was done, she did not bear a grudge, and accepted an apology at face value. That her disappearance might be a deliberate act did not sit well with any in the room.

Many miles away, Lucia was trying to fathom why someone was pounding on her skull with a sharp object, while at the same time jostling her rather vigorously. She was lying on her back and, groaning, she tried to move, only to realise she was firmly restrained.

Forcing her eyes open, she squinted, ignoring the stabbing pain this elicited, but could not see anything, unable to determine whether it was just really dark or she was covered in a thick blanket.

Panic began to filter through Lucia's very groggy consciousness when she realised her arms and legs were bound and her mouth was gagged. Memories of the arena reared up, and she had to swallow several times to curb threatening nausea.

Inhaling long slow breaths through her nose, she attempted to work out where she was, and what was happening to her. Tentatively, she relaxed her mind and let her thoughts reach out, meeting those of a nearby horse. Posing the question, Lucia received images of being trussed up like a chicken at the market, shoved into a large wooden cage affixed to a cart, then covered with an old sack. This explained the pinned sensation and the rattling.

Desperate to determine where they were heading, Lucia sensed the creature seemed unsure. Carefully probing the mare's memory, she was able to ascertain they were on a road, which eventually terminated at the silver and lead mines at Castulo, about a week's ride from Emerita.

Her stomach plummeted, she knew a little about these mines. The Roman thugs — for that was the politest description she had heard — operating them, were notoriously ruthless taskmasters. The slaves forced to work there, lived, or rather barely existed, in appalling conditions, labouring in virtual darkness to retrieve the precious metals. Thousands died every year, simply replaced by another batch — their lives meaningless.

If that was her destination, her life was already forfeit. There would be no escape. Writhing in an attempt to loosen her bonds, Lucia tried to recall how she ended up in this mess. The last thing she remembered with any clarity was placing her hand into that of the tramp-like man from whom she agreed to buy a horse. Then, nothing until a few moments ago. Her period of insensibility cannot have been too long, for it was still dark — unless she had been unconscious for longer than a day, which was unlikely.

Her wriggling was futile; the bonds were tight and had been wrapped right around her body. She would have to find another way. Her thoughts flew to Rufius. By now he would know she was missing, and her heart sank at the distress her disappearance would cause.

Her other concern was who had done this? Why had she been kidnapped? Were there others with her in this wagon, or was she the only one? Was Ovidius behind it? He was the most logical culprit. She knew of no one else who bore her a grudge. These thoughts tumbled through her throbbing head, but it was better to keep thinking, for if she stopped she would likely give in to a screaming tantrum.

Hours, or so it seemed, later, the rattling slowed and then ceased. She felt the wagon rock as the driver, she presumed, hopped down. From the side of her head, the cloth was drawn away, and Lucia blinked. Above her, through the criss-cross of a wooden frame, presumably the cage, she noted it was dawn, the soft grey light not too harsh on her eyes after being in darkness for so long.

A man she did not recognise climbed up into the back of the wagon. Unlatching the cage, and resting one hand on the wooden side bar, he leaned down, so close to her face she could see the spittle at the side of his mouth, his breath enough to slay one of the bears in the bestiariorum.

"You are awake? I imagine you are thirsty and hungry."

Lucia would have gaped had she not been gagged, so had to make do with simply widening her eyes at him. He undid the cloth around her mouth. Lucia spat out the stray bits of thread stuck to her lips and tried to speak, but her mouth was too dry.

She shook her head, a big mistake, for the action brought the sickness back with a vengeance. Lucia moaned her agony, and the man must have realised what was happening, for he turned her onto her side, lifted her shoulders and held her steady while she vomited helplessly and wretchedly over the edge of the wagon.

The stranger stroked her back in a comforting gesture, so at odds with the situation, Lucia began to wonder whether she could appeal to his better nature and persuade him to release her. Eventually the bout of sickness passed, and he assisted her into a sitting position.

The dull grey of the early dawn was morphing into shades of pink and gold. Lucia glanced around and breathed in the clean air. The countryside was unfamiliar — a bit rugged, with sparse grass and scrubby trees.

"Where are we?" she croaked. The man did not speak, but he did lift a water pouch made of animal hide to her mouth, tipping it so she could swallow some of the cool liquid therein.

Lucia spluttered, the water spilling down her front, but she did not care, it was so refreshing. "Thank you," she said when he removed the pouch. He made no comment. Lucia tried smiling but he remained expressionless. "Excuse me, sir," she ventured. "Might you tell me where we are going, and why I am bound?"

His eyes bored into her and it was all she could do not to squirm.

"Castulo."

"Do you have orders to hand me over to the mine owners?" she searched his face and noticing a tightening of his jaw as his gaze slid away, giving her the answer. "Why? Why would you do this? What have I ever done to you?" she paused. "I trust you have been paid handsomely to abduct the wife of an army official, one who is close friends with the procurator," she said almost absently. There was no reply.

Lucia looked out over the landscape as she spoke, but out of the corner of her eye she saw him frown and rub his chin thoughtfully. Taking a chance she continued.

"Do you have a wife, children?"

Unable to help himself, he nodded, staring intently at her.

"How would you feel, should one or all of them disappear in the dead of night with no explanation? Where would you even begin to start searching for them? Maybe you care so little for them you are happy they have gone, no more sounds of children playing, no wife to greet you with a kiss at the end of the day." Lucia stopped. Rufius' face swam across her vision and it was all she could do not to break down and cry.

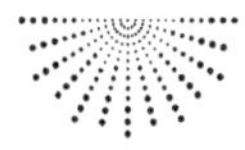

CHAPTER NINETEEN

The man, whose name was Agapito, initially only half-listened to this tiny woman. He was used to his captives pleading for release, treating her comments with disinterest, bordering on scepticism.

Something, and when he looked back on the incident later he could never define what it was, impelled him to rethink his assessment of her. Raking an indifferent gaze over her, Agapito recognised that the woman's clothing was of good quality, her skin was soft and smooth, her hands — although lightly calloused — were not those of someone who lived a labour-intensive life, and her hair was thick and glossy.

The more he studied her, the more he had to acknowledge that she did not look like a slave at all.

Agapito usually transported groups of slaves, purchased in bulk, from the markets to where ever their buyers wanted them sending — homes, mines, farms. This was a completely different assignment.

A Roman, well dressed and with an entourage, approached him, explaining he needed an escaped slave returning to the mines near Castulo. Agapito was grateful for the lucrative commission, until the man brought her to him as darkness fell the previous evening, bound, gagged, and wrapped in a sack.

Although not the brightest of men, Agapito did not agree with ill treatment of women, whatever their station in life. To see so small a female in such straits gnawed at his innate sense of compassion, made worse when he noticed she was unconscious, and the side of her head was coated in not-quite-dried blood.

In Agapito's mind, you simply did not strike a woman. Furthermore, he had a reputation to consider. He was acknowledged as being one of the more considerate drivers. Trying to extricate himself from the assignment, Agapito argued it was not in his purview to convey anyone so firmly restrained — blithely ignoring the fact any slaves he transported were always caged.

The man was insistent, however, saying it was imperative she be returned to her owner. Apparently, the woman was a serial escapee, and the reason she was bound and gagged was because she fought with them when they attempted to recapture her.

Agapito remained suspicious, but the man offered a ridiculously large sum, and, in the end, coin overrode instinct.

Lucia watched as he processed her words. Maybe there was a slim chance she might persuade him to free her, but it would take some time.

"Would it be too much to ask that you loosen my bonds?" she entreated. "My arms and legs are almost numb, and my head aches so badly I can scarcely see. Surely you must see I am in no fit state to run."

Agapito ran his eyes over her, noting the exhaustion and pain etched on her face, the dark bruises under her eyes, her hair tangled, and matted with blood from a wound no one had thought to clean. Her feet were blue with cold, and she was shivering. Something akin to disgust at his behaviour made his chest constrict, and he mentally kicked himself for letting greed to squash his better judgement.

Pulling out a large blade, he leaned over her.

If possible, Lucia blanched more, a terrified whimper stealing over her lips, even as she clamped them shut.

"Fear not, domina. I have no mind to harm you. I do not get paid if you are dead upon delivery." With this rather morbid attempt at humour, he sliced through the rope holding her fast.

The sudden release made Lucia feel rather giddy, and as though her arms were floating. She could not prevent a giggle at so peculiar a response, at the same time aware the pain in her head was distorting her acumen.

"Thank you, sir. Oh, that is so much better." An odd tingling spread from her toes and fingertips, along her limbs when the blood, no longer restricted, began to course through her veins. As the numbness retreated, she stretched, flexing her muscles, then rubbed her arms to get some heat into them. "Where's my cloak," she wondered out loud.

The man crouching in front of her shrugged. "You did not have one when he carried you to my stable last evening, or any footwear for that matter."

Lucia twisted around, scanning the bed of the wagon and spying an old horse blanket, grabbed for it through the bars of the cage. Snatching it up, she hugged it around her chilled body. The smell of horse and the odd prickly bit of straw, inconsequential compared with the warmth it provided.

Confident his captive was not about to flee, Agapito hopped down from the wagon, going to the front where, tucked under the driver's seat, two large baskets filled with food, and a large flagon of water could be found. Unstrapping one of the baskets, he carried it over to the side of the road and placed it on a flattish rock.

He helped Lucia down, holding her steady until her legs stopped trembling, before assisting her over to the rock, the solicitous gesture contrary to the situation. Thanking him, she sank down onto cold stone, taking the hunk of bread he handed to her.

Lucia's head continued to pound, and the queasiness lingered. The thought of food made her stomach rebel, but she knew she had to eat, if she had any chance of either escaping her captor or persuading him to free her voluntarily, she needed all her faculties. She nibbled on the bread, trying to come up with a plan.

"Would you be so kind as to give me your name, sir?" she asked. "We are stuck together, presumably for days, until you hand me over to whoever paid for me. We might as well make the best of it."

"Agapito" the man muttered.

"I am Lucia." She smiled, but he noticed it did not reach her eyes.

Over the last few hours, long before Lucia awoke, Agapito's conscience had begun pestering him. Now, in the cold light of a winter's morning, he was becoming increasingly uncomfortable at the idea of delivering this fragile-looking woman to the overseer at the mine. A man named Calvus Bruccius, whose reputation for cruelty was not exaggerated.

Agapito was not a stupid man. He knew what Calvus would do with Lucia. She was beautiful, despite her current bedraggled appearance. Rather than send her down the mines and work her to death, Calvus, and probably his cronies, would use her body to quench their lust, without care or qualms, taking their fill until, tiring of her, would simply dispose of her by any method he chose. Her life was worthless now.

Studying his face, the sense of foreboding Lucia already felt, increased. It was clear Agapito knew her fate. Still she sought to soothe him, while clinging to the possibility, however remote, that he might let her go

"'Tis not your fault."

Her soft voice distracted Agapito from his dark thoughts. He looked at the small hand pressed on his arm, then back up to her weary face.

"You have no knowledge of who I am, and I daresay you were given a good reason for conveying a bound woman to Castulo." Almost as an aside, she added, "You have an interesting name. I believe it derives from the Greek *agapetos*, which means beloved. An ancient and honourable name."

He threw her a sharp look, but her expression was bland. A few minutes of silence ensued.

Lucia turned to face him. "Please tell me how all this came about."

Agapito frowned, uncertain why she cared.

Lucia's mouth twisted in a sad smile. "'Tis clear someone wants me dead, and this way my demise is less traceable than having me killed in Emerita. That said, I imagine my husband will not stop until he finds me." She heaved a deep sigh, thoughts of Rufius clamouring in her head, hating that she had caused such upset. "I pity any man who tries to prevent him."

Recalling she said her husband had some status, Agapito asked, "Who is your husband?"

"Gaius Rufius Atellus, he..."

"No, that cannot be," Agapito interrupted in consternation. "No, *no*, **no**! Rufius is one of my customers."

Lucia's forehead creased in bewilderment, wishing the drumming in her skull would go away. "My husband does *not* deal in slaves," she countered acerbically.

"No, you misunderstand," he interjected before she could remonstrate further. "I am an ostler. This," waving his hand about, "transporting slaves, is work I undertake during quiet periods. Once the season for chariot races and gladiatorial games is over, I often have weeks; months even, with little income. About two years ago, someone asked whether I would be interested in conveying all manner of goods, yes including slaves, to outlying areas, farms, mines, and the like. It pays good coin, more than I make being an ostler."

Agapito did not know why he was telling Lucia this, but something about her engendered trust. It was an unsettling sensation, but he felt compelled to clarify that he was not inherently wicked.

Lucia tried to concentrate on what he was saying, but the pain in her head was reaching monumental proportions. She felt it imperative to stay awake and upright. She needed to work out how to escape, and she wanted Rufius more than she had ever wanted anything in her life. Forcing her attention back to Agapito, Lucia squinted at him. Keeping her eyes open was becoming such an effort.

"Gaius Rufius hires my horses for some of his staff. If they need to conduct inspections of the roads and bridges and any construction outside the centre of Emerita, it is quicker if they go on horseback. To walk would take too long. Something about those who demand reports disliking delays. I had no inkling..." he trailed off, the enormity of what he was involved with hitting home.

"Agapito, please describe to me, the man who commissioned this little assignment," Lucia asked, her words deliberate and oddly slurred, as though she was having trouble forming them, or had drunk too much calda.

Knowing the latter was not possible, Agapito searched her face, which was contorted with pain. He feared the wound on her head was more severe than he had been given to understand. Regardless of what eventuated, the morally indignant internal voice, which continued to nag at Agapito, insisted he tend to Lucia immediately.

"Before I do, let me clean your head," he beseeched.

"Clean my head?" Lucia stared at him, completely confused now. *Was her head dirty?* "It does hurt. A lot. Why does it need cleaning?" She touched the side of her head, agony lanced through her and she hissed. *By all the Gods, that was a mistake.* Her fingers felt sticky. Bringing her hand in front of her face, Lucia stared at her palm, desperately trying to make sense of the past three minutes, never mind the past twenty-four hours. "Why is my palm bloody?" she asked, holding it up to show him. "Maybe I should wa…" her words trailed off and she made to stand up. Everything slewed and the vista in front of her became distorted and fragmented. "Agapi—" she keeled over, landing on the dirt in a graceless heap.

To his credit, Agapito reacted with haste. Gathering Lucia up, he carried her some distance until he came upon a little stream. Using an almost clean cloth, he gently washed the blood from her head, and rinsed her hair, appalled when he saw the gash behind her ear.

He shook his head, realising how grievously she suffered; yet not once had she complained. *Although,* he tried to convince himself, *knowing what she was about to face, maybe she considered a sore head was the least of her worries.*

Lucia did not regain consciousness for a protracted

period, and when she did it was to a beautiful day. Above her, a cheerful sun shone brightly in a sky of pale blue, and the air was chill, but clear. In the far distance, she discerned a hint of clouds heralding rain, but they were no threat.

"Lucia? Can you hear me?"

Lucia turned her head, gingerly, to see Agapito kneeling beside her. Raising herself up on her elbows, she scanned her surroundings. They had not moved, this was the place where they stopped to eat.

"Why are we still here?" she asked, annoyed at how weak she sounded.

"I cannot continue this journey. I cannot hand you over to Calvus Bruccius, no matter my monetary gain. My wife will never forgive me if I complete this mission." Agapito hung his head, mortified that greed had overcome compassion. He raised tormented eyes to hers, "Please forgive me, Lucia. I wanted to wait until you awoke, to make sure you are fit to travel, so I can take you home."

"W-what…?" she gawked at him, a kernel of hope taking root.

He repeated his intention, adding, "I do not care to be deceived. Had his explanation been the truth, I would have no hesitation in returning you to Calvus, but this… this is treachery. He wishes you dead for no reason I can think of. The man is a murderer."

Harsh words, and Lucia thought she knew who had precipitated this. A conversation with Rufius weeks ago flickering into her mind. Ovidius was behind her abduction, of that Lucia was absolutely certain, but what was his long-term objective? Was it to torment Rufius, or was there something else going on?

"Agapito, before I was so impolite as to swoon," her whimsy making the ostler smile just a little, "I asked you to describe the man who insisted you take me to Calvus Bruccius. Please do so now. I think I know who it was, but I need confirmation."

"He is a little taller than I. A portly and balding gentleman, with the bearing of someone who was once a soldier but is no longer. His expression seems permanently soured, as though life dealt him a bad hand, and rather than make the best of it, has allowed it to rule his every action."

Lucia nodded. Agapito was describing Ovidius to perfection. She pictured the rotund veteran, his sneering lips, cold eyes, and discontented countenance. A shudder ran through her, nothing to do with the wintry air. It was imperative she return to Emerita, for now the feeling of dread revolved around Rufius, and what evil Ovidius might have planned for him.

CHAPTER TWENTY

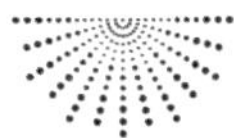

The trenchant efforts of those searching for Lucia, in and around Emerita, were met with failure. Throughout the long and miserable night, they trod deserted streets; banged on doors, questioned anyone they could rouse from their beds, or whom they came across. Spoke with countless people to determine whether they had seen or heard anything that might help them find Lucia, and pursued every possible lead, even those which were clearly fanciful.

Rufius was becoming desperate; accepting Lucia had either been kidnapped, or worse, killed and left where no one would find her. He clung to the belief it was the former, at least it gave him some hope, for his heart felt as though it was being slowly shredded.

Marius and Marcellus were pillars of strength, coordinating the multitude of volunteers into search parties and, using the town like a grid reference, sent them out to check in a logical sequence of sections. It was approaching dawn, when a soldier from the garrison rushed in waving a filthy and sodden piece of material.

"Gaius Rufius, Gaius Rufius, I found this…" Gasping for

breath, the man slithered to a halt in front of the table where Marius and Rufius were pouring over a map of the city, working out their next plan of action. He sank onto a convenient chair, sucking air into his lungs.

"Frugi, what? What is it?"

Frugi — centurion, and trusted friend of Rufius — heaved the dark cloth onto the table, where it landed with a squelchy thud. Rufius unfolded it, his heart hammering, he already knew whose it was, he recognised the bright square of material sewn into the inside, the little pocket where she kept her coin, but he wanted Marius to see it too. Just to prove his brain was not playing tricks with his eyes.

Marius twitched a corner of the ruined cloak, and then turned to Rufius. "It is Lucia's," he breathed, his tones disbelieving. "Why would she shed her clo—" he stopped. Lucia would *not* shed her cloak. Last evening had been wretched, far too cold to walk the streets without an outer garment. That begged the question, why had the two been separated. "Frugi, where did you find this?" he asked the still gasping soldier.

"In the field, over the bridge, where the horses graze." Waving his hand in the general direction of said field.

Marius and Rufius locked eyes, and spoke in unison.

"*Ovidius!*"

The antipathy, with which Rufius spat the man's name, shocked those in the room who did not know the history between the two men. Marius smiled grimly. This did not bode well for the dissolute veteran. Rufius had many more influential friends and colleagues than Ovidius, the latter well known for his unscrupulous dealings.

As succinctly as possible, Rufius outlined why Ovidius might target Lucia, concluding with, "If he thinks he can get to me through Lucia, he will. I do not like to suspect such dastardly behaviour from a fellow soldier, but it maybe that

Ovidius is taken by a hatred, a madness he cannot control. All I care about is Lucia's safe return. My next port of call will be Ovidius' domus regardless of the early hour. If he has harmed…" Rufius bit off his last words, his expression flinty.

"You shall not go alone, Gaius Rufius. Lucia's disappearance affects us all, and I would rather there be witnesses to the man's skulduggery." Marcellus interjected, his tones implacable. Rufius nodded wearily, fear for Lucia churning in his gut like rancid *garum*. He was too tired to argue, he just wanted something, anything, to confirm Lucia was alive.

The group around the table, Rufius, Marcellus, Marius, Frugi and six other soldiers plotted their strategy. This morning, their visit to Ovidius would appear nothing more than a general enquiry into a missing woman.

Rufius would not make the approach. His relationship with Ovidius was too volatile. Frugi was chosen. An affable soldier who, despite his rank, appeared naïve. It was a persona he cultivated because it encouraged people to cough up more information than they realised when he interrogated them.

Frugi would question the whole street along which Ovidius had his villa. By not singling him out, they hoped their quarry might remain unaware of their suspicions, and that if they were circumspect in the way they broached the topic, he might let slip something he otherwise would never dream of sharing. Any snippet, however inconsequential it might appear, they were able to garner from Ovidius would be investigated.

Marcellus advised Rufius to go home and get some rest. "You will be of little use to your wife if you collapse from exhaustion," the lanista groused.

"I will sleep when she is safe, not until. How you expect me to rest when you are all toiling under the same debility is beyond my comprehension. Come, let us partake of some sustenance before we set out." Rufius indicated the platter of food thoughtfully organised by one of his subordinates.

Hot drinks and the tasty fare revived them somewhat, and shortly thereafter, while the remaining search parties continued their efforts, in another area of the town, Rufius and his coterie set out.

The rain had eased during the last hour and a weak sun peeked over the horizon, chasing away the long grey shadows, as vaporous fingers of translucent light crept up the mellow stone walls of Emerita. The streets still ran from the force of the deluge. The morning light refracting through the water, created beautiful reflections — had any of those splashing through it cared to look.

They reached Ovidius' villa in less than half an hour. It was on a peaceful, tree-lined street on the outskirts of the town, although still within the walls. While the majority waited out of sight, four soldiers began knocking at doors, rousing a rush of servants to answer the loud banging before it disturbed the household.

Those answering the doors were grilled, stout denials heard and — a titillating morsel of gossip sensed — explanations were demanded in return. Frugi and his three comrades made a good show of being terribly apologetic and completely mystified that their superiors deemed it essential to wake households in order to ask about some heedless woman who had gone missing.

As agreed, Frugi strolled up the short pathway bordered by neatly trimmed bushes, to Ovidius' front door. Sending up a prayer to Fortuna that she would bless his task on this chill morning, Frugi raised his fist and thumped the solid wooden door.

Far beyond the confines of the town, two travellers were gradually retracing their steps. Now clean, Lucia's head was bandaged, after a fashion, using a strip of material torn from her dress. Agapito settled Lucia as comfortably as possible on the seat beside him, wrapping the voluminous blanket around her.

Unfortunately for Lucia, the jarring motion of the wagon as it rumbled over the huge stones forming the road, provoked a frequent recurrence of her earlier sickness. In the end, Agapito made the decision to halt and wait until the bout passed.

Much as she hated to do so, Lucia crawled into the cage on the back of the wagon, and lay down, using a bundle of old rags to cushion her aching head. This way, Agapito was able to increase their pace, aiming to be back at Emerita by nightfall.

Unwilling to make Lucia's journey any more arduous than it already was, Agapito stopped every hour or so. It slowed their progress considerably, but the ostler was becoming more and more concerned about Lucia's state of health. She seemed to be floating in and out of consciousness, and he definitely did *not* want her to die while in his care.

At every break, he assisted her carefully down from the wagon, and found somewhere for her to sit. He offered refreshment, but Lucia had no appetite, the thought of food making her fractious stomach roil.

Despite an urgency to get home, Lucia accepted Agapito was trying to do his best for her. She did not fuss, content to enjoy the serenity of their surroundings. The day remained bright, the air cool but bearable, and although clouds were amassing, they were no threat. In fact, Lucia mused, had she been with Rufius, without a spectacular headache or needing to concentrate to form a cohesive sentence, the day would have been idyllic.

The day slid, or rather rattled, by, the sun tracking across the sky and around the eighth hour, Agapito pointed; in the distance Lucia could make out a change in the terrain. It was subtle, they were miles away, but she knew it was Emerita. Forgetting her headache, forgetting her anxiety, she flung her arms around her erstwhile kidnapper, and kissed his weathered cheek.

"Oh, we're nearly home! Agapito, thank you, thank you from the bottom of my heart. You cannot imagine what your decision means to me. Twice my life has been reprieved; I do believe the gods might be feeling just a little benevolent. You, who could have ignored your heart and handed me over to a corrupt supervisor with nary a care, saved me, and I will never forget your kindness."

She sank back in her seat, unaware Agapito had undergone his own epiphany, and that the last twelve hours had wrought a change in him he could not have foreseen had the Fates slapped him in the face with it.

Ignoring the ever-present thumping in her skull, Lucia leaned forward, her anticipation at seeing her adored husband again, a dream she thought hopelessly lost.

Hours earlier, in a tranquil suburb in Emerita, Frugi waited less than patiently for his summons to be answered. After knocking a third time, the door was yanked open, and a very disgruntled slave glowered at the person who gave him so rude an awakening.

"My apologies," said Frugi, not sounding particularly contrite. "We are looking for a missing person. A young woman…" he went on to describe Lucia without providing her name. The slave remained politely puzzled, but gave no indication he had ever seen her. Pressing the slave for several minutes, Frugi was convinced Lucia had never been within a Roman mile of this villa. Trudging back along the street he met up with the rest of the group.

"I am sorry, Gaius Rufius, I do not think Lucia has been here, ever. I am adept at reading expressions and can tell when a person holds back information. These people know nothing." Frugi's tones were conciliatory; saddened that he was the one to dash what seemed their last hope.

"Where can she be?" muttered Rufius, pacing in his agitation. "She cannot just vanish into thin air. I think we have to go back to her last known whereabouts. We should go to where you found her cloak and start from there. That is all we have to go on. Maybe there is something else, something we missed." He continued to march up and down, the others watching in sympathy.

They were about to leave, when a door in a wall near where they were standing creaked open. A curly head peeped around and scanned the street. When it spotted the group, a slight figure tiptoed out, closing the door silently. It was a young woman, maybe a year or two older than Lucia. She approached them cautiously, and her demeanour had all the men on high alert.

"Are you looking for Hostus Ovidius?" she asked in undertones and glanced over her shoulder as though worried someone might overhear.

Rufius closed the gap between them and spoke in, what he hoped was, a calm and soothing manner. "Yes, we are. We think he might be able to help us in an investigation. Do you know where he is?"

The girl shook her head. "He disappeared last afternoon, around the tenth hour and we have not seen him since. He was very angry, but also..." she paused, searching for the right words, "…excited, as though he had received fortuitous news. He did not tell Mother where he was going and has not returned." She shrugged, then almost conspiratorially, added, "I am glad he's gone. It is a respite. He hurts Mother, but she refuses to confide in anyone."

Intrigued at the prospect of gleaning something pertinent without having to ask, the group pricked up their ears, and waited patiently, their expressions showing nothing but mild encouragement.

The girl sighed… "He married mother six years ago, I believe for her inheritance and this villa, more than any real affection. At first, he was polite and considerate, but of late he has become morose and…" she paused again "… rather brutal. He is curt when addressing my siblings and myself and is cruel to Mother both by words and actions. She lost one husband, my father, to sickness and I believe she would rather suffer this man's tyranny than the ignominy of standing in front of witnesses and demanding a divorce. Moreover, I think he would deny her petition, or at least find a way to take the money father left her."

She shrugged, then, almost as an afterthought. "This may be why I have yet to marry. I prefer to remain unwed than be treated with such contempt. Neither do I wish to leave my mother to his tender mercies. There is only me, my sisters have already left to be with their husbands. He is an odious man." Her tone one of utter loathing.

"I am truly sorry your family are suffering from his actions. I assure you, should you manage to persuade your mother to cut the ties biding her to Hostus Ovidius, I can round up seven witnesses, compassionate to her situation." Rufius sought to comfort the girl's disquiet. "I apologise for being forthright, but might I ask whether Ovidius owns, or is responsible for any other properties?"

The girl pondered this for a few moments, but to their chagrin, was unable to offer any further information.

"I shall ascertain what else I am able though," she pledged, seeing the disappointment in their faces, perplexed at their reaction. "What has he done?" she ventured, suddenly registering how peculiar it was, so many men arriving in a quiet street at this early hour.

Rufius decided to be honest. After what she had revealed, the young woman deserved to know. "Maybe nothing, but it concerns the disappearance of my wife. We think he may have some knowledge of what happened to her."

The girl paled. "If he is involved, I pity both you and her." An odd comment, but one which sent ice right through Rufius. "How can I find you?" she added. Rufius provided his address, saying if he was not there, a member of his household would take the information from her.

"Thank you…" he raised a questioning eyebrow

"Aurelia Ulpiana," she replied, with a proud tilt of her head. Clearly she had not taken her adoptive father's family name. "With Mother's permission I retained my father's name," she said in answer to their tacit enquiry. "It seems my intuition regarding Ovidius was correct."

"Thank you, Aurelia Ulpiana, please do not hesitate to seek me out if you are able to discover anything pertinent." Rufius bowed, and with Aurelia's assurances ringing in their ears, the group took their leave, despondent that they were no closer to finding Lucia.

CHAPTER TWENTY-ONE

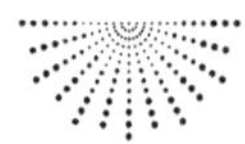

The day ticked by with ever-increasing slowness for those who continued the search for Lucia. Then, around the ninth hour, they had a breakthrough. Aurelia appeared at the house of Rufius, with some information. It seemed Ovidius owned a farm, which was located about seven miles beyond the city walls. Apprised of Rufius' suspicions, Aurelia's mother, Decima Icilia found the strength to shed the invisible fetters by which Ovidius kept her cowed. The idea another might suffer physical harm at his hands, unconscionable.

Apparently, Ovidius gained the farm in lieu of payment for a debt. He had told his wife it was neglected, and not worth repairing, hoping to sell it at an exorbitant rate to a gullible buyer. Although he had owned it at least four years, she said he rarely bothered visiting, because it was off the beaten track.

Listening to Aurelia, Rufius realised this farm was a convenient place for Ovidius to hide, or to hide someone else.

"I must investigate the possibility he is holding Lucia at this farm," Rufius declared. "I will go alone. If it is in so isolated a location, a large contingent of men would not go unnoticed. I should be able to slip in unseen."

"Now, Rufius, do not be hasty," spluttered Marcellus. "If Ovidius truly wishes to wreak his revenge on you, to arrive without reinforcements plays right into his hands. No, to rush in is short sighted. He may expect you to uncover his whereabouts, and be prepared. He will not be alone, more than likely he is surrounded by his toadies ready to do his dirty work.

"Rufius, you are a soldier you know not to charge headlong into a situation you cannot control. To save Lucia is imperative, but I do not imagine she wants to see you die in the attempt." Rufius started to interrupt. Marcellus held up his hand. "Trust me, my friend, all we need is a new plan of action."

Grudgingly, Rufius had to admit Marcellus was right. Thanking Aurelia, who slipped quietly away after pleading to be informed of the final outcome, Rufius was persuaded to return to the Gladiators' School. In dribs and drabs, groups of men were beginning to appear, after another day's fruitless search. Marcellus waited until all had gathered and told them everything they gleaned from Aurelia.

"Yes, we should check out this farm. Descending *en masse* however would doubtless tip our hand to Ovidius. We want to keep him guessing. Currently, he thinks he has the advantage, and I prefer not to disabuse him of that. I suggest Rufius goes in seemingly alone, to see whether he can persuade Ovidius to disclose Lucia's whereabouts. We follow at a safe distance. That Rufius appears to be unaccompanied should lull Ovidius, and any henchmen, into a false sense of security. We think Ovidius' motive is revenge, if so I expect he will happily spill his guts regarding Lucia, if for no other reason than to cause Rufius here distress."

Marcellus' dark eyes under beetling brows, pinned the others in the room until they nodded their understanding.

"If he has hurt Lucia. I shall have no alternative but to kill him," Rufius interposed, his bland, almost airy tone in stark contrast with his words and the rage clearly seething just below the surface.

"Hopefully, it will not come to that, dominus," soothed Marius. He peered out of the door at the fading light. "Shall we reconvene here in the morning? It is too late to locate an isolated homestead in the dark."

Reluctantly, the others agreed. Marius was correct. To attempt to scout out a farm, on the scant information provided and in the dark, was lunacy. Saying goodnight, the company made their weary and various ways home, frustrated and heartsore, that after searching for a night and a day, all they had was a cloak and the possibility of a maybe.

Rufius thanked Marcellus, before following Marius into the quiet streets. Grey dusk hung over the city, the air becoming frigid. Rufius walked in silence, and his steward knew better than to disturb his thoughts. As they entered the domus, Rufius voiced his appreciation for all Marius had done, and then dismissed him for the evening.

"Thank you, Marius. Your support has been invaluable. I am too tired to eat, and think it is best to get some rest. I suggest you do the same. I have no doubt, tomorrow will be exacting."

Marius grinned his acknowledgement, affirming he would wake his master at the first hour should it prove necessary. Rufius smiled in return, and clapped Marius on the shoulder.

"Goodnight, my friend," he said before trudging slowly to his cubiculum. Once there, he sank heavily onto the bed, his shoulders sagging. Lucia was everywhere in this room.

She was in the bright bed coverings and the wall hanging. She was in the lovingly made dresses and tunics with their colourful edges, her hint of defiance against the monotone colours preferred by so many. She was in the pile of footwear kicked haphazardly under a chair. She was in the fine-toothed, delicate hair comb; neatly placed on the small table under the simple yet elegant reflecting dish.

Rufius felt a sharp twinge in the region of his heart. Pushing himself upright, he wandered across the room and picked up the comb, turning it over and over in his hands as though so simple a gesture would magically bring her back. He looked up, to see his image staring back at him, from a face he scarcely recognised.

Peering into the circle of polished metal, Rufius was shocked by his dishevelled appearance. Filling a large bowl with water, he stripped off and indulged in a thorough wash, then took the time to shave, and trim his hair. For a soldier, even a veteran, lazy grooming was unacceptable, and went against long years of self-discipline honed by his time in the army.

When reunited with Lucia, Rufius was determined not to be scruffy. Satisfied, he was about to slide between the cold sheets, when that familiar foreboding overtook him. *What if Lucia was being tortured? What if she was locked up in a room without light or enough air? What if going to sleep this night meant the difference between her life and death.*

Rufius began to pace the room restlessly, images of his beautiful wife flickering through his mind. *No, it could not wait. He had to get to that farm.* Quietly, he dragged a clean tunic over his head, followed by thick *braccae* – the warm woollen trousers favoured during the winter months.

A heavy cloak and boots, and he was ready. Upon reaching the atrium, Rufius paused, ruminating over how best to proceed. Before anything else, it was imperative he find the location of the farm. Nodding to himself, he crept out of house, and made haste to his workshop. Rooting through his collection of maps, he quickly located and unrolled the one delineating the area surrounding the town, and spent several moments studying it carefully.

The map covered a ten mile radius, depicting every route in and out of Emerita, most of which had to be monitored and maintained, hence the reason for the level of detail. Tracing the spiderweb of roads and tracks leading out of the town, he easily spotted the sporadic smallholdings scattered around the countryside.

Rufius rejected the majority of them immediately because they were too close the road, but a couple caught his attention. He narrowed it down to the one he reckoned to be the most likely prospect — a farm nestled in a little dip, quite some distance from the road, and therefore, probably unseen. It was worth checking, and was better than lying in bed not sleeping, worrying about what Ovidius might be doing to Lucia.

Hurrying back along moonlit streets, a thought struck him and, instead of heading straight to the stables, Rufius slipped soundlessly into the main house and along to the tablinum. Lighting an oil lamp, he pulled a wax tablet from a pile on the corner of his desk. Scratching away with his stylus, Rufius drafted a short but detailed missive to the procurator, Quintus Antonius Valerius.

If the worst came to pass, he wanted the official to know of his suspicions. Setting it aside, knowing it would be delivered at first light, Rufius tidied the desk, got to his feet and blew out the lamp.

With a dexterity refined by years of practice, Rufius had Ares saddled in seconds, the stallion evincing little surprise at having his slumber interrupted in the middle of the night. After checking to make sure their movements were not detected, man and horse left the house with the stealth of apparitions, and vanished into the night, the darkness swallowing them as though neither had ever been there.

Less than an hour later, a wagon rolled to a halt outside Rufius' domus. Agapito roused Lucia, helping her down from the back of the vehicle. She leaned against the wagon while Agapito hammered on the door. Seconds ticked by, then the door swung open, and Flavia peeked out, holding an oil lamp.

A muttered conversation then Flavia turned, shouting to someone within. Marius appeared. Lucia tried to smile, but it was too hard. The steward took one look at her and caught her up, carrying her indoors and through to the triclinium, yelling for food and a hot beverage.

When they passed Agapito, Lucia grasped his sleeve pulling him inside with her. Unsure of his reception, bearing in mind his part in this sorry tale, the ostler hovered at the entrance to the triclinium.

"Marius, Agapito needs refreshments also. He saved my life." Lucia did not elaborate, not yet. The telling was complicated, and she wanted her mouth and her brain to be in accordance when she did. "Rufius, please I must see Rufius…" Marius nodded and laying her carefully on one of the couches, rushed out. "Agapito, come in and take a seat. You should eat before you go home," Lucia invited, and not really knowing how to refuse, Agapito did as he was bidden.

The thunder of footsteps heralded Marius' return. He all but fell into the room, his expression bewildered.

"He is gone."

"What do you mean, he's gone?" Lucia was struggling to make sense of anything, the steward's words bouncing around her head.

"Just that, he is gone. He said he was going to try to sleep, before we…" Marius paused. Did he tell Lucia what had transpired? She had to know sooner or later, but the bandage around her head and her white face told its own story. Lucia needed a medicus and quickly, everything else would have to wait.

"Scaro," he yelled, and moments later the lad tumbled into the triclinium, dopey from sleep.

"Sir?" he asked, his mouth falling open in astonishment when he saw Lucia. "Oh, mistress, how glad I am to see you delivered home safely. The gods are smiling on us this night."

Lucia summoned up a smile for the boy, inordinately uplifted by the reception of the household, while Marius instructed him to fetch Salonius. Scaro bowed and dashed out. Seconds later, they heard the door bang as he fled into the street.

"Marius, please where is Rufius. You may as well tell me while we await Salonius."

Seeing the sense in Lucia's argument, Marius went on to brief her in as few words as possible, the events of the previous twenty-four hours. Agapito listened in growing horror, his participation in this debacle leaving him in a state of abject remorse. Spotting his unease, Lucia reached out to press her hand on his arm.

"Agapito, please do not blame yourself. You were as oblivious to Ovidius' intentions as everyone else. He hoodwinked my husband, and seemingly half the garrison of Emerita, not to mention the lanista and presumably whoever granted him the position of market overseer. No one would expect such behaviour from a pillar of the community. His duplicity is no one's fault but his own. Ovidius will answer to his crimes in this life, or the next."

Marius looked baffled, prompting Lucia to try to explain Agapito's role in this debacle.

"So, I have returned just as Rufius decided to head out to this farm. Do I have this correct?"

Marius nodded at her question.

Lucia sighed. "This is reminiscent of the play Rufius took me to see at the theatre last week. Sadly, I doubt the ending will be so amusing." Desperate for a proper bath, something to dull the stabbing pain in her head, and then maybe follow her husband on his wild goose chase, Lucia made to stand.

"Please wait for Salonius," Marius entreated. "He will be here in but a moment."

Lucia capitulated — in truth she felt wholly unwell. Flavia came in with food and hot calda, and the three fell upon it as though ravenous. Lucia had not eaten properly since being abducted; Marius was hungry from a day of searching, and Agapito ate simply because it was there.

Shortly thereafter, Salonius stuck his head through the doorway. Scaro's request that he attend the Atellus house urgently had been babbled without much consideration for comprehension. Something about his mistress returning but she looked terrible — pale and shivery, and her head was wrapped in a dirty cloth.

With experienced eyes, the medicus scrutinised Lucia, before asking whether she minded him examining her head.

Knowing she had little choice, Marius would doubtless sit on her if she refused, Lucia consented.

Unwrapping the makeshift bandage, Salonius prodded and probed the laceration. Lucia could feel nausea threatening once more, grateful when Agapito, recognising her greying pallor, murmured to Marius that a bowl might be judicious. A timely suggestion, because Lucia was violently sick at the same instant a bowl miraculously appeared under her chin.

Salonius continued unmoved, cleaning the wound and applying a healing salve. The subtle aroma of frankincense and the more pungent one of arnica permeated the room, the blend oddly soothing.

Eventually, he completed his ministrations and bound Lucia's poor aching head in strips of clean cloth. Adding a pinch of a powder to a fresh goblet of calda, he swirled it around until it dissolved

"Drink this, my dear," he instructed. "It will ease the pain, and help you sleep." As Lucia could have happily swallowed poison at that moment, she made no demur, gulping the mixture, her nose crinkling at the sour taste. "I will return in the morning to check on you," he remarked, before turning to Marius and adding, "send for me if you have any concerns."

Marius assured Salonius he would have no hesitation.

"Where is Rufius?" the medicus asked. "He has been combing the town for you." Patting Lucia's hand. Marius explained and Salonius tutted. "That boy, always so headstrong." Making both Lucia and Marius smile, at his referring to a man of six and thirty years, as a boy. "I shall leave you to your rest, Lucia. Do not fret about your husband, he will return to you soon."

Heaving his bulk off the couch, Salonius chatted with

Marius about signs of Lucia deteriorating, while the steward walked the affable doctor to the door.

Lucia was sliding into oblivion again. It would not do, she had to find Rufius. He was walking into a trap. Whatever Salonius dispensed, however, was stronger than her willpower because before Marius came back into the room, Lucia was asleep.

CHAPTER TWENTY-TWO

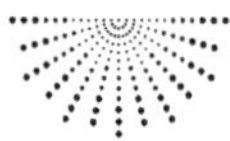

As ever when the heart is at stake, timing is everything and, unbeknownst to those at the domus, less than an hour separated Rufius' decision to locate the farm and Lucia's return. Had these events coincided, the outcome would have been vastly different. Instead, while Salonius was tending to Lucia, Rufius was galloping across one of the bridges leading from the town.

In case anyone was watching the house, Rufius opted to walk Ares along the rear alleyway, and out onto a backstreet before mounting. This had the added benefit of not disturbing either his household or their neighbours. Trotting through the town, he waited until they were almost at the bridge, and then gave the stallion his head. Ares streaked out, his powerful body rippling under Rufius, covering the miles with speed.

. . .

The narrow trail from the road would be missed unless one was looking carefully. Almost hidden behind two bushy trees, on a night less clear, Rufius would have ridden straight past. Luck was on his side — a bright moon heightened the shadows, and he was able to pick out the gap with comparative ease. Slowing Ares to a walk, Rufius made his way steadily along the track, the horse's hooves muffled by the mud, not dried after the recent rainstorm.

Aware extreme caution was now required, he slid off the horse at a reasonable distance from the house, looping the reins securely over a convenient branch. "Wait here old friend," he murmured, patting Ares' flank. Ares nickered, blew in Rufius' ear, and pawed the ground before transferring his attention to the leaves fluttering tantalisingly close to his nose.

Creeping towards the farmhouse, Rufius scanned his surroundings, continually. Trees and bushes, so recognisable in daylight, took on a sinister aspect, bending towards him in the stiffening breeze, and in his exhausted state, appeared like formless horrors from the underworld.

Shaking his head to clear it of such absurdity, Rufius continued down the slight slope, following the edge of an ancient olive grove, grateful for its cover. By the time he reached the far side, he was so close to the outbuildings he was in the shadows thrown from them.

Thanking the gods, he inched forward, pausing every few steps to listen intently for anything he could not ascribe to nature. All he heard was the rustle of trees, and the odd hoot from an owl.

Hugging the wooden wall of the closest building, Rufius tried to work out which was the main dwelling. A large courtyard was circled by several low structures, but at the far side, a larger building caught his eye.

Constructed from local stone with a tiled roof, it was

clearly built for longevity and protection from the weather — cool in summer warm in winter. Unwilling to risk crossing the open space, Rufius doubled back on himself and edged around the outbuildings, pausing every few steps to listen — the lack of sound, unnerving. Tension tightened his shoulders, and he rolled them, twisting his head from side to side in an attempt to loosen the knots.

Coming to a door, he pushed, surprised to find it was well oiled, opening easily and silently. Too late he spied three figures looming up at him from the corners of the dim room. Before he could react, they set upon him, using fists and feet to subdue.

His last conscious thought was a curse to the gods for abandoning him.

Rufius' luck had just run out.

In the early hours of the morning Lucia awoke, groggy and momentarily confused as to her whereabouts. Peering around, she realised with relief, she was at home, in her own bed, and safe. She recalled Marius' words about Rufius and his intentions.

Forgetting her injured head, Lucia shot out of bed, only to be halted when a bout of dizziness plagued her. Growling her frustration, she waited until it passed, then went through her usual ablutions with more haste than care. Dragging a clean and warm dress — oh what bliss — over her head, she fastened it with a bright belt.

Picking up her small satchel, Lucia retrieved her *pugio*, the small dagger Rufius gave her months ago when unsure what, if anything, the threat against her might be or where it was coming from. Without telling Rufius, Lucia had immediately secreted it away in her cubiculum, unwilling to carry a weapon, but was glad of it now. Sliding it into an internal pocket of her bag, she surveyed the bedchamber looking for something imbued with Rufius' scent. His tunics and togas were too bulky.

Staring at the bed while ruminating over all possibilities, Lucia's gaze fell upon the folded linen cloths over their pillows. Pulling Rufius' free, she tucked it neatly into the satchel, before slipping her feet into sturdy boots and shrugging into her woollen cloak.

She dashed along to the kitchen, and then slowed her steps to tiptoe in, hoping no one else was about, only to find Scaro curled up on a bedroll in front of the fire. Snuggled in his arms lay a scrawny dog.

Lucia recognised it as being the one, which lurked in the alley behind the house and, despite her urgency, paused at the sight, pressing her lips together so as not to chuckle and wake the pair. Both were snoring, both sported the same untameable hair — or fur in the dog's case — and both looked more comfortable than she would have believed possible on a stone flagged floor; the mat on which they lay, scarcely enough to ward off the cold.

The dog opened one bleary eye, pinning her with its stare, the end of its scrawny tail thumping on the floor. Perceiving no threat, and clearly not being offered any food, the creature went straight back to sleep. Skirting the two slumbering beauties, Lucia spotted a sweet bun on the table, which she ate in three bites, washing it down with several mouthfuls of cold calda. About to retrace her steps, she bit down on a startled squeak when a small hand tugged on her cloak.

"Mistress, you should not be out of bed, the medicus said you were to rest." Scaro spoke in sleepy reproach.

Lucia ruffled his hair. "I know, Scaro, but the master is in danger and, knowing this, I cannot lie abed. When Marius wakes, you may tell him you saw me. I am away to the bestiariorum. I have a plan, of which I hope Marcellus will approve. Keep my secret until the household wakes, and you may keep that hound!"

Scaro's cheeky face lit up at the prospect of keeping the mutt. "Thank you, mistress. I promise he will be a good boy.

Lucia smiled at his eager face. "Do you have a name?"

Scaro shook his head. "I did not dare to name him when he was not mine.

"Are you sure no one else has a claim on this dog?" she pried, gently.

"No, absolutely not, mistress," he assured her. "I asked all around the neighbourhood, no one wants him, they throw stones to make him run away." Scaro scrubbed his face when he said this — that someone would deliberately harm any creature, hurt his trusting soul.

Lucia pondered this for precious seconds, aware time was ticking by. "How about Sirius?" she suggested, recalling one of the manuscripts in Rufius' tablinum. "He was the faithful canine companion of Orion, and the most famous dog in Greek mythology. Scaro and Sirius sounds like a good part-nership."

Scaro beamed his agreement.

"Now that's settled, I must hurry. Remember, please give me at least until dawn breaks before you tell Marius," knowing Scaro would be torn between what she asked him to do and what he knew Rufius would expect of him. "I will take every care, Scaro," drawing him close for a quick hug, "but I must find Rufius."

Scaro dipped his head, and then, almost faster than Lucia could blink, grabbed two *libae* Ana's tasty honey cakes, from the shelf, along with a hunk of bread, quickly wrapping them in a cloth before handing them to Lucia.

"In case you or the master get hungry," he said, his faith that Lucia would find Rufius, touching.

"Thank you, Scaro, now no more delays." Lucia shoved the food into the small satchel, hurrying out of the kitchen and along the passage to where Eos was stabled. She noticed Ares' empty loosebox and had to blink away pesky tears. *This is no time to cry, girl*, she admonished herself.

Forgoing the saddle, Lucia quickly fastened the bridle and reins, then as she mounted Eos, reached out with her mind, melding with that of the mare, explaining what they were going to do. Eos pranced skittishly at the idea, but Lucia soothed, assuring her she would not be on the menu of a large and possibly hungry predator.

Within minutes they were at the Gladiators' School. Lucia dismounted and, ignoring the uncivil hour, banged on the door and kept banging until a drowsy guard opened it.

It was Gallio.

He gawked and then rubbed his eyes to make sure he wasn't seeing things.

"Mistress Atella. Is it really you? By all the Gods how are you here? We have been..." he bit off the rest of his sentence, ushering Lucia into the slightly less cold atrium, still shaking his head in disbelief.

Sending up a prayer of thanks it was someone she considered a friend, Lucia begged him to rouse Marcellus. "Please hurry, I know the hour is late and you must all be exhausted. Marius informed me of the search, my apologies for causing such concern, but I have work to do this night and I need the lanista's help."

Something in Lucia's tone had Gallio almost running along the colonnaded walkway to the lanista's rooms, his sandals slapping on the stones. Lucia heard the thud of a fist against wood, and a grumbled conversation. Just when she thought her petition was to be denied, Marcellus appeared, his grey hair was sticking out at all angles, his tunic — doubtless pulled on in a hurry — was wrinkled, and his expression a blend of shock, relief, and confusion.

"Lucia, my dear, what happened? Where have you been? The school, nay half the town has been searching for you."

"I know, and I am truly sorry. It is a long story and I will tell you all of it presently. Suffice it to say, Ovidius was behind it, Rufius does not know I am returned and has gone chasing after him. I am about to ask you to consent to me taking Feronia…" Marcellus paled then bright colour suffused his cheeks and he started to splutter, but Lucia did not give him chance to voice a denial "…before you say anything, I believe she will lead me to Rufius and protect us both. Marcellus, I cannot find him without her. I have an item which bears his scent, allowing Feronia to track him."

Marcellus remained unconvinced that releasing a huge she-wolf into the care of this slip of a woman, who currently looked half dead and incapable of controlling the beast, was the most judicious idea. He folded his arms, studying Lucia impassively; taking in her bruised features and bandaged head.

"If I hand her into your care, you will free her, and I am uncertain that is in the best interest of either Feronia or the general public. Lucia, Feronia knows nothing beyond the confines of the bestiariorum and the arena. She was a pup when brought to me, she does not know how to be a true wolf."

"I give you my word, I will bring her back with me. Please trust me." Lucia was starting to hop up and down in agitation, her need to get to Rufius outweighing all other considerations. "Marcellus, I am begging you." She opened her palms in entreaty, her beautiful grey-green eyes huge in her tired face. "He will die… I cannot let him die…" she trailed off, blinking away those annoying tears which continued to lurk just under the surface.

Lucia knew it was because she was injured, and exhausted, and more than a little terrified, but that did not mean she was about to succumb to such feminine frailty.

"How will you even find the farmhouse? We do not know where it is. I do not know whether Gaius Rufius located it, he could easily end up somewhere totally unconnected to Ovidius."

"Feronia will track him," Lucia assured Marcellus, her faith in the abilities of the she-wolf, absolute. "I have brought something Rufius uses regularly, once she gets a whiff of his scent she will lead me straight to him."

Marcellus heaved a sigh, Lucia would never forgive him if he did not agree, and for a man used to being the brunt of contempt, found he could not bear the thought she would treat him with disdain.

Inclining his grizzled head, he turned and stalked towards the bestiariorum. Lucia scampered after him, followed by Gallio who was still trying to get his head around what was going on. Passing between the enclosures, Lucia caught the familiar and, to her, soothing smell of warm animals — who slept on, undisturbed by the presence of humans — and clean straw.

She inhaled deeply, the action steadying her. Upon reaching Feronia's enclosure, Lucia asked both men to step aside.

"I must ask her permission to enter and also state my case. She may yet refuse."

Marcellus frowned. "Are you sure this is the best plan? It will delay our rescue mission. Would it not be better to assemble a contingent of men from here and the garrison, and come with you? That way we and by we, I mean my fellow soldiers and me, not you, definitely not you. Rufius would…" Marcellus did not want to contemplate what Rufius would do if he thought Lucia was placing herself in more danger, "…*we* can simply storm the farmhouse?"

"No, Ovidius will expect that. I imagine he already has guards stationed around the property who will warn him long before you can get to Rufius. His intent is to kill my husband, in revenge for being discharged from the army all those years ago. What began as anger at a perceived wrong has morphed into an all-consuming hatred, warping his mind. That he believes he can get away with selling me into slavery and killing Rufius demonstrates how far into madness he has descended."

Marcellus gawked at Lucia. "Selling you into slavery…" he raised his eyes to the roof, wondering whether life would ever be normal again.

CHAPTER TWENTY-THREE

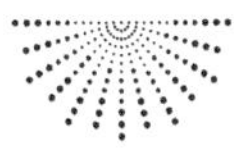

"We have no time to discuss this. I must speak with Feronia." Lucia did not wait for permission, and passing through the first gate, she knelt on the straw. Relaxing, Lucia emptied her mind and let her thoughts flow out, seeking those of the she-wolf. *Great Alpha, may I enter?* She waited. A drowsy response filtered through, granting permission.

So far so good. Lucia stood, and slipped through the second gate, ensuring both latches were secure. Dropping back onto her knees she sent her plea. *My mate is in danger. One, whom reason has forsaken, holds him captive intent on killing him. I come to petition your help.*

A long low growl emanated from the shelter. Images flooded Lucia's head, a series of questions she answered as best she could. There was a long silence, Lucia was almost screaming with impatience, but took care not to let her inner turmoil infiltrate her thoughts. In the darkness, she became aware of movement, she heard a shuffle and then a grey shadow slunk out of the cave. Lucia remained on her knees head bent, her position one of supplication, waiting.

Feronia padded closer, Lucia felt her hair lift as the wolf huffed a breath, then a cold nose nuzzled her ear, a large head came to rest on her shoulder. Trembling with effort, Lucia thanked the she-wolf, and through their link shared her fears for Rufius, as well as her plan to rescue him. Minutes ticked by until finally, Feronia agreed, standing patiently while Lucia unlatched the gate.

"Marcellus," she called softly to the lanista, before opening the main gate. "I cannot prevent you from following. I daresay Scaro has already apprised Marius of my scheme, but I beg you, give me one hour before you come after me.

Accord Feronia and I this chance. Ovidius does not yet have cold-blooded murder on his hands, maybe there is hope. If confronted by a horde of angry soldiers, however, his actions may take a deadly turn, something I wish to avoid at all costs." Lucia held Marcellus' gaze.

The lanista nodded. "Be careful, Lucia," was all he said, moving away so Feronia did not either take fright or take a nip.

Placing her hand on the wolf's neck, burying her fingers in the thick ruff, Lucia led the wolf through the gate and out of the bestiariorum. Their minds still connected, Lucia explained about Eos, her pleas that Feronia not eat her mare, amusing the wolf. Before mounting Eos, Lucia pulled the swatch of material from her satchel. Holding it out, Lucia informed Feronia it held the scent of her mate. The she-wolf sniffed, snuffled, then lifted her head and bayed. The sound echoed throughout the town, unsettling those who heard.

It seemed a portent of doom.

Rufius was dreaming, it was a warm day, Lucia was beside him and they were strolling along the edge of a field of ripe wheat. The sun was shining, almost too brightly, and the breeze was strong enough that the wheat was undulating, like a golden sea.

His wife was chattering about this and that, nothing of particular significance, but her words flowed over him, her soft voice a balm. He reached for her hand entwining their fingers, drawing her against him for a long kiss.

"We are alone, my love," his tone inviting, watching as Lucia twisted in his embrace to check their surrounds. As far as the eye could see there was nothing, not a soul to be seen, not a sheep, not a cow, not even a building. Gripping his hand and leading him right into the field, Lucia pulled him down, pushing him onto his back, the wheat closing around them, in a flaxen screen.

Grinning saucily, she lifted her dress over her head, the sight of her naked slenderness sending a rush of blood to his loins. Bending over him, she slowly and sinuously, moved up his body, her mouth and her hands sending his heart rate soaring. He was also naked but did not recall removing his tunic. He sucked in a sharp breath, Lucia's hair spilled over his body, chestnut ringlets teasing his heated flesh.

As he reached for her, the picture shimmered and changed. Confused Rufius stared down at Lucia, who was now lying across him at an odd angle. Her dark curls had become rivulets of blood, coiling out from a body covered in deep gouges. With a trembling hand, he lifted her chin, her eyeless sockets accused, her lifeblood drained.

Rufius roared his despair.

Someone was shaking him. A grating voice hissed near his ear, but the words were distorted. Desperate to recapture the dream as though it would tell him what happened, tell him who killed his beloved Lucia,

Rufius ignored the voice, but it was insistent. Then a hand slapped his face. Grudgingly, he attempted to open his eyes, only to realise one was so puffed up it was nigh on impossible to raise his eyelid, and the other was not much better. He tried to speak, but his mouth was swollen and his lips sore.

He made do with a frustrated groan.

"Welcome, Gaius Rufius. Honoured guest. To appear uninvited in the middle of the night is less than polite, but I am of a mind to forgive your transgressions, just this once."

A vicious prod to his ribs sent pain jarring through Rufius' side. *What, in Hades, was going on? Where was he? Who was talking?* Squinting through the lowered lid of his good eye, Rufius took stock of his predicament.

To his never-ending humiliation, he registered that he was naked and had been strung up. His wrists were bound, and the rope was, presumably, hooked over something above his head, forcing him to balance on the balls of his feet.

His ankles were shackled, the heavy chain weighing him down, stretching his bruised and battered body to its limits, and every time he moved, the ropes around his wrists chafed, biting into his skin.

Cursing his shoddy luck, Rufius steadied his breathing, wondering whether he had any hope of escape. It didn't feel promising, but maybe the bindings were not very strong. He wriggled his hands experimentally, but the rope remained tight.

"There is no escape." The voice informed him, disinterestedly. "Your woman is lost; her fate sealed the moment she met you. I imagine she will prove useful to Calvus Bruccius for a time, then he will no doubt dispose of her, as he does all his… whores."

Rufius felt a terrible anger begin to simmer. He knew the reputation of the aforementioned overseer; the man was barbaric. Closing his eyes, he tried to regain control of his emotions. Tried to banish the images crowding his mind, of Lucia being brutalised for the pleasure of a sadist.

"Why?" he rasped. "Why hurt her? What has she ever done to you?"

"She has done nothing to me, Gaius Rufius, but she is important to you." In a tone indicating this should be patently obvious. "She is of no consequence now. You, however, you are here and at my mercy. I am looking forward to breaking you."

Something Lucia said to him after one of her nightmares popped into Rufius' mind — that her death would be his downfall. If she was indeed dead, his life had no meaning, so Ovidius could do his worst. On the other hand, unless Bruccius had travelled to Emerita to buy Lucia — unlikely, because he never did his own dirty work — she was relatively safe until she was handed over at Castulo.

Hope kindled.

Rufius swallowed, and strove for calm, letting his senses rove. He smelt smoke, heard the crackle of flames and, angling his head, he spied the corner of a raised fire pit. Was the lunatic going to burn him to death? Seconds later, he was to discover the reason for the fire.

Out of the corner of his good eye, Rufius saw a gentle explosion of sparks, immediately followed by an intense stabbing pain, as Ovidius prodded him with the white-hot tip of something sharp, probably a sword. Determined not to give his tormentor the satisfaction of hearing his scream, Rufius clenched his teeth.

Two, three, at least four times, Ovidius repeated his actions, until the pain became too much for his hostage, who slumped in his fetters, blessed oblivion staking its claim.

Replacing the sword in the fire, Ovidius added a curiously forged, three-pronged farming implement. In his twisted mind, death by evisceration seemed a fitting and inglorious end to his erstwhile commander. Scrutinising the unconscious man for several moments, his face sinister in the light from the dancing flames, Ovidius smiled and left the room.

Not far away, Lucia, Eos, and Feronia were closing in. The great wolf tracked Rufius from the domus, unerringly, to the farm. As Rufius had done hours before, Lucia spied the narrow trail between the trees, leading from the road to the farm.

Unsure who might be lying in wait, she dismounted and walked through the olive grove, soon coming upon Ares who was steadily munching grass. The stallion nickered his recognition, and Lucia spoke softly to him, stroking his regal nose, while extracting what information she could, which was scant.

Looping Eos' reigns over the same branch, Lucia sank onto the cool grass, contemplating her next move. She had no doubt Feronia would eliminate any threat, but at what cost?

Dawn was stealing over the horizon. Inch by inch, as though a veil was being drawn back, inky darkness paled to muted greys, the silvery pink glow warming the underside of a smattering of clouds, heralding the sunrise.

Other than these few wisps, the sky was clear, although the wind remained blustery, which was both a hindrance and an advantage. No one would hear her approach, but it would also mask the sound of impending danger.

Absently stroking Feronia's back, Lucia opened her mind, the two communing without restriction. Plans and counter plans, risks and hazards bounced between them in a flurry of images.

First, she needed to find Rufius. Was he already here? If so where, and was he in danger? Lucia could not rid her head of Ovidius' face, cackling in unhinged glee at the thought of Rufius seeing her death and being unable to prevent it.

Rationally, she knew it was just a bad dream, but in the gloom of the breaking day, and although the circumstances were somewhat reversed, the truth of it hung in the air.

Feronia nuzzled Lucia's neck, laying her head on the woman's shoulder, breath warm against her throat, prompting Lucia to appreciate the trust she shared with this wild beast.

Her head was aching badly, and giving in to a moment's respite, she rested her cheek against that of the wolf. Lucia had the uncanny impression that Feronia's strength and power was flowing into her body, diminishing the ache, and imbuing her with the courage to face what could be her worst nightmare.

Worse than being sold to a crude boor, worse than dying in the arena — for this time she was the witness not the victim, and if she failed… *no*…failure was inconceivable.

Lucia pulled herself together, straightened her shoulders, and sent a thought to Feronia.

Come, my Alpha. It is time.

The wolf growled her response, the low rumble, like distant thunder, heightening anticipation. Standing, Lucia reached into the satchel and withdrew the dagger, before hanging the bag over the same branch through which the reins were hooked. The less she carried the better.

Scanning the area, she spied a collection of buildings a little way ahead, nestled sleepily in the dip, the welcoming aspect lulling the unwary. There was no sign of movement, but Lucia was not fooled. Ovidius would not leave his compound unguarded.

Crouching low to the ground, Lucia led the way towards the nearest building. In the dim light, she misstepped, slithering down the gentle slope to the edge of the tree line, landing in an inelegant heap just inside the cover of the sprawling olives.

Annoyed with herself, Lucia discerned Feronia chuckling — if a wolf could chuckle — at her ungainly conduct, while she padded surefooted to join her, wresting a childish response from Lucia, which involved a tongue and a sort of *thbpbpthpt* sound.

The utter incongruity of the situation caused Lucia to stuff her hand in her mouth, biting off a burst of irreverent laughter. Aware hysteria lurked on the periphery of her senses, Lucia made a concerted effort to regain control.

Now was not the time for hilarity.

Quiet as ghosts, Feronia and Lucia made their approach,

pausing every few paces to scan their surroundings, and for Feronia to scent the air. Smoke curled up through two of the roofs. Clearly, these two building were inhabited, but to what extent? Was Rufius in one of them? Almost certainly.

Edging nearer, Lucia hurried to hide against the wooden outbuildings, Feronia at her heels, the early morning shadows continuing to conceal their presence. Feronia whined quietly, unease threading through both human and wolf. While Lucia was pondering her next move, the frigid air was rent by an agonised bellow.

It was Rufius.

CHAPTER TWENTY-FOUR

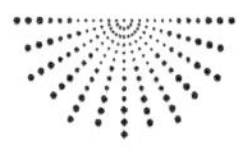

Lucia's chest pinched as the cry resounded across the farmyard, the raw agony almost palpable. Sucking in a breath, she inched forward until able to peer around the corner of the building they were sheltering behind. In front of her, six variously sized structures were positioned in a loose circle.

Directly opposite — a large sturdy, stone and tile construction, a single wooden door in the centre of the wall, and four shuttered windows evenly spaced along the façade — tendrils of smoke rising from both chimneys marking it as the main domicile. *Was that where Ovidius and his henchmen waited?*

As far as Lucia could discern there was no one guarding the property, and Feronia had given no indication anyone else was abroad. Ovidius must be supremely confident that Rufius had arrived without backup.

To her left — a couple of small outhouses built from thin wooden panels resembling, to Lucia's relatively inexperienced eye, storage huts and she dismissed them as being inconsequential. On the right — a larger wooden building, which Lucia surmised was probably a barn. The solid walls only went up a third of the height of the building; the upper portion being open slats topped by a precarious looking roof. Not somewhere you would hold a person captive.

That left the building she was hiding behind, and the one to her right. Craning her neck, Lucia stared at the solid wooden walls above her. Of substantial height, it looked to offer suitable protection from the elements but then as her eyes roved around the little complex, she noticed smoke coiling up from the roof of the remaining structure. It seemed significant that in so small a number of farm buildings, two of them required a fire.

Feronia whined again, bumping her shoulder into Lucia's side. Turning, Lucia was transfixed by the wolf's amber gaze, which bored into hers. Opening her mind, she restored their connection, although so in tune had they become, it was no longer necessary. Nodding at the unspoken question in Feronia's eyes, the pair crossed the small gap between the buildings, following the wall to the far corner, peeking around to check for anyone who might be watching for them.

Lucia stood for several moments, assessing the situation. Rufius was inside this building. Someone was hurting him, but how many more would she face? Were there several smaller rooms or one large one? Would the door screech on its hinges when she opened it? How long would it be before Marcellus and Marius arrived? Despite her brave words at the school, Lucia wished she had listened to the lanista and waited for him to organise a contingent of soldiers, so there was more than just a wolf with her — however monstrous that wolf might be.

At about the same moment Lucia took an ungainly tumble down the hill, Rufius stirred, the muscles in his arms, screaming from the tortuous angle by which he was strung up. Forcing his aching legs to take his weight, he welcomed the brief respite, and flexed his fingers in an attempt to counteract the numbness slowly paralysing his arms.

The room was cooler; the roaring blaze had dwindled to glowing embers. Perhaps Ovidius was finished branding him. Rufius tried to see what damage the man had inflicted, but it proved impossible. Ovidius struck him several times on his lower abdomen and across his back, out of his line of sight, which was maybe no bad thing.

Rufius shuddered in recollection. He had managed to maintain his silence but it was a close thing. The smell of seared skin as Ovidius pressed the scorching sword against his flesh was sickening, the pain — indescribable, while the glare from the flaming weapon lit the room. Now, other than the smouldering fire, all was in darkness.

Rufius listened, but all that met his ears was the sound of his own breathing, nothing to suggest another's presence. Inhaling slowly, he tried to shift into a less uncomfortable position, but what relief he was able to achieve was relative. The old wound in his leg was beginning to throb, and he knew he would not be able to put his weight on it for much longer.

The oppressive stillness was broken by the slap of footsteps along the passageway, and Rufius steeled himself. He accepted this was his death, he just prayed to the gods that it would be quick.

Ovidius entered the room, a sneer curling his lip. "Good morning, Gaius Rufius. I trust you slept well."

Rufius did not deign to reply, he just stared at the overseer, his face unreadable.

"I was considering bringing you some food, but it seems rather a waste when you will shortly be begging a ride from the ferryman." Flicking a denarius up and down as he spoke. "Fret not, I shall place the requisite coin under your tongue. I would rather your shade did not return."

Interesting, thought Rufius, *he fears the dead*. Watching Ovidius, he tried to predict the man's next move, but he was volatile and erratic. One minute he was striding up and down the room waving his hands and decrying the army, the senate, Emerita's officials — pretty much everyone. The next, he was quietly stoking up the fire, wedging a large log into the middle of the pit, thrusting the sword, and another metal object, into the flames.

Rufius closed his eyes, wishing he could have seen Lucia one last time. Her elfin face gazing up at him, her mischievous smile when she was prevaricating over something, her astonishing eyes enchanting him. So focused was he on conjuring her up, he missed the sizzle of sparks as Ovidius withdrew the sword from the blaze. Heat seared into his side, the shock wrenching an animalistic scream from the depths of his soul.

Gasping, Rufius blinked back unexpected tears, shaking his head to clear the muffled roaring which was dulling his senses, desperately clinging to sanity and consciousness. Water cascaded over him, which although refreshing in its coolness, stung his blistered skin. His vision cleared, sharpened, and he braced himself for the next assault.

"Apologise, Gaius Rufius. Apologise and hand over all your assets, your home, your servants, and your coin, and I may consider a reprieve." Tapping the sword on the rim of the fire pit.

Rufius goggled at Ovidius, and through lips almost sealed shut from swelling and dried blood, asked him to repeat his words.

Ovidius obliged, adding, "It seems fair compensation. You took everything from me, now I shall take everything from you. I expect you presume all the extra and unforeseen damage throughout the town to be accidental?" he crowed in glee. "It was I, you stupid fool, and you did not know. It kept you occupied, so you missed things unfolding right under your nose." Pausing for dramatic effect, he concluded. "I shall get it anyway. I have ways and means of getting what I want, just ask your wife."

Rufius could scarcely comprehend the depths of the man's madness. The levels of implication within Ovidius' words were repugnant. Slowly and deliberately, Rufius outlined why he would never willingly hand over anything to one so depraved.

"You killed without compunction or conscience. Your idea of justice was to crucify the perpetrators without trial, simply because you could. Now, I hear you mistreat your wife and her daughters. That you believe you are entitled to appropriate anything of mine upon my death, merely demonstrates how deranged you have become. You left me no choice, Ovidius; before I set out I drafted a missive, which will be handed to Quintus Antonius today. Even if you kill me, he will know of your treachery."

· · ·

Ovidius glared at Rufius, the mania distorting his mind and his hatred for the man hanging in front of him like a beast about to be slaughtered, becoming all-consuming. His fury burned hotter than the sword in the flames.

"It matters not. You are done, *commander*," he spat the last word. "By the time anyone discovers you are here, you will be nothing but bones, and I will be gone." Lifting the other implement from the fire, he toyed with it; twisting it around and making sure Rufius could see what he held.

The three prongs looked like massive claws and Rufius was reminded of Feronia, bitterly aware that the dangerous beast among them was not a wolf at all. There was only one reason anyone would use such a weapon.

A brave man, Rufius had faced much during his time in the army, but this merciless violence was beyond his experience. Even in battle, sworn enemies retained some empathy, and if a man had to die, it was done quickly and without malice. This also explained why he hated the spectacle of the arena; death in any of its forms was not entertaining at all.

Rufius tried to bank down the horror, his mind winging to Lucia, and her description of that afternoon in the amphitheatre. This must be akin to how she felt; to know you are about to be shredded, gutted like a fish by creatures with no empathy for their victims was chilling, and the stuff of never-ending nightmares.

Ovidius was muttering to himself, thrusting the iron in and out of the flames, twisting it this way and that, trying to ascertain how hot it was.

Rufius shut his eyes again.

There was nothing he could do now.

Marcellus, completely ignoring Lucia's request to delay an hour before he followed her, began gathering his most trusted guards, the instant she departed. All were serving or veteran soldiers. Hunting villains was what they lived for, and far preferable to watching over criminals and prisoners of war at the Gladiators' School.

Most had been involved in the search for Lucia, the majority were exhausted, yet without exception — once apprised of the developing situation — all clamoured to be included, relishing the idea of a good skirmish. While appreciating their enthusiasm, Marcellus pointed out this was impossible, for the school and bestiariorum could not be left unguarded.

Those he left in charge at the school, however, were tasked with preparing for a possible influx of injured personnel — friend or foe. Controlled chaos ensued, in the midst of which they heard a clatter of hooves and a moment later, Marius appeared waving a tablet and a piece of papyrus.

"Scaro woke me, gabbling something about Lucia going after Rufius. She asked him to wait an hour, but he was frightened for her, and came to tell me her intentions." The steward sounded flustered.

"She has already been here and taken Feronia. I know…" at the incredulous look on Marius' face, "…but I could not deny her request. The wolf will protect Lucia, I imagine, with her life."

Marius shook his head, and then continued, "Before coming, I checked around the domus and found this tablet, to be delivered to the procurator at the first hour. In light of its contents, I do not think I should wait. On a whim, I rode by way of Rufius' workshops and spotted this on one of the tables." After handing the tablet to Marcellus, who scanned it quickly, Marius unrolled the papyrus, revealing a map.

The two men pored over it, easily identifying the farm Rufius spotted hours earlier.

"This must be it; there is nothing else in the vicinity fitting Aurelia's description. We have to investigate," Marius postulated, "and I must apprise the procurator immediately. The information contained therein," indicating the tablet, "is too crucial to withhold any longer."

Marcellus concurred. "I agree, but please hurry, I fear for the lives of both Rufius and Lucia. Whatever Quintus Antonius decides, I shall set out forthwith. There is an insidious madness afoot. It is like a runaway wagon, totally beyond our control, and will only stop when it crashes. I doubt we can prevent the collision, but if we get there in time, maybe we can soften the landing and avert a tragedy. We *must* ensure no more blood is spilled at this man's hands. He cannot be allowed to escape."

Marius dashed out into the darkness. Quintus Antonius' abode was only one street away from the school, and by the time he returned, Marcellus and his contingent were waiting in the courtyard — armed, mounted, and raring to go.

"What news from the procurator?" Marcellus asked when Marius skidded to a halt next to him.

"We are to hasten to the farm, he has already sent a message to the garrison, and will organise half a centuria to follow us. He does not think it likely Ovidius has a large posse of henchmen, but feels it sensible to assume the worst."

Marcellus saw the sense in that and nodded as he clicked his horse. Marius mounted the stallion he had borrowed from Rufius' stables, presuming his master would approve, and joined Marcellus at the head of the line. The din created by several horses trotting through the quiet streets, deafening in the slumbering town, goading more than one resident, blissfully unaware of the reason, to grumble about the inconsiderate behaviour of thoughtless louts.

They were less than an hour behind Lucia.

While Marcellus, Marius and their detachment of soldiers rode into a day slowly dawning, Lucia and Feronia were at the door to the building in which Lucia surmised Rufius was being held. It was standing ajar, so the pair slipped through the gap, soundlessly. This brought them into a passageway, running the full length of the building. From where they stood, Lucia could see four doors. Three were wide open but one, at the far end, was closed.

That must be where Rufius was being held, the only thing emanating from the remaining rooms was gloom and silence. *Where were Ovidius' accomplices? He could not subdue Rufius singlehandedly.* Motioning towards the end of the corridor, Lucia took two steps then paused, struck by a devilish idea.

"Ovidius thinks he has sent me to my death," she mused out loud. "Granted, I would not be at Castulo yet, but he is not to know whether I died from my injury."

Feronia… facing the huge creature, Lucia spoke into her mind… *I think a touch of ghostly retribution is called for, what say you?*

Feronia's upper lip curled back in a parody of a smile, and Lucia grinned back, a wicked gleam in her eyes. *I do believe we deserve a little fun,* she continued and sent a series of images to the watching wolf.

Feronia tossed her head and moved forwards, scenting the musty air, the metallic tang of blood, sweat, and fear assaulting her sensitive nose. Growling low in her chest, the sound vibrating around the narrow wooden corridor, she sent her agreement back to Lucia.

Listening intently, Lucia heard curious noises emanating from the other side of the wooden walls. She was unable to discern what they were, but doubted they related to anything pleasant. Upon reaching the door, Lucia peered through the cracks.

Opposite, she could see a large fire burning on a kind of raised, square, freestanding hearth. Ovidius was standing over it, jabbing something into the flames. To her right, she spied Rufius and clapped a hand over her mouth to prevent her own scream from gurgling up.

Her beloved was hanging from his wrists, his naked body covered in blood, bruises, and what appeared to be savage blisters; his face so swollen he was scarcely recognisable.

For one heart-stopping moment she thought he was dead. Then she noticed careful movement as he tried, presumably, to adjust his body into a less awkward position — her stomach clenched, and her fury seethed.

Taking a steadying breath, Lucia asked Feronia to growl and to continue growling until she gave the signal to stop. *Long and low, like a hum,* she elaborated, *I will speak over it; hopefully it will strike terror into his evil heart.*

The wolf did as her human companion requested, emitting a rumbling sound. It rolled round the wooden building, vibrating like distant thunder, and the air crackled.

Lucia began to speak.

CHAPTER TWENTY-FIVE

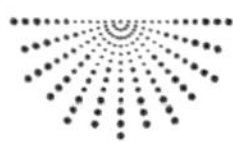

Ovidius was about to taunt his victim again, when something made him stop stoking the fire. He cocked his head and listened. No, he could discern nothing untoward. Deciding he must be imagining things, he turned his attention back to heating the blade of the sword.

Then he heard the voice.

"Hostus Ovidius Caecus." There was a pause then his name was repeated, barely audible over a peculiar rumble, which had just begun. Ovidius contemplated the possibility of an earthquake, but the ground was not shifting under him. Puzzled, he frowned, and again was about to dismiss it as fancy, when...

"Your day of judgement is nigh. Too often have you blamed others for your own failings. Too often have you punished those least deserving of your cruelty. You are a thief, a liar, a cheat, a bully, a kidnapper, and a murderer... murderer..." the last word drawn out slowly, dying away like an echo.

Busy fiddling with his instruments of torture, Ovidius

was suddenly held immobile. His eyes tracked around the room, unsure what was going on.

To Rufius, it was like the music of the gods. The sweet harmony of her voice wove around his mutilated body, caressing his heart, and reviving his soul. Lucia was alive.

Forcing his lids open, he scanned the decrepit space, but she was not there. For one irrational moment he wondered, in his desperation to see her one last time, whether he had conjured her up from the flames in the fire pit.

Then her voice came again, and even though he could not see her, Rufius knew she was no shade.

He waited.

"You would sell me to Calvus Bruccius?" the voice accused. "You orchestrate my abduction, by having me tricked, knocked unconscious, trussed up like a chicken, and then handed off, without shame."

There came a long melancholy sigh, it blended with the rumble, creating a mournful wail. Ice trickled down Ovidius' spine as the hairs went up on the back of his neck, and he gripped the three-pronged weapon.

"You think to kill one already dead?" the voice mocked. "Oh dear, you have much to learn about the afterlife. The gods do not smile on those who flout their rules. I was dying when you handed me over, he could not save me, though he tried. He just left me there in the sun, for the wild things to scavenge. Now you will not get paid, and Calvus Bruccius is missing a promised slave. Think of how this will besmirch your reputation, not to mention the lost coin. So sad."

Had he been able to summon up the energy, Rufius would have laughed at Lucia's dolorous tones. He did, however, manage a satisfied humph.

The singsong voice went on; listing all the things Ovidius would answer for, not least that he was currently preparing to murder another. Lucia let her voice strengthen, her displeasure apparent, spurring Ovidius to stutter his reasons, his excuses, and his justification.

"Pray, cease your yapping. You cannot retract what is done. The omens foretell your doom…" she intoned, and then paused as though contemplating, concluding softly, "…however… perhaps there is a way to redeem yourself."

"What, what must I do?" Terror spiralling through his gut, Ovidius, now virtually grovelling in the dirt, gibbered hysterically. He begged for clemency; he would do anything, anything to appease the gods.

A craven coward, Ovidius had no desire to meet his death at the hands of a malevolent shade. Distractedly, he released his grip on the tool, and it fell back into the fire, as he repeated his plea. "Please, whatever it is, I am willing to do it."

Silence met his entreaty.

Hesitantly, Ovidius rose to his feet, disconcerted. *Had he imagined it? Had the gods really abandoned him? It was this farm; he knew it was too isolated. It was probably just the wind in the trees.* His imagination ran riot.

The quiet hung like a pall, and another icy finger trailed its way down Ovidius' spine. He shivered.

From her vantage point, Lucia prepared to fire her last salvo. Whatever happened she was going into that room, but she wanted to mitigate any chance of the veteran soldier inflicting further damage on Rufius.

Drawing herself up to her full, albeit diminutive, height, Lucia, nodding to Feronia who growled louder, put forward her demand in stentorian tones.

"Release your prisoner. Or you shall surely die!"

Ovidius gawked and, fumbling in his panic, began to unshackle Rufius. It took precious moments, he was working alone — it had taken three men to hook the rope over the beam and lift the unconscious man into his current position. Rufius was exceedingly tall, with a powerful physique — not easy for one person to manoeuvre. He weighed too much for the portly overseer, who although tall and once as brawny as Rufius, was no longer fit.

Huffing and puffing with effort, when the rope suddenly loosened, Ovidius simply dropped him. Rufius crumpled, his muscles spasming at the abrupt change, unable to hold him upright. He hit the floor with a thud, exhaling an agonised groan, his face contorted in pain.

Lucia hissed her wrath at this cavalier treatment of her husband, the sound slicing through air thick with tension.

The possibility he might have miscalculated began to gnaw at the fringe of Ovidius' broken mind. Sweat dripping off him, he apologised profusely, gabbling frantically over his words, still hoping for a reprieve.

From beyond the confines of the room there was no response.

Rufius winced as he tried to get his circulation going — arms and legs numb from being strung up for so many hours. Knowing his impetuous wife, he guessed she would probably burst through the door at any moment, and he needed to be upright, ready to do what he could to protect her from this lunatic.

Managing to roll onto his side, he tucked his legs under him and using the floor as leverage, twisted into a seated position. Leaning his battered body against a wooden post, he rubbed his wrists and arms, flexing his fingers, ignoring the peculiar tingling, and throbbing soreness this engendered.

The oppressive silence unnerved Ovidius. Terror of the unknown, of facing the living dead, clawed at his throat, prompting him to edge stealthily backwards, to the raised fire pit. Without conscious awareness, he reached behind him for either of the two weapons lying in the flames, yelping when his fingers came into contact with the hilt of the sword.

After so long in the fire, the blade was hotter than the spits on which animals were roasted — the forged handle, scorching. The sudden jerk of his hand knocked the weapon onto the floor, where it landed with a dull thud, sparks skittering over the dust, loud in the deathly stillness.

Ovidius froze.

Peeking through the cracks, Lucia studied Ovidius, guessing he was just intimidated enough to be caught off balance. At the same moment the sword hit the floor, she gave Feronia the signal, and the two launched themselves with such force that the door gave up any desire to maintain its solidity and exploded in a shower of splintered wood.

Lucia, the pounding in her head causing her some vision disturbance, was tired of playing games. This ended now.

Storming into the room, her hair swirling around her head — reminiscent of Medusa's snakes, and wielding her small dagger, Lucia cursed Ovidius. Her condemnation included what Rufius presumed to be colourful Vettone obscenities. Certainly, he had never heard most of them in all his long years in the army, her invective, masterful and relentless.

The overseer fell back against her verbal onslaught, his body brushing the fire pit. The heat from the flames and the abject relief that the voice did not belong to a vengeful ghoul come to haunt him, provoked a disastrous reaction.

Feronia circled the edge of the room, her eyes fixed on Ovidius, her baleful glare and unceasing growl shattering the last vestiges of sanity clinging to the far depths of Ovidius' mind.

"You would kill my husband?" Lucia shrieked. "You reprehensible, low-life blaggard. How dare you presume to be judge and executioner to a man who has only ever sought to save and protect. You who steals, perverts, and vilifies, believe yourself a suitable arbitrator?" A humourless laugh tumbled over her lips while she berated Ovidius. Feronia paced, her leonine head swinging between Lucia and the overseer — ever-watchful amber eyes missing nothing.

While Ovidius was focused on Lucia, Rufius pushed himself to his feet. It was a painstakingly slow business, in part because of his injuries and continuing stiffness, in part so he did not catch Ovidius' attention. If he could just encourage his legs and arms to follow instructions he might be able to summon up the energy to tackle Ovidius to the floor and subdue him.

❧

When they looked back on it later, it was difficult to recall, exactly, who moved first. Lucia and Ovidius were facing off to one side of the room. Feronia was advancing without seeming to, her astute mind, maybe recognising that this maniac was even more dangerous now because he had nothing to lose, prickled in warning. Rufius was resting against the post. Outside, the pale winter sun broke through the grey dawn. A single ray illuminated the bizarre tableau, and momentarily dazzled Lucia.

She flinched, ducking her head to avoid the glare, blinking rapidly.

It was all Ovidius needed. In that instant, he grabbed the three-pronged tool and lunged at Rufius. Despite being blinded by the sunbeam, Lucia anticipated his intent, and with an enraged yell, hurled herself between the two, swinging her dagger wildly.

Simultaneously, she heard her husband's shouted warning, as he tried to stop her, and felt the scalding metal brand her skin. Just as suddenly it was gone, when in a flash of grey, Feronia darted forward.

The she-wolf pounced, snarling and gnashing her teeth. With a thunderous roar, she clamped her massive jaw around Ovidius' neck, his astonished screech reduced to a ghastly gurgle as Feronia ripped out his throat. Blood exploded from the wound, arcing in warm frothy jets as Ovidius' heart continued to pump urgently. A spontaneous reflex by the organ tasked with keeping a body alive; its necessity fading rapidly.

Arms flailing, his death inevitable, Ovidius struck, the

vicious weapon still gripped in his hand, slicing through the wolf's chest. Relaxing her jaw, Feronia lifted her head and bayed, the same long ululating unearthly howl last heard months ago, and a lifetime away. As her blood mingled with that of the dying overseer, Feronia ripped open his torso, effectively eviscerating him, leaving no chance of survival.

A gutless man, Hostus Ovidius Caecus died as he lived, the irony of that not lost on Rufius. Singularly indifferent to the grisly mess, he took a step towards the huddle of woman and wolf on the floor, and then hesitated. Desperate to embrace his wife, to check her for injuries, to hold her and never let go, Rufius was unwilling to intrude on so heart-breaking a farewell.

Lucia fell onto her knees next to the great wolf; doing anything she could to staunch the bleeding. Weeping uncontrollably, she held the devastating wound closed, begging for help, pleading for someone to save Feronia. Images flooded her mind. Memories of shared moments, the wolf's gratitude for her liberation, fleeting though it was, and her glee in killing the man who had caused so much anguish.

"Please don't die," Lucia sobbed. "You are dear to me. I cannot lose you."

Let me go, my friend. I am old. My body was already weakening. Had I stayed with the pack, I would have to fight to remain Alpha. Here, I die saving you and your mate. It is an honourable death.

Lucia curled herself around the fatally injured creature, cradling her head, stroking fur already becoming stiff, begging her not to give up. Feronia lifted her head and stared straight into Lucia's eyes — luminous amber on sage green. Silent communication flickered between them, and as Lucia watched, the tawny glow began to dim.

I smell freedom. Feronia's 'tone' one of astonishment, drawing a hint of a chuckle from Lucia.

It is time.

Swallowing her sorrow, Lucia summoned up a smile. Kissing the long snout, she gently fondled the proud ears, rocking Feronia as though the massive she-wolf was a mere cub. Nestling her head on Lucia's shoulder, Feronia whined a little, huffed a weary sigh, and died.

Their minds melded, Lucia felt her leave. Their connection severed, leaving nothing but a vast emptiness.

"Nooooooooooooooooooooooooooooooooooooo." Her desolate wail reverberated around the complex of buildings, bouncing off the structures to come back in lilting echoes. A fresh bout of tears overtook her. Ignoring the excruciating spasms lancing through him with every movement, Rufius hunkered down on the dusty and bloodstained ground, gathered his wife against him, and scattered feather-light kisses over her face.

"Lucia my love, she saved your life. I know it is heartbreaking, but her death was honourable," unknowingly repeating Feronia's thoughts.

Lucia tried to reply but her throat was clogged with sobs, and what was there to say? Rufius was correct. Feronia died a noble death, protecting the only person who truly understood her. Rufius was still speaking, but she could not make any sense of his words, they seemed to be drifting to her from a great distance.

Grief, fear, and pain were taking their toll, rendering Lucia incapable of comprehending what was real and what was illusion. The only certainty being that she was safely wrapped in her husband's arms, with a dead wolf at her feet.

Lucia heard herself make a funny little sound, and everything went black.

CHAPTER TWENTY-SIX

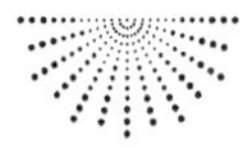

Mere moments later, a flurry of people tumbled into the room only to pause, held motionless by the spectacle that met their eyes.

In a room liberally splattered with blood, veteran soldier, and city official, Gaius Rufius Atellus, thankfully alive, although naked and looking very much worse for wear was sitting on the filthy floor.

His unconscious wife, Lucia Atella, was in his arms, the grubby bandage on her head coming unravelled. A huge wolf, which appeared to have been gutted, lay alongside Hostus Ovidius Caecus, similarly disembowelled, his head lolling at an impossible angle — the reason clear upon closer inspection.

"Gaius Rufius…"

"Dominus…"

"Rufius…"

"What in Hades happened?"

A barrage of questions was fired at Rufius, who lifted his hand as though to hold them back. As quickly and succinctly as he was able, through cracked, sore, and swollen lips, he explained what had occurred from the moment he left the house the previous night until this moment.

"I cannot tell you what Lucia endured, for she appeared less than half of one hour ago. I think Ovidius caught her with a hot iron, and her head seems injured." His brow creased in confusion, having no idea how that came about.

"I think the blood is that of Ovidius and the wolf, but I cannot be certain. Feronia died saving Lucia's life, and it all became too much for my wife, who, probably to her own mortification, although I shall never remind her of it, fainted." Rufius spoke in tones suggesting only mild interest, completely at odds with the gruesome scene.

As a man, the crowd moved, willing hands helping up Rufius, who refused to relinquish his hold on Lucia. Someone tucked an old sack around Rufius' waist, more to stave off the morning chill than in concern for his dignity. Others began the unpleasant task of tidying the bodies of the wolf and Ovidius as best they could.

The latter would be returned to the city, his widow given the option of burying him. When it looked as though the men would simply whisk Feronia way to be tossed in a pit, as was typical for animals killed in the arena, Rufius interposed. His voice hoarse as he fought to suppress fatigue, stress, and acute discomfort.

"Please, Feronia deserves to be treated with utmost respect, and she will be granted a heroine's burial. I shall arrange an appropriate tomb, whether she is cremated or inhumed."

Those involved in the removal of the two corpses halted, and one of them scurried off to find something suitable to wrap around the wolf.

"As you wish, Gaius Rufius," Marcellus said as though soothing a factious child, while making sure the two men assisting Rufius into the daylight did not jar him. "Now, please sit here while we organise a medicus and a wagon. My men are quite capable of handling this little mess…" the incongruity of the lanista's statement, tugged a ghost of a smile from Rufius, "…and I do believe we are about to be joined by some of your garrison. Enjoy the sunshine." Marcellus grinned, glad the shadow darkening his friends' lives was finally banished, relief making him suddenly light of heart and possibly a trifle giddy.

Rufius grinned back, albeit wearily, while his escorts helped him and his precious armful to a long wooden bench perched against the adjoining building. Holding him steady, they lowered him carefully onto the cool wood. Lucia stirred, yawned, pushed her head under his chin, settled against him more comfortably and fell into a natural sleep.

Rufius kissed the top of her head, and sent a prayer of thanks to Fortuna for smiling on them, for granting them another chance at life. Between them, they had suffered enough near-death encounters to last several lifetimes, and he trusted Fate would be kind enough to allow them to live out the rest of their existence in relative peace.

Just as Marcellus predicted, it was not long before another contingent of men rode into the courtyard, led by Quintus Antonius Valerius. The procurator was off his horse almost before the group came to a complete standstill, rushing over to where Rufius was sitting.

"My friend, what…?" his question died on his lips as he noticed a number of Marcellus' men coming out of a building, carrying two bodies, one of which was a massive grey wolf. Aghast, he brought his gaze back to Rufius, narrowing his eyes at the state of the couple. "Rufius?"

Rufius shuffled along the bench, making some space and, once Quintus Antonius was seated, repeated his tale. "I do not know what Lucia has suffered. I only discovered she was alive seconds before she and Feronia hurtled into that room," he concluded, cocking his head in the direction of the barn-like structure. "She fainted and, although roused momentarily, I think she is now asleep and I would rather not disturb her for a while."

Antonius nodded his understanding and asked a few pertinent questions, before striding over to where Marcellus was discussing something with Marius and offered to take over.

"I expect you both have duties to which you should attend. This," waving his hand around, "is part of my purview." He contemplated the ramshackle collection of buildings, his brow furrowed. "I shall instruct my soldiers to search this complex thoroughly and, once cleared of anything important, I do believe I will raze it to the ground. Too much evil lurks here. The very buildings are imbued with it. Even with the death of Ovidius, his malevolence lingers."

Unaware of how poetic he sounded, Antonius, beamed benignly at the two men and then began shouting orders at the contingent who had accompanied him.

Rufius watched as, with a speed that never failed to impress him, the regulated efficiency, typical of the Roman Army turned chaos into order. He was so engrossed by it all, he did not hear Salonius approaching and winced when the affable medicus rested a hand on his shoulder, in tacit announcement of his presence.

"My apologies, Gaius Rufius, Quintus Antonius indicated that my presence was a necessity. It seems he was correct."

"Naught a proper bath and some ointment cannot cure," Rufius replied, stiffly. Salonius folded his arms and stared at him until Rufius shifted uncomfortably under his gimlet gaze.

"I might be getting on in years, but I am not an imbecile and my eyes rarely deceive me. Let me at least check you over. A more thorough evaluation of your injuries must wait until we get you both home, and into cleaner surroundings." He glanced around with distaste, taking in the deplorable state of the little farmstead, not to mention the deplorable state of his two patients.

"Please check Lucia first. Ovidius slashed at her when she got between us…"

Salonius raised a quizzical eyebrow, so for the third time in less than an hour Rufius told his tale while grudgingly, it must be admitted, submitting to a cursory examination.

Lucia woke while the medicus was checking her over, momentarily bemused by the sound of so many people talking over and around her. Her head was aching badly, and her arm stung. She mumbled something, only to be gently hushed by Rufius and Salonius.

"Let Salonius do his job, my love. Soon we shall be home, where I imagine you might appreciate a proper bath." Referring to the capacious tub she folded herself bodily into, as opposed to the public baths he and his fellow Romans frequented. He was pleased to see a smile curving her lips.

"A bath would be quite perfect," she agreed, already thinking about which scented oil she would add, an effective diversion from darker thoughts.

Salonius completed his check-up, and Antonius declared himself satisfied his men had investigated every nook and cranny of the farm. Their extensive search uncovered nothing except two rickety-looking wagons in one of the outbuildings. Of Ovidius' three accomplices who set upon Rufius, there was no trace.

It was presumed they absconded when it became apparent their continued association with Ovidius might lead to an untimely end. One of the soldiers, dispatched to collect Eos and Ares, found them waiting patiently where they had been left, at the far side of the olive grove. He also retrieved Lucia's satchel, which he spotted swinging from a branch, the soldier led the animals down the hill to the farm. The two horses, serenely indifferent to the overnight upheaval, were now placidly munching on some hay, adding to the surprisingly domestic backdrop.

Not long after, and despite Rufius' assertion he was fit enough to ride home, he and Lucia were persuaded onto the back of one of the wagons, one without a cage, to Lucia's relief. Antonius, thoughtfully, had placed several blankets on the hard, wooden base, making the journey a little more comfortable.

The other wagon was for transporting the bodies of Feronia and Ovidius

The sun was climbing to its zenith, a few hardy birds twittered, seeking what food they could in the middle of winter. The mood among those returning to Emerita was relaxed, carefree almost, as though an intolerable burden had been lifted — which for some it had. Even the air seemed fresher, the sun brighter, evoking the aftermath of a wild storm, when everything is washed clean.

One of the soldiers began to whistle a popular tune, and soon the whole company joined in. An enthusiastic performance outweighed any lack of harmony, the disparate assortment of voices blending effortlessly, as though with so simple a composition, grim memories would be extinguished, and in their place, the hope for a future untarnished.

Lucia slept most of the way home, rousing just as the wagon rolled into their street. When they pulled to a halt, the front

door of the domus opened and a crowd of people tumbled out, the joy on their faces at the safe return of their master and mistress a balm to Rufius and Lucia. Marius helped the couple down, escorting them into the cool atrium, fending off the questions flying from all angles.

Laughing, Rufius held up a hand and they fell quiet. "I will be happy to give you all the gory details, and trust me, they are very gory, but first my wife needs some medical attention—"

"As do you," a deep voice interrupted.

"—and, as the good medicus here reminds me, so do I. Please be patient. It has been a tortuous ordeal, neither of us is unscathed, but it could have been worse. Give us time to rest, after which, we shall gather in the triclinium, whereupon I, we both, promise to share the sorry tale."

And with that the household had to be content, because Salonius shooed Lucia and Rufius along to their cubiculum. Another, far more detailed examination was undertaken. Flavia and Tullia were summoned to fetch water, bowls, and cloths and assist the medicus in cleaning the several wounds and blistered burns. It was a slow process, especially with the blisters, because the skin had a tendency to peel if a cloth was pressed too firmly, but in order to clean the area a little pressure was required.

In the end, Salonius suggested they soak several unused sponges in the mixture he had concocted and place the sodden article on the blister, without pressing down. The mixture would drain out of the sponge over the wound, hopefully rinsing away any stray bits of dust and dirt.

Tullia and Flavia were appalled at the idea of applying sponges, considering them unclean even when new — their use normally being to wipe a person's backside after morning ablutions. Salonius assured them these new ones were as clean as the cloths, but to appease them, asked for a bucket of boiling water, which he poured over the sponges prior to use. Slightly mollified, the women got back to work and eventually pronounced themselves happy with their efforts.

Salonius administered a liniment, infused with frankincense and myrrh, to every laceration, and a milk and honey ointment to each burn, before bandaging all those requiring it. Lucia's head needed tending to, and Salonius persuaded her into a draft containing poppy juice, to induce a restful slumber.

As the medicus was finishing up, he noticed Lucia was already fast asleep, the draft working quickly. Rufius was not far behind but he refused the same mixture, claiming he needed his wits about him, in truth he hated the after-effects of the opiate.

By the sixth hour, the house was quiet, Lucia and Rufius were asleep, and the staff had returned to their regular duties. A sense of suppressed excitement hung in the air, however, for there was still the small matter of a titillating story.

Elsewhere in the town, Marcellus and his assistants, rather later than normal began their daily routine. Thankfully, during the coldest of the winter months there were no games to prepare for, but there was always training for the men, and the feeding of the animals as well as their enclosures mucking out — all time-consuming chores.

Marcellus stood for long moments outside the wolves' pen, speculating whether the rest of the pack realised their leader was not coming back. The group seemed restless but not distressed, maybe the animals were somehow aware of Feronia's death, or maybe they adapted more quickly than humans.

Shrugging, there was nothing he could do. Perhaps when Lucia was feeling better, he would ask her to commune with the pack, to explain what occurred at the farm. Marcellus shook his head, chuckling at the absurdity of his thoughts.

Less than a year ago, had anyone told him he would meet someone who could converse with wild creatures, he would have laughed them out of the school, yet here he was, actually looking forward to the next time it would happen. Still chuckling, he pushed all that out of his mind and continued with his tasks.

In a modest office, not far from the Gladiators' School, Quintus Antonius Valerius was sitting at his desk staring into space. This would almost certainly be his penultimate report before departing Emerita. He had been recalled to the capital of Empire, his tenure complete.

Looking forward to seeing his wife, Claudia, and getting reacquainted with their close-knit group of friends, he realised he would miss this small town, and the untamed countryside surrounding it.

Antonius disliked the hustle and bustle of city life, the opposite of his wife, who although had visited twice, preferred the vibrant lifestyle of Rome to this unassuming backwater. A wry smile pulled at his lips, imagining her reaction when he told of recent events. Unassuming indeed.

His new position within the Imperial administration sounded interesting, if not slightly unnerving. Political machinations were the bane of his life, and something he definitely had *not* missed living so far from Rome. The new emperor, Gaius Julius Caesar Germanicus, better known as Caligula, had succeeded his uncle Tiberius Claudius Nero in the early months of the year.

Antonius, who had met Tiberius once or twice immediately prior to the latter's remove to Capri, was saddened to learn of the death of the once meritorious ruler. As for Caligula, who initially showed every indication of being a virtuous and moderate emperor was now rumoured to be afflicted by an underlying mania. Antonius suspected life in Rome would be even more bizarre than that of Emerita, which would be quite an achievement after these last few months.

Tapping his stylus, Antonius brought his mind back to the present and wrote his account of the incident, knowing it would need to be added to, once he had more details.

Describing the necessity of using the garrison for a civilian matter required prudent language and, mindful of how easily documents could be misinterpreted by those seeking to undermine an official, Antonius took his time making sure the wording was unambiguous.

The day continued as though the drama at a humble farm in the picturesque countryside had never happened.

CHAPTER TWENTY-SEVEN

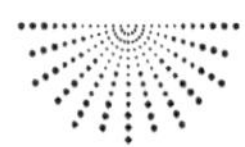

The day was nearly over by the time Lucia and Rufius woke. Under strict orders from Salonius, the household did not disturb the couple, going about their daily chores as unobtrusively as possible.

The sun was already setting when Lucia roused, aware of a weight across her stomach. Delicious warmth spread through her and, ignoring her protesting muscles and the dull throb in her head, twisted around until she was facing Rufius.

Her husband was almost unrecognisable. His poor face was mangled, and his lips split, but to Lucia he was the most beautiful sight. After the ugly escalation of violence confronting them throughout these last few days, she continued to be astonished they both survived.

Unable to help herself, she smoothed a gentle hand along his stubbled jaw, careful not to catch any of the abrasions, and around the soft shell of his ear into his shaggy hair.

Would he forgive her thoughtless behaviour? Would he want her to remain as his wife after all he had suffered for her? She did not deserve it, but by all the Gods, she hoped he did — his arm around her waist, tucking her against him while he slept, suggested he did. She was not sure she could live without him. Yes, she would eat and sleep and breathe, but it would be an existence, not a life.

The sheer raw strength of her love for Rufius was powerful enough to make her whole body tingle, just by looking at him. A love she never expected or looked for, but once found could never be erased. Stretching up, she brushed his lips with hers and as she drew back, met his sleepy gaze.

Time stopped.

Or so it seemed.

Lucia watched Rufius study her pale features. His dark brown eyes held her captive, but this was a prison she had no intention of escaping — unless he wanted to release her. She wanted to tell him how much she loved him, how sorry she was for being the reason he was hurt, but words refused to form.

A large hand slid up her body, making her shiver in anticipation, despite all the aches and pains they both suffered. Over her hip, tracing the curve of her waist, skimming her breast, coming to rest at the base of her throat. His thumb stroked the erratic pulse fluttering there, before curling around the back of her neck, fingers entangling in her wild chestnut curls.

He rested his forehead on hers.

"Lucia…" her name merely a whisper.

"*Mi dilecte,*" her murmured endearment as tangible as a caress.

"I thought I'd lost you, I thought…" he stopped. The fear she was dead or worse, locked up, being tortured, only to discover she had been sold to a ruthless mine operator, rose like bile in his throat. He swallowed, shifted his position, and sucked in breath, wincing when his injuries chafed.

"Please forgive me, Rufius. I had no mind to put you through such distress." Lucia paused, then desperate to confess, to get it all out in the open, continued, "It was my own fault, I should have trusted my instinct, but I did not, and look at the consequences. I cannot bear knowing you were so cruelly treated because of me and understand completely if you deem my presence in your life too disruptive. I can easily leave, it would take me moments to collect my belong—" a finger on her lips halted her stream of words.

"Lucia, my love, you think I would put you aside?" His voice was impassive, giving Lucia no clue as to his mood. The same finger slid under her chin, tilting it so Rufius could see her expression in the waning light. Lucia nodded, keeping her eyelids downcast, unable to meet his gaze, dreading the censure she expected to see. "Lucia, please look at me."

Slowly she raised her eyes and blinked. Rufius was smiling, maybe a little sadly, but his eyes burned with emotion.

"My beautiful wife, there is nothing to forgive, and why you would ever imagine I might want to live without you is beyond me. It was not your fault I was ambushed… hush and listen," when Lucia tried to interrupt with a strenuous denial.

Rufius explained what led to his decision to go to the farm alone. "You were not the only one who did not pay heed to instinct. I was not prepared to delay the search for the farm until the morning. That *he* might have abducted and taken you there for his own vile ends was more than I could handle, to wait might have had fatal consequences." Wilfully disregarding the fact that, notwithstanding his best efforts, it did — albeit with an unforeseen twist.

"I did not, could not, wait. I slipped out of the house unnoticed, went to my workshop where I scoured one of my maps until I found what I presumed to be the farm and headed directly there. Being cognisant of all the dangers and risks on any mission is fundamental to any successful military campaign. I tried to prepare for every eventuality, but I forgot I was working against one without rational thought. They caught me off guard and…" Rufius stopped, his jaw working, tortuous hours in a dusty barn crowding into his mind.

"Please tell me it all." Lucia's persuasive tones jolted him back to the present,

"I am not sure I should, it was… disagreeable." A monumental understatement.

"Yet you will expect to hear what happened to me." Gently chiding. "What did you say many moons ago, when entreating me to tell about my day in the arena? Talking about it will help you come to terms with it, is what you said, and your words are true. To share your experience, however traumatic, loosens its grip on your heart and mind, and the process of healing can begin. I doubt such sage advice has changed between then and now."

She grinned suddenly, and it lit her face, sparking an involuntary response within Rufius, so sensuous it was indecent. *Damn his aching body.*

Lifting up on her elbow, Lucia scattered butterfly-soft kisses over his sore face. "Tell me."

The moment her lips touched his skin, he lost the fight. Well, to be fair, he lost the fight the instant he saw her tied to a stake — but occasionally he attempted to maintain the upper hand. Her lips however, stole his sanity, so he gave in and, trying to skirt over the more lurid details, Rufius imparted the rest of his tale.

There was a long silence. Lucia, appalled at what her husband endured was humbled, and her heart sore. Rufius was not about to let her off the hook and, wise to her sensitive soul, sought to divert her by demanding she reciprocate. Lucia gathered her thoughts and lay back on her pillow. Her eyes were on the ceiling, but she was seeing a whole different scene.

"It was beginning to rain. I was coming home from the bestiariorum, when a rather disreputable looking man who begged me to come and check his horse waylaid me. My intuition told me to ignore his plea and get home as quickly as possible. I wish I had listened to it." Ruefully. "He sounded so desolate, and I did not want a sick horse left unattended in the encroaching bad weather and the cold night. He took me to a field and when I stroked the mare, who by the way we need to rescue, poor dear, she has been badly neglected..." going on to describe the horse's woes.

Rufius chuckled at how quickly she could go off on a tangent. Lying on his side, elbow on the pillow, he rested his head on one hand, while seeking her hand with the other, entwining their fingers. "You were stroking the horse," he reminded.

"Oh yes, sorry, when I did I was assailed with horrible images of cruelty by the man beside me. Trying not to show my anxiety, I demanded he let me buy her. I offered a ridiculous sum. He agreed, and put out his hand, saying you shake hands to seal a deal. I have never heard of such a thing, but did not wish to upset him, possibly voiding the agreement. I put my hand out. Instead of shaking it, he dragged me closer to him, and then everything is a blank until I woke up in a cart miles from home."

Lucia divulged what transpired on the lonely road to Castulo. How Agapito realised he had been deceived and his decision to bring her home. "I think I arrived back here not long after you left. I know Marius had no idea you were gone because he came to find you. I wanted to come straight after you, but everyone insisted I wait until Salonius had checked me over, and he made it very clear I was in no fit state for anything except bed. I think he added something to the brew he persuaded me to drink, because almost immediately I was asleep." Her disgruntled expression prompted another chuckle from her husband.

Lucia gave Rufius a full description of the events leading up to her explosive entry into the room he was trussed up in. Rufius listened, his mouth agape, astonished at her tenacity, courage, and sheer dumb luck. She faltered, her words dwindling, as she came to the moment Feronia and she arrived at the door.

"When I saw what he had done, what he was about to do, my heart stopped. For one horrible moment I thought you were dead, and my world began to disintegrate. Then I spotted movement, as though you were attempting to relieve the stretch on your muscles, and I knew there was a chance." She paused. "I struggle to comprehend that it only happened this morning. It feels surreal. How did we survive?"

Rufius lifted their joined hands and kissed her knuckles, still scuffed from her adventures.

"You do not need to continue, my love. From this point our stories almost coincide, except you lost Feronia. A heroic act by one who had no cause to trust or protect humans. I am sorry she died."

Lucia felt tears forming again. *Not again,* she thought wearily, *I did not think I had anything left to cry.* Swallowing her sobs, and changing the subject, she asked gruffly, "Do you suppose we are expected to get up?" Twisting her head, she noticed it was already dark outside, and although hours since she ate anything, she wasn't hungry. All she wanted to do was stay in the comfortable bed, in the arms of her husband.

"When did you last eat?" Rufius read her thoughts.

She shrugged. "I do not recall, but I am not hungry. The thought of food…" she shook her head, "…no, my stomach is not quite ready. All I want to do is stay here with you, away from the world and all its drama, just for a little longer." Smiling shyly.

Rufius stared down into her wan face, stroked a finger along her cheek, and slid off the bed.

Lucia frowned at him. *Really, she had just said she wanted to stay here with him, and he gets up...humph,* not the reaction she hoped for.

"I am only going to find us some sustenance, and we can eat it in bed." He winked, and hobbled painfully out of the room. Halfway along the colonnaded walkway, he met Marius, who stood in front of him, effectively blocking his path.

"Dominus, please return to your cubiculum. I was coming to see whether you required anything. Clearly, I am too late," Marius chastised, his expression one of resigned amusement.

"I hoped to beg some food. Neither of us feels up to the rigmarole of dressing, and eating in the triclinium, and Lucia thinks she is not hungry, but we have not eaten for hours. Might you be so kind as to bring us a platter and if possible, two goblets of calda?" Opening his palms, his tones contrite.

Marius grinned, and saying he would be back forthwith, retraced his steps towards the kitchen. Rufius made his slow way back to the bedchamber sinking back onto the thick bedcovers in relief.

"Marius was coming to check on us. He is organising some food."

Lucia tried to make herself look presentable, but accepted it was a losing battle and opted to burrow under the bedclothes when Marius appeared several moments later. The steward was carrying a tray on which stood two steaming cups of calda and a large platter of food that smelt heavenly. Lucia's stomach growled, contradicting her claim she was not hungry and making the two men laugh.

All of a sudden, a lightness of spirit suffused those in the room and, inexplicably, Lucia and Rufius felt revitalised. Unbidden their eyes met, each recognising the subtle fluctuation.

It was as though all the elements and emotions of their lives had been tossed in the air, to reform and flutter back to earth in a new pattern. A steadfast and indissoluble pattern, which would endure throughout this lifetime and into the next.

Yes, they both suffered to a greater or lesser extent, it would take time to heal, and doubtless there were questions to deal with, but their discussion and the realisation the threat had been permanently, if not rather hideously, averted, expunged the strain both, unknowingly, were living under.

Marius, astute enough to know when three was a crowd, said his goodnights.

"Please do not hesitate to call if there is anything, anything at all you require," he implored before disappearing along the dark passage, his sandals slapping rhythmically on the flagged floor.

Rufius grinned at Lucia, who patted the bed.

"Come join me, my love. How very decadent, eating in bed and what a shame we are not well enough to make the most of it," smiling primly, at the same time as biting into a warm honeyed roll, the sweet juice running down her chin. Barking a laugh, Rufius, leaned forward, gingerly, to catch the sticky honey with his finger, licking it clean in a most lascivious manner. Lucia joined in his laughter as they settled down to enjoy the tasty repast.

Sipping their hot drinks, they chatted some more, but before long sleep sang its seductive melody, aided by the powder Marius had stirred into their drinks at Salonius' instruction. Within minutes of Rufius blowing out the oil lamp, both were deep in slumber, for once without dreams.

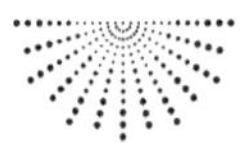

CHAPTER TWENTY-EIGHT

The following day Salonius bustled in to re-examine his patients. Rufius' body was a mass of bruises, contusions, and blisters, eliciting plenty of tutting and hissing from the medicus. He was meticulous — cleaning, applying various salves, and redressing the multitude of injuries.

"I believe you have several cracked if not broken ribs, young man." He peered at Rufius, who grinned foolishly at being called a young man. The medicus grinned back and continued, "The bandages around your chest are more to stop sudden movements than for any other reason. There is no ointment to heal such damage, although arnica massaged in should alleviate some of the discomfort. I shall leave a jar with instructions for its use." He looked at Lucia, who confirmed she was familiar with the remedy.

Finishing off, he transferred his attentions to Lucia. First he unbound and rinsed her head wound, then checked both it, her several lacerations, and the burns on her arm and side for contamination. Eventually, Salonius pronounced himself satisfied, affirming he would return regularly until certain they were healing normally, but to send Scaro if anything changed or either felt unwell.

"You are both very lucky and, thankfully, being healthy youngsters the pair of you will likely heal more quickly than most." He informed them in his habitually absentminded fashion, while packing his bag, tidily arranging his instruments, and pots of noxious smelling balms and drafts.

"Please stay for prandium. Flavia tells me Ana is poaching fish, your favourite…" Lucia dangled her invitation.

"Hmmm, I should get home, patients you know…"

"Please, Salonius…" she cajoled with a sweet smile.

Salonius patted Lucia's hand. "Thank you, my dear, I accept. My wife is out doing good deeds today, so I daresay any refreshment will be sparse at home." Tucking Lucia's arm through his, the genial medicus strolled through to the triclinium, chattering about this and that.

A goblet or two of mulsum was a delightful accompaniment to a hearty meal, and encouraged relaxed chatter. Their gossip made a pleasant interlude, and it was mid-afternoon before Salonius took his leave.

When the door closed behind the amiable medicus, Rufius decided it would be a suitable time to indulge his staff's craving for a juicy story. Once he managed to corral them into the triclinium, which took some doing, he divulged the salient details — embellishment definitely not necessary.

To his amusement, they questioned him exhaustively, determined to extract every morsel. He answered with good humour, aware they wanted to claim intimate knowledge to their friends and neighbours, all of whom would be hankering to hear the sordid details. Feronia's role as both protector and killer was received with remarkable aplomb;

the household no longer surprised by anything Lucia was embroiled in.

After the tale was told, and the staff satisfied, the two at the centre of it all spent the remainder of the day quietly, following Salonius' orders and resting, both tucked up in bed much earlier than was their habit.

Three days later, Quintus Antonius Valerius called. The procurator wanted to make his farewells privately and arrived without his usual retinue. Rufius and Lucia received him in the triclinium and, over hot calda and some sweet rolls, furnished him with a complete picture of Ovidius' machinations. Rufius explained about the overseer's harsh behaviour in Pannonia, and subsequent discharge from the army.

"It seems, because I was the one who reported him to my superiors, he held me responsible for his misfortunes from that day forward," Rufius elaborated. "You know what my suppositions were regarding that day in the arena," inclining his head slightly, towards Lucia. Antonius nodded. "I have since come to the conclusion that was simply coincidence, but once Ovidius realised I was the one who rescued the woman who dared reject his overtures, he decided she was a good target. To hurt Lucia was to hurt me."

He shrugged, nonchalantly, but Lucia wasn't fooled. Her hand crept into his, squeezing gently, her expression, bleak.

Rufius smiled down at her. "I must confess a reluctant admiration for his tenacity. He schemed, and cheated, and lied until he had created an intricate web of deceit, so convoluted it was almost impossible to trace any threat back to him. A shrewd operator, indeed, his plot only foiled because Agapito decided to heed his conscience and bring my wife home. Had he not, this debacle would have had a far different ending. That, and Lucia's decision to involve Feronia. That wolf…" Rufius shook his head, Feronia's selfless conduct, continued to confound him.

Lucia interjected with her own opinions, but when it came down to it, the actions of Ovidius were those of a madman. A dead madman whose reasoning, however preposterous, went with him to the grave. They could really only speculate as to whether one or several perceived slights triggered his descent into lunacy.

While the two men were talking, Lucia was beset by the oddest notion, their chatter flowed around her, but she felt detached and all sound was muted. The more she considered the concept nudging at her, the more she realised that what she had presumed to be fantasy was, in fact, the truth, and although unable to fathom why, she knew without a shadow of a doubt that this was the moment.

So engrossed were they in their conversation, neither man noticed her slip out of the room to return moments later, carrying a small leather pouch. After resuming her seat as though naught had happened and, while awaiting a lull in the discussion, Lucia pondered her words.

It was important he understood why.

The room fell quiet and, seizing her chance, Lucia spoke. "I apologise for interrupting, but wonder whether I might beg a moment of your time?" Puzzled, they assured her she was doing no such thing. She thanked them and smiled but to the two watching, the gesture seemed reserved, as though uncertain of her reception.

Lucia stood, smoothed non-existent wrinkles from her dress, then before her nerves failed her, faced the procurator and launched in. "Quintus Antonius Valerius, although we met only recently, I know you to be an honourable man. One who is also compassionate, tolerant, and principled. Twice, to my knowledge, you have used your position to save me, as well as my husband."

Even more confused, both men stared, unsure where this was going.

Ignoring their bemusement expressions, she forged ahead, her gaze fixed on Antonius. "You were also generous enough to stand in my father's stead on the day of our marriage, a gesture I shall never forget. I was, still am in all honesty, ignorant of your Roman marriage ceremony, it baffles me, however there was a small part of the ritual of which I was only recently apprised. Perhaps because my father is dead, perhaps because I am half-Vettone," she paused, "whatever the reason, no one thought to mention it to me at the time, and is something I wish to rectify."

Lucia lifted the leather pouch, undid the drawstring and withdrew the gemstone.

Holding it aloft on the palm of her hand, she advanced two steps. A shaft of sunlight through the window high on the wall, behind the couch on which the procurator was sitting, illuminated the ruby, scattering twinkling red sparkles around the room.

Silence surrounded the three.

Lucia bowed her head slightly. "Quintus Antonius, your kindness, your humanity, and your noble spirit are qualities rarely found in those who wield power, and have made you a popular, revered, and trustworthy official. In a lesser man, such accolades might cause a certain arrogance, yet you remain reticent and humble, and someone I am privileged to call a friend."

She rolled the ruby in her hand, contemplatively.

"I digress. I understand a Roman bride would return to her father the locket bestowed at birth. Regrettably, I do not have a birth gift, but my father presented this gemstone to my mother on the day they married. He loved her dearly, and when he died he took part of her with him. She gave it me shortly before she followed him to the afterlife. She knew she was dying, and I remember being angry because I could not save her. I wanted to sell the ruby and use the coin to pay for a physician." She smiled sadly, her vision turned inward.

Shaking her head, she resumed. "Mother took my hand, 'Lucia,' she said, 'treasure of my heart, no coin can help me now, it is time for me to join your father. I have missed him these long years.' I cried because she did not want to stay for me. I was still a child; how would I cope without her?"

She shrugged ruefully. "Then she said the strangest thing, that my father believed the ruby to be special, because of the manner in which he received it. Apparently, a man whose life he saved gave it to him. I always thought it fanciful, probably more acceptable than the truth, but mother was adamant. The man said my father was merely a guardian, that the ruby would touch seven lives before it came into the possession of the person for whom it was intended, but Fate would smile on those who shielded it.

"Until recently, I thought the whole story preposterous, incredible, and invented to please Mother. Of late however, I reconsidered its veracity. While the ruby has been in my keeping, I faced many challenges and, somehow with the love and care of others, I have prevailed. I met my Rufius, and have been welcomed into this community warmly.

"My heart tells me it is time to let the ruby go, and because you have been instrumental in my continued good fortune, in place of a birth gift, I entrust this to you. If you are indeed its fifth guardian, you will know what to do."

Lucia took one more step and gave the glistening gemstone to the stunned procurator.

His jaw dropped.

"L-Lucia," he stammered, completely at a loss for words, "I cannot... this is... your inheritance... I have not..." Antonius clamped his lips shut, willing his mouth to catch to his brain.

Lucia moved to sit next to Rufius, who took her hand and pressed a kiss to her forehead. Their eyes met, and he nodded, almost imperceptibly, in tacit agreement. Lucia released a long sigh. She did not know what motivated her decision, but the instant she placed the ruby in Antonius' hand, she knew it was the right one. Presumably, Fate had a plan.

Lucia shook her head and smiled at Antonius. "This is not my inheritance. I cannot claim ownership of something of which I am merely a custodian. The ruby is destined to come to you, of that I am quite certain."

'Thank you, Lucia Atella; I shall safeguard this until my heart dictates otherwise. I admit to being rather sceptical about Fate, or the will of the Gods, which I know is... unorthodox for a Roman. In this case, I am inclined to accept sometimes there is a force at work among us greater than our comprehension. Here in this small town, I have witnessed things I believed impossible. So who am I to question the destiny of this ruby? I am honoured to have met you both, and rest assured, even without this gift, you will always be in my heart."

Rufius, sensing the discussion was becoming emotional, called for more refreshments. While they waited, he asked an innocuous question about Antonius' travel plans, which kept their conversation on a lighter note for the remainder of the procurator's visit.

During the days that followed, Rufius visited Decima Icilia, Ovidius' widow to make sure she and Aurelia were not left destitute. As he had promised Aurelia, Rufius gave the two women an update as to what occurred at the farm. It was a softened, somewhat condensed version of events, neither needed to suffer further distress as a result of the man's actions, and their appreciation for his compassion was apparent.

Rufius also arranged for the funeral rites to be observed, but at the request of the widow, forwent the laying out of the body. Quietly, and without fuss, Rufius organised for Ovidius to be cremated under cover of darkness, his ashes collected into a nondescript urn, and placed in one of the lesser-frequented *columbaria*. Icilia was tempted to have them drop his body in one of the *puticuli*, or dumping pits, where he would be left to rot, or be picked apart by carrion birds, but she could not quite bring herself to do so.

As the year turned, Icilia was often seen around the town on the arm of an affable widower, her contented smile, testament to her new-found happiness.

In contrast, Feronia was buried with full ceremony, in the manner of a military hero or woman of extraordinary status. She was washed, her wound stitched, and a coin placed in her mouth, so she could pay Charon, the ferryman.

On the day of the funeral, Feronia was carried in regal procession, led by Rufius, Lucia, Marius, and Marcellus. Even Antonius attended, his last 'official' engagement before he departed for Rome.

The simple casket was flanked by those who worked in the Gladiators' School, along with friends and neighbours of the Atellus family, as well as a troupe of musicians. Lucia did feel moved to murmur, in aside to Rufius, that the great she-wolf would have been highly amused by such pomp; bearing in mind her sole purpose was to kill. No murderer was treated with such respect.

For Lucia, although the day was poignant — full of memory and more than a little sorrow, it also closed a chapter of her life. Feronia's funeral rites, the last item on the long list of matters to be dealt with as a consequence of Ovidius' perfidy.

Marcellus, his perception of what was normal now altered out of all recognition, returned to his orderly routine. The simple husbandry of gladiators and animals, a welcome respite from chasing down lunatics.

The horse, Lucia was determined to buy the night she was abducted, was rescued and restored to full health in the Atellus stable

Agapito confessed his part in the debacle, to Rufius. The latter assured him that although he might wish to trust his gut *before* they were twelve hours away from Emerita, he *had* tended to Lucia's wounds the best he could, and returned her home as quickly as was feasible.

At Lucia's insistence, and after discussion with both the procurator and the legatus, Agapito was offered the position of assistant stablehand at the garrison. This meant, along with his own business, he would never lack for work and would now be busy all year round.

Agapito — who had admitted his involvement to Erlea, his unsuspecting wife, and whose declaration he was unworthy of such largesse, was pooh poohed by Lucia — never regretted his decision to defy Ovidius.

Lucia, being Lucia, inveigled herself into his life,

becoming fast friends with Erlea, and honorary aunt to their three children.

As per Antonius' orders, the farm was razed, and within weeks nature began to encroach, the disquieting tale surrounding it nothing more than a rumour, and soon forgotten by everyone… well almost everyone.

Those, whose lives were transformed forever by the events of that fateful day, would never forget.

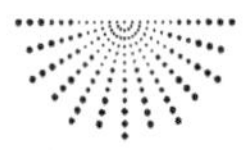

How does one move on after such a calamitous event? How do you pick up the pieces of a life someone was determined to destroy?

For a little while, in the wake of the catastrophe, Lucia struggled. Her visits to the bestiariorum dwindled because she missed seeing Feronia, the wolf's absence a constant reminder.

She developed a tendency to glance over her shoulder, to flinch at any unexpected sound or movement, and for a time, refused to leave the domus without being accompanied by Rufius or Marius.

Lucia knew her behaviour to be irrational but was powerless to curb it. Her loom was her solace, and she channelled her feelings of helplessness into a new collection of pieces. As always exquisitely woven, but now her designs seemed to reflect the conflict within — almost discordant.

Interestingly, they proved extremely popular, and she was inundated with requests. She worked every day and, after spending a little time with Rufius over the evening meal, long into each night. Her husband frequently awoke in the hours before dawn to find her gone from their bed, only to hear the muffled clack of the loom as she vented her insomnia on the intricacies of a new pattern.

Salonius assured Rufius that Lucia's reaction was quite natural, and to give her the time and space she needed to process everything. As a general rule, Lucia was a pragmatic young woman; it was simply that her innate sense of trust had taken a beating.

Rufius was a patient man, however, making sure he was there, listening when she needed to talk, providing a shoulder to cry on, and a pair of strong arms to hold her close. Slowly but surely as the days began to lengthen and the promise of spring teased at the last vestiges of winter, the cheerful, happy-go-lucky vivacious attitude, that was quin-tessentially Lucia, began to re-emerge.

The year turned, and by the end of spring, Lucia was in high demand. The popularity of her weaving and painting continued to increase with commissions rolling in, Rufius and she contemplating the possibility of expanding her burgeoning business.

Marcellus, in what he hoped was his most winsome manner, begged Lucia to monitor the various animals at the bestiariorum; the season of gladiatorial games was in full swing, and injuries were commonplace. Despite her ongoing abhorrence at, what was in her opinion, the callous exploitation of wild beasts, Lucia was not about to let any suffer.

The story of Feronia had spread far and wide, encour-aging the inhabitants of Emerita to trust Lucia's intuition where their livestock was concerned, and she was often approached for her advice on all manner of problems relating to their animals — from sheep, to cattle to horses, and the occasional dog.

As Lucia anticipated, Sirius was soon a fixture in the Atellus household. Initially, Rufius was convinced the creature would bring with him fleas and disease, but Lucia ensured Sirius was regularly bathed, and suggested he might be quite useful as a guard dog.

Despite his reservations, Rufius was often heard discussing important business matters with Sirius, who listened attentively, head cocked to one side for all the world as though he could offer an erudite opinion.

Sirius proved to be very much the gentleman or rather, gentledog. Never jumping, always polite — well, as polite as a dog sorely tested with treats could be — and only barked when he believed his family were in mortal peril.

To be fair, occasionally he thought this stretched to the numerous twittering birds that enjoyed bathing in the courtyard fountain, but for the most part he was a most obedient canine.

Rufius, in his capacity as supervisor of the town's infrastructure was never at a loss for work. The roads, pipes, drains, and bridges; the three aqueducts, and civic buildings such as the amphitheatre, the two *fora* and the theatre, not to mention insulae, houses, villas, and baths, all required constant inspection and maintenance.

The inexplicable acts of sabotage died with Ovidius, and Rufius made no further reference to the incidents, consigning them to the past. He and his growing team worked hard, but their city reflected their diligence and they were righteously proud of their efforts.

With so much to keep them occupied, Lucia and Rufius made a concerted effort to spend time together. Afternoons walking through the leafy streets, evenings sitting outside their favourite thermopolium chatting with friends. Rufius began to talk about the possibility of visiting the small village outside Rome, where his family was from and where his parents still lived.

Lucia was hesitant. Perhaps she was not the choice the senior Atellus' would prefer for their only son. Rufius grinned when she explained her reluctance, pointing out, had he not been wounded he would still be in the military and therefore ineligible to marry.

"My parents will love you as much as I do," he said and kissed her soundly, curtailing the discussion for the time being.

Lucia pushed it to the back of her mind, to be dealt with should the matter ever arise again. Truth be told, she secretly wanted to meet Rufius' parents. She wanted to know everything about him, and they would be able to tell her what he was like as a child and a young man before he joined the army at eighteen. Like pieces of a puzzle, she needed the last few to complete the picture. Maybe one day.

Summer blazed down on Emerita, the days were long and hot, and one morning, while working in the cool of the domus, Lucia realised she had known Rufius a whole year. She was vague about the actual date because the way Romans calculated their years meant little to her.

Lucia had never been taught, and now saw no reason to learn anything other than the basics. She got up with the sun, and went to bed when she was tired, measuring the passing of the year by the changing seasons. To Lucia's recollection, the day she ended up in the arena had been the last gladiatorial games before the summer hiatus, and this year's equivalent had taken place three days previously.

A whole year! On the one hand it was a mere handspan of time, on the other it seemed as though he had been part of her life forever. Such an auspicious occasion demanded a celebration. She pondered over what sort of gift might be suitable, and planned a picnic. Taking Ana into her confidence, the pair came up with Rufius' favourite treats, and she did not find it too hard to persuade her husband to put aside a whole day to spend with her.

Inspiration for the gift struck later that same afternoon, as Lucia was sorting out her pile of sketches. In the process of separating them into themes, she came across the picture of Rufius she drew shortly after he rescued her. Sitting back on her heels, Lucia held the papyrus, one finger tracing the image.

It was obvious, even then, that she was irrevocably in love with him. The way she captured the crinkles at the corners of his eyes, the slight crease in his brow, the hint of a smile curving his lips softening his rather austere features, and his thick dark hair, rather dishevelled and slightly longer than military regulations allowed — but he *was* retired. Her heart stuttered.

She recalled his comment that day, when he picked her drawing up from the floor… 'It is a shame I do not have one of you'. Beaming with happiness, Lucia realised exactly what she could give him.

Scouting around the riverbank, she came across a lovely flat piece of pale grey stone, not too large and very smooth. Taking care Rufius would not come upon her unexpectedly, Lucia set to work.

It was challenging trying to reproduce her own likeness,

but she persevered, and eventually believed she had captured the image she wanted. Needing to be sure, she showed it to Marius, and asked for his opinion. The steward's expression was enough of an answer.

"*Lucia!*" he exclaimed in awed tones. "That is… how did you… how are you able…?" Marius stopped and took a breath, stunned by Lucia's talent. "I am astonished, it is so lifelike." His eyes and mouth formed perfect 'O's.

"Thank you, Marius, that is the reaction I was hoping for. Please do not tell Rufius. I want to surprise him."

"Your secret is safe with me, domina. He will be ecstatic."

Lucia grinned and went to hide the piece until the day of the picnic.

Two days later, a basket tucked under one arm, and holding Lucia's hand, Rufius strolled along sunny streets to the outskirts of Emerita. Crossing the beautiful stone bridge, the pair soon reached their favourite spot on the grassy banks of the Albarregas in the shadow of the huge aqueduct.

It was quiet here, away from the more popular leisure spots. Most folk preferred the wider and more easily accessible spaces along the River Anas at the other side of the town, meaning it was unlikely they would be disturbed.

Opening the basket, Rufius lifted out a colourful rug and placed it on the grass. Making themselves comfortable, they chatted about this and that, catching up on their respective weeks. Lucia dug about in the basket and withdrew some little tarts full of stewed pears, and sweet wine cakes — the smell of cinnamon making their mouths water. After pouring two cups of mulsum, they each leaned on one elbow and enjoyed the food.

While they sipped their drinks, Lucia sat up and began to

fidget. Despite her spirited temperament, she was normally quite a peaceful companion, compelling Rufius to wonder what bothered her.

"What is it, my love?" he asked gently, reaching out to still her hands, which she was wringing in her lap. She looked across at him, scanning his beloved face, and down his throat, to his chest. Her eyes raked over his tanned skin following the angles of his body to the honed musculature of his legs, as he reclined on the rug. An image of them making love popped into her mind and she felt her heart rate speed up, heat washing up her cheeks.

"Lucia…?"

She calmed her breathing. Her heart rate — well there was *no* chance of calming that, not when all she wanted to do was divest Rufius of his tunic, with all haste, and ravish him. A strangled gurgle of laughter slipped over her lips at her wanton thoughts, and she tried to concentrate on what she was trying to say. Rufius was staring at her, eyes crinkled with mirth, his brow creased. The similarity to her sketch, uncanny.

"*Mi dilecte.*" The endearment rolled off her tongue, sweeter than the rolls they had just eaten. "I think it is about a year since we first met. The circumstances were… harrowing, yet fortuitous. I believe that day — the day a man of courage and principle, who did not know the woman tied to a stake but cared enough to rescue her from certain death — was our prelude to fate. The chances of so many stars aligning at that precise moment, incalculable. We were on different paths, neither looking to change the status quo, happy with our lives. It seems Fortune had other ideas."

She smiled and stretched over to brush her lips against his. Rufius groaned and caught her against him, their kiss quickly becoming heated. Before they became completely consumed by their ardour, Lucia pushed herself away.

"Please," she gasped, breathless, "let me finish."

Rufius grinned and opened his palm, indicating she should proceed. Although taking her hand and rubbing his thumb over her fingers was not at all conducive to Lucia being able to maintain her composure, or indeed her concentration.

Tutting, she continued. "As I was saying," frowning in mock annoyance, making him grin all the more, "Fortune had a different plan. Almost immediately, I realised, although indebted to you for saving my life, my feelings, my emotions bore absolutely no resemblance to gratitude. It was clear you had an affection for me, but I presumed it was merely compassion for my regrettable situation. When you told me you loved me," she sighed her mind winging back to the murmured words in the afterglow of passion, "now that was a gift I never anticipated, but was all the more cherished because of it. I love you, Gaius Rufius Atellus, I do not think I can ever find the words to tell you how much, so I tried to capture it for you."

Puzzled, Rufius watched her delve into the basket.

Lucia scrabbled under the food, seeking the long flat item, carefully hidden prior to the basket being filled. Sliding it out, wrapped in a piece of cloth woven especially, she handed it to her husband.

"Lucia, what is this?"

"Well, you need to open it to find out." She smiled a little uncertainly. *Had she done him justice?* Marius seemed to think so, but it was Rufius' reaction she wanted to see.

· · ·

Rufius peeled back the soft fabric, to reveal a piece of flat grey stone, on which his wife had painted the most incredible image. It was the two of them, almost in profile, their faces slightly angled to the viewer. Her portrayal was so realistic he had to blink to reassure himself they weren't actually alive.

Lucia and he were gazing into each other's eyes. Two of his fingers looked to be stroking along her jawline, while her thumb rested on the corner of his mouth as though about to trace his lower lip — a favourite gesture of hers. Their mirrored expressions shone with devotion. The rendition was extraordinary. The love, which had gone into its creation, undeniable.

"Lucia, I am lost for words. This is astonishing, your artistry, your skill is known to me, but this, this surpasses everything you have ever done." He held it against his heart. "I asked you, once. I asked for a keepsake, something with your image etched onto it, and you were so surprised at my request." There was a long pause as his eyes were drawn back to the picture. "You remembered." He stared at their portraits, shaking his head in disbelief.

"There is little you say that I forget, my love," Lucia murmured. "Everything you do, everything you say is, like this image is onto stone, forever imprinted into my soul. I—" what ever she was about to say was muffled under Rufius' mouth as, placing the etching safely in the basket, he hauled his wife against him and kissed her senseless.

Ardour cooled for now, they curled up together, happy and relaxed, resuming their easy chatter. The combined sounds of animals in the field at the other side of the river, the twitter of birds and the lazy drone of insects were hypnotic, and within minutes, Rufius and Lucia were asleep.

It was a warm summer's day, and Rufius was half-reclining on a colourfully woven mat, by the river, just outside Emerita. At his feet — a basket overflowing with food, alongside him — a beautiful woman dozed.

Hair, the colour of aged wine, tumbled in riotous abandon around slim shoulders, her clothing was mussed, and her face flushed. He knew without a doubt they had been kissing, he could taste her on his lips and hers were swollen.

His heart thudded and, wholly unable to help himself, leaned close to kiss her again. Her eyes fluttered open, glorious grey-green, framed by sooty lashes, and she stared at him until he questioned whether he was falling into her gaze.

"Rufius…" his name slipped out on a sigh, and she lifted herself up on one elbow, hair streaming behind her in chestnut rivulets.

Pressing her lips to his, she stroked one hand across his chest, over his waist, and on down, coming to rest on his thigh. *Surely, she must feel his need for her*? Inquisitive fingers crept under his tunic, gliding over his skin, her touch a brand. He shuddered as her hand encircled him, at the same time as she brought her gaze up to his face, eyes glinting wickedly in the sunlight.

"Make love to me, Rufius," she purred.

This time, Rufius realised he wasn't dreaming…

If this was indeed, a prelude to fate, imagine the next chapter.

CHAPTER THIRTY

ROME AD 40

Quintus Antonius Valerius approached the bed. His wife, Claudia, lay fast asleep her face flushed, her dark hair, tousled and still slightly damp was splayed over the pillow, stark against the pale linen. She was exhausted, yet to Antonius she had never looked more beautiful. Rather than disturb her, he pulled up a chair and made himself comfortable, content to watch over his wife until she woke.

In an ornate wooden crib just in front of his feet, a tiny scrap of humanity snuffled.

His son.

The birth had been long and painful. Several times throughout the night, Claudia cursed her husband for implanting her with his seed, refusing to let him leave the room, even though the midwife assured Claudia his presence was neither essential nor warranted.

Claudia informed the midwife in no uncertain terms, her

husband was with her at the beginning of this, and by all the gods he would be with her at the end. She begged him to hold her hand, which she squeezed more tightly with every contraction; he was still not entirely sure she hadn't broken it.

Antonius knew part of her reasoning was fear. Death in childbirth was common, and it did not distinguish between rich and poor, young and not so young. Claudia, a healthy woman of twenty and six, was considered past her prime for having children.

Although for much of their early marriage, Antonius was away from Rome, they wed for love, something they affirmed with gratifying frequency whenever he was able to arrange leave, or Claudia visited. As they were so far without issue, it seemed they were not to be blessed with a family.

When Claudia told him she had conceived, he was over-joyed, and spent the next two months cosseting his wife until she thought she might scream from his attentiveness. Used to a modicum of independence, Claudia chafed at the restrictions he demanded she abide by.

Eventually, her threat that if he did not let her breathe, she might find a way to prevent him ever procreating again, persuaded him to relax his over-protective constraints. The remaining months of her confinement — as pleasant as could be expected.

Almost twenty-four hours ago, her pains began. According to the midwife, everything progressed normally, but as the pains came closer together Claudia's strength began to fail. Antonius, terrified he would lose his wife, did everything he could to encourage her and help, even rubbing a rather peculiar scented warm oil over her swollen abdomen, something which was supposed to offer some relief — Claudia was sceptical, but grudgingly admitted, once massaged in, it *did* ease the discomfort a little.

Finally, when Antonius was certain his wife was about to expire, a small squawking bundle of arms and legs slithered into the world, clearly furious at being expelled unceremoniously into the cold air from its warm cocoon. The midwife caught the wriggling mass and dealt with it as Antonius supposed she always did. To his eye she did look to be rather rough with so tiny an infant, but forbore to comment.

Antonius lifted his wife, carrying her from the birthing chair to the freshly made bed. Several old sheets covered the clean ones, to be burned once Claudia was bathed, dried, and healing balm applied. Seconds later, the baby was swaddled and handed to his exhausted mother. Antonius had never felt anything like the swelling of his heart when Claudia looked at the child.

"It is a boy," the midwife said in practical tones, "nurse him for a moment, while I clean you up. Then you must rest. I'll organise a wet nurse."

"No!" Claudia put out a hand and touched the woman's arm. "No, I shall nourish him myself." Then to her husband, "We have a son." The wonderment in her voice brought tears to Antonius' eyes.

"We do, I am so proud of you my love, you are braver than an army of soldiers facing a horde of barbarians."

"I thought that particular battle was never going to end, that he would never be born, but now he is here, the struggle to birth him is but a distant memory. Quite extraordinary." She smiled up at Antonius. She sighed a long weary sigh and reached up to cup his cheek. "I love you, my husband."

He kissed the top of her head, tucking a wayward strand of hair behind her ear. "I love you more, my wife."

A few moments later she was asleep. Antonius gently lifted the babe from her arms and held him quite naturally as though practiced at holding tiny infants.

"My son, my first born. You are healthy, and my beloved

Claudia, your mother, survived the ordeal. Today the Gods smiled on us." He paused and gazed into the scrunched up drowsy face. "I have an inkling you are destined for a life which will take you farther than any of us could imagine." He laid the child in the crib and covered him with a soft blanket.

Now it was several hours later and, ignoring the midwife's suggestion he leave Claudia to rest, Antonius found he could not bear to be apart from her or the babe.

He had been sitting for quite some time, contemplating what to name his son, when he felt a gentle hand on his arm. Twisting in his seat, he saw Claudia was awake and watching him, tired but content.

"What tiresome thoughts are crossing your mind, my love?" she asked. "You look as though all the weight of the world is bearing down on your shoulders."

Smiling, he took her hand and entwined their fingers. "You realise, of course, that our lives are no longer our own? We have this little mite who shall rely on us for everything until suddenly he takes off into the wide blue yonder, never to look back."

"Maybe so, but just think of the joy we shall share as he grows and matures from baby through childhood, adolescence into manhood. You can be the strong disciplinarian, I shall be the one who spoils him, who tends to his little worries, and who encourages him to fly."

They both laughed knowing their roles would be reversed. Claudia might be the one to soothe and calm, but she would also be the one who refused to stand for any nonsense. Antonius was a tranquil soul, firm when required, but more teacher than taskmaster, and Claudia knew her son, and any other children they might be fortunate to have, would wrap him around their tiny fingers.

Antonius lifted the fractious baby from his soft nest and gave him to his mother. The midwife had explained how the child should suckle at her breast, and after several false starts, he latched on, to Claudia's everlasting relief.

"We should decide on a name, my love," Antonius ventured, still in awe of this perfect human in miniature.

"I thought Antonius…

"No, it does not fit him. I was thinking maybe Lucius Maxentius?" Maxentius was Claudia's father's name but none in either family was named Lucius.

"Lucius?" Claudia queried, puzzled.

Antonius withdrew a small leather pouch from his pocket. "This was given to me in Emerita, by a young woman who escaped death three times that I know of. Twice, I was instrumental in her rescue."

His wife knew something of what occurred, in a small town in the far-flung province of Lusitania. Antonius included odd snippets in his many letters home, but he had not told Claudia everything.

He did not identify those involved. If working within the Imperial administration had taught him anything, it was that one could never be sure whether there might be repercussions, and it was always prudent to avoid committing names to documents. Moreover, once he departed Emerita, the events of that year seemed outlandish, and maybe best forgotten. He could not forget, however — he had the ruby.

Antonius revealed to his wife the whole of the strange story. How a diminutive young woman who possessed an uncanny ability to commune with animals, first came to his attention in the arena, how she calmed the beasts, and of the events that followed. Her love for Rufius, and her determination to save him from a madman.

He took care to let it be known there was absolutely no romantic entanglement, and Claudia was secure in her husband's love. Antonius knew the tales sounded fantastical and, had he not been witness to most of them, would have declared them to be falsehoods. But he *had* witnessed them, and they had upon him left an indelible mark.

"Is this why you were so subdued on your return from Hispania?" Claudia asked gently, taking his hand and entwining their fingers.

"In part, for I enjoyed my tenure there, though I missed you. Anyway, Lucia, that is her name, gave me this just before my departure, saying she believed it was destined to come into my possession. On this day, in honour of the birth of my son and to your courage, I entrust it to you."

Claudia tipped the pouch and its contents fell onto her lap. A large ruby, not quite a teardrop, not quite an oval, something in between lay on the white sheet, tiny shards of red light sprinkled across the bed where the light caught its facets. It seemed to pulse, as though a living, breathing organism.

There was a long silence.

"My beloved husband, this is indeed a rare gem, and I shall treasure it while it remains in my care, which, inexplicably, I sense is fleeting. This is why you chose Lucius? You wish to immortalise the name of this woman, Lucia, whose life so impacted yours by calling our son Lucius?"

"I cannot explain, my love, but somehow it feels as though our destinies became entwined. That my time in Emerita was a prelude to events, to a fate not yet imagined. Fanciful it may be, but I beg you to grant me this request for our son's name."

Antonius' eyes held Claudia's, the immeasurable he bore her, warming their green depths. Claudia smiled and squeezed his fingers. Lifting her son who protested at being separated from the comfort of her breast, she whispered…

"Welcome to the world, Lucius Maxentius Valerius. You are named for one who has faced many challenges and overcome them. Your fate will surely be remarkable."

MASADA AD 71

Lucius Maxentius Valerius unhooked his cloak from where it always hung by the door and laid it on the bed. There at the neck, the bright gemstone twinkled against the darker material of the garment. He unfastened the clasp, and sat on the bed, still completely overwhelmed by the knowledge he was now a father. Yesterday, his beautiful Hannah had given birth to a daughter, whom they named Claudia after his mother.

Maxentius had been terrified Hannah would die during childbirth. At no time during the last nine months had she said anything, presumably not wanting to worry him, but he was not ignorant of the dangers, and to lose her would be the death of him. Never in his wildest imagination did he expect to find and fall in love with someone who made him feel as though without her he would forget to breathe.

When the horde of Zealots had stormed the Roman outpost at Masada five years previously, Maxentius, garrison commander, had been badly wounded. Three days later, Hannah had found him and his two comrades clinging to life, and demanded she be allowed to treat their wounds.

One she was unable to save, but Marcus — his second-in-command — and he had survived, slowly becoming part of this isolated enclave. Any attempt to flee would mean certain death, but the moment he had laid eyes on Hannah, escape was the last thing on his mind.

When he discovered she loved him too, Maxentius' life was complete. Despite everything stacked against them — the least of which being that Maxentius was a serving Roman soldier and thus, a sworn enemy of those who now held him captive — they had married. He was of the belief, whatever challenges they faced, as long as they were together, they could surmount them.

He turned the clasp in his hand, rubbing his thumb over the glistening stone. It was a large ruby, dark at the centre, paler at the edges, its shape not quite oval and not quite teardrop, somewhere in between. It nestled in an intricate surround of gold, which had been swirled and twisted around the stone.

Maxentius knew the history of this clasp. It was a tale which his father had told Maxentius and his sister Antonia many times when they were growing up. It featured a woman named Lucia who apparently possessed the ability to commune with animals, a veteran Roman soldier and a wolf. A series of traumatic events, which began with a rescue and culminated in a kidnapping and two deaths, sounded fantastical to the two children, but Antonius swore every word was true. He had been given the ruby in gratitude for his part in saving Lucia twice.

His father had gifted the ruby to his mother upon his, Maxentius', birth and he was named for the Lucia of the story. His mother, in her turn had arranged for it to be fashioned into the ornate clasp, which she gave him on the day he was officially accepted into the army.

For months he had wanted to present it to Hannah, in replacement of a pin she lost after being hurt by one of the rebels, but there was never a perfect moment, and he was afraid it would remind her of the reason she lost her other clasp.

Today, his intuition told him the time was right, and although not given to fancy, Maxentius could not help but feel that the ruby was always supposed to end up in Hannah's possession.

He stared at the gemstone, which seemed to glow and pulse, almost as though it had a heartbeat. With a wry smile, he shook his head; clearly, becoming a father had addled his senses. Standing, he replaced his cloak on its hook, and retraced his steps through their suite of rooms to where Hannah was nursing their daughter.

Sitting by the huge window, Hannah Valerius was lost in contemplation. The stunning vista beyond the citadel, which normally mesmerised her, barely registered today because her attention was wholly focused on the tiny infant asleep in her arms. Hannah did not think she would ever stop being amazed that she had given birth to this beautiful child.

At the sound of a familiar footfall, she turned her head, admiring the tall man who filled the archway.

"She looks so comfortable, cradled in your arms," Maxentius murmured, unwilling to disturb the peace. Hannah smiled, as he came and sat on the window ledge, no reply necessary.

"I have something I wish to give you, in honour of this

day," and with a small flourish, placed the clasp in his wife's hand. "This was given to me by my mother who had it made for my entrance into the army. It was blessed by one of the three major *flamines* — an important priest in my world — and has held my cloak securely for many years. Now, I want you to have it. It will replace the pin you lost and is something you can pass onto our daughter when she is old enough to know our story."

Astounded, Hannah gazed at the clasp, and then raised her eyes to her husband. "Max, this is too much, it is gorgeous. How could you part with it?" she asked, in a voice full of wonder, while her fingers traced the delicate yet surprisingly strong design.

"It is something I have wanted to give you for many moons but had no wish to remind you of why you need a new pin. This very auspicious occasion called for something extraordinary and I would like you to have it."

While they sat, Maxentius shared the story of how his father came by the ruby finishing up by saying, "My father told me this gem would touch seven lives before it came into the possession of the one for whom it was intended. He was the fifth guardian," he stared into Hannah's eyes. "I believe that person is you. You are the eighth holder of the ruby."

About to refute his claim, something about his words gave Hannah pause. Her life, everything which had led her to this moment was as fantastical as this story. *Did she want to argue with Fate? Not a chance.*

She studied the beautiful clasp. "Thank you, my love. I will treasure this always not only because it came from you, but also because of its history. I promise to guard it well."

Maxentius smiled, a tender, loving smile, and Hannah reached out to cup his cheek, her fingers stroking along his jawline.

"My love, how did we get so lucky?" she asked.

Maxentius turned his head and kissed her palm, before bending closer to brush her lips, then sat with his wife while she fed their child.

"I do not believe luck had anything to do with this, my love. This was Fate."

EXCEPT FROM THE POMEGRANATE TREE

HANNAH'S HEIRLOOM - BOOK ONE

I t was the shimmering heat which started it all, making me aware of a subtle shift in the air. It was hot that day; warmer than any day we'd had so far, and unusually so for the time of year. Hot enough for the occasional mirage, cobweb like, to form and dissolve in front of me. Sitting on a desolate outcrop letting my imagination run riot, taking in the ruins and the majesty of what remained, voices from the past whirling around me, I understood why people think they see ghosts.

Sheltered from the blazing sun, I was perched on a stone ledge, the wall behind pressing into my back. The breeze was soughing across the top of the plateau, down into its cracks and fissures. So atmospheric, it made me believe I could call them up; that the long dead souls of this place would simply manifest from the dust beneath my feet, so close did they seem.

Absently fingering the crumpled letter spread out over a dog-eared book in my lap, I began to contemplate the reason why I had come here in the first place and what on earth I thought I was going to find.

. . .

But I get ahead of myself. You don't even know who I am or why I'm rambling about a lump of rock. My name is Hannah, the rocky outcrop is Herod's great desert fortress of Masada, the dog-eared book is Josephus' *The Jewish War* and my Gran wrote the letter.

Okay, so it's a curious mix and, I hear you say, not particularly compelling. You could be right, but something was stirring as if all these, seemingly unrelated, things had to come together, at this one place for a reason. What that reason was, I had no idea, yet had the uneasy feeling I couldn't stop it and by the time it was over I would not be the same.

Yes, I know what you're thinking — it's the sun and the heat messing with my mind — I agree, it's possible, even as a child, my parents reckoned I had too vivid an imagination. I overheard one of my aunts telling my mother, I was fey. As a child, who loved reading about swashbuckling heroes and damsels in distress — often losing myself in their world — being fey sounded very cool. Plus, I assumed all kids did the same, especially as my heritage, typical of so many born in Britain, blends the romance of the French and the Celts with the pragmatism of ancient Germanic tribes.

This sensation was different, more tangible, as though the past was about to come into the present revealing its secrets and nothing in my imagination could prepare me for what I would uncover. *Was I apprehensive?* Of course, despite how implausible it sounds, but we'll see where the days take us.

More to the point, let's get back to how I got here in the first place. My life, to date, has been fairly ordinary. First school, then university, after which, I was lucky enough to land a job with a museum in their classical antiquities department.

A dream role, I spend my days cataloguing ancient artefacts and help with the preparation of new displays and exhibitions. I have a lovely group of friends and enjoy an active social life, pretty much your typical single girl.

About six months ago I received a letter from my Gran. It threw me a little — she has been dead for over ten years but, apparently, this date for its delivery was at her instruction. I had read the letter hundreds of times and still didn't really understand it. The words made no sense. One thing *was* clear, I had to come here, to this stark corner of the world, to Masada.

Yes, I know, who hops on a plane and travels to a remote ruined fortress in the middle of an Israeli desert, on the strength of a few sentences in a ten-year-old letter? I bet you're thinking I'm an idiot.

Well maybe I am, but I need to unravel this. Maybe it's nothing, just a letter from an old lady. In which case, what have I lost? I'll have had an interesting holiday at a world heritage site — but what if it *was* something? Was I prepared not to take the risk? No, I was not! You want to know what's in the letter? Well it's probably for the best, then you'll know what I mean.

My darling Hannah,

As it has been with all of us, you will have received this on your twenty fifth birthday. The age at which you are becoming quite the adult yet retain some of your childhood wonder and imagination. I hope you will never lose that part of yourself.

Said to have been a gift from a grateful soldier during the siege at Masada, this clasp has been passed down through the generations of our family. Created in ancient times as a talisman, whispers of enchantment have always surrounded it. Personally, I think this was more likely a way to protect it from those whose curiosity may have got the better of them. I believe the power of the clasp lies in its history.

    It is your turn now - guard it well.
    Your loving Gran.

See, what was I supposed to do with this information — *guard it well* — it was a brooch! Who would know the history of this brooch or clasp or whatever it was and how on earth would I be able to trace it with nothing more than a letter, oh and the clasp itself? *Masada* — seriously — how is that even possible?

To be fair, the clasp is gorgeous, an unusually shaped, dark-red stone, not quite a teardrop and not quite an oval, something in between. It looks like a ruby but I'm not really sure, set into a finely wrought design of some precious metal with a pin on the back to hold it in place. I'd like to think the metal is gold, but I can't imagine how it would have survived without being sold, stolen or melted down. It has a burnished look and I often speculated whether it was more likely bronze, which could explain its longevity.

I remember as a child, Gran let me use it when I played dress ups with my sister, and I would rub the stone pretending it was magic. Now I'm not sure I dare even hold it.

Where was I? Oh yes — the trip. Once I decided I probably needed to go to where it all started, the timing of my visit to Masada was prompted further by the fact my friend, Max Vallier, would be spending a month or so on the current excavations. He'd been out two or three times before and loved it, reckoning it was one of those sites which get under your skin and you have to keep coming back.

Max, an engineer by profession, also loves archaeology and has found — to his continuing delight — what can be discovered through the excavation of ancient structures often proves useful in modern engineering. That he was already planning to come over here when I got the letter, seemed too good to be true.

What else can I tell you about Max? His family are wealthy and claim to trace their history back a long way, to the Romans if I recall correctly and, although from old money, are not snooty or snobbish. We have known each other for years; I think I was fourteen when we first met. We talk all the time and really enjoy each other's company. I'd say he's probably my best friend.

Max suggested, since I wanted to visit, we tie our trips together. Neither of us would have to travel alone, and we had someone with whom we could enjoy any spare time. He even managed to get me a room to myself — okay, more like a bunk, with a desk, but it had its own bathroom — in the digs, where he and the other archaeologists were staying. How could I say no?

Now here we are, six months later — all our planning and organising done — actually on the top of the rock at Masada.

We've been here a few days. I've already helped out on some of the plots and done my fair share of exploring the whole of this fortress as well as the remains of the Roman camps below. If I move slightly, I can see Max carefully uncovering a mosaic in one of the rooms.

The other archaeologists are spread out around the site. Their work is often interrupted by tourists who wander the plateau inspecting the excavations, asking numerous questions and gasping in astonishment, while snapping away with their cameras.

❦

As I said, it is warmer than usual, but not unbearably hot. The sun is high, and more mirages materialise across hard-baked ground. Thankfully, the breeze keeps the temperature almost comfortable, and I am in the shade.

From my vantage point I can see the Dead Sea glistening in the distance, luring the parched traveller with its restorative blueness, yet entirely undrinkable. This land, which seems so hostile, is able to produce colourful flowers of unknown origin, which are scattered over the vast outcrop, the result of an unusually stormy winter.

The archaeologists tell me, in ancient times, the water from these rare wet winters not only filled the massive cisterns carved into the rock, but also supported a variety of growing things, from vegetables to flowers — even small fruit trees. Remarkable, given the dry arid landscape flowing out around me.

Several pomegranate trees, planted by a group of archaeologists during a Jewish festival in the early days of excavation, provide welcome shade, and somehow manage to survive the harsh conditions on the plateau.

I leant back against the wall, soaking it all in. The incredible view with its ever-changing colours, and the long history of this rock called Masada.

It was the shimmering heat that started it all!

ABOUT THE AUTHOR

Rosie Chapel lives in Perth, Australia with her hubby and three furkids. When not writing, she loves catching up with friends, burying herself in a book (or three), discovering the wonders of Western Australia, or — and the best — a quiet evening at home with her husband, enjoying a glass of wine and a movie.

Website: www.rosiechapel.com

The Pomegranate Tree

Hannah's Heirloom - Book One

Hoping to trace the origins of an ancient ruby clasp, a gift from her long dead grandmother, Hannah Wilson travels to the fortress of Masada with her best friend, Max. Strange dreams concerning a rebel ambush begin to haunt Hannah and following a tragic accident, she slips into the world of Ancient Masada.

A woman out of time, Hannah must rely on her instincts and her knowledge of what will befall this citadel to survive. Will she escape, or is she doomed to die along with hundreds of others as Masada falls – and what does any of this have to do with an ancient ruby clasp?

Echoes of Stone and Fire

Hannah's Heirloom - Book Two

Pompeii - a vibrant city lost in time following the AD79 eruption of Vesuvius. Now rediscovered, archaeologists yearn for an opportunity to uncover the town's past. Some things, however, are best left alone - revealing the secrets hidden beneath the stones could prove perilous. Hannah and Max are brought to Pompeii by a surprise invitation to join an excavation team who are trying to uncover the city's long history.

After entering an excavated house that bears a Hebrew inscription, Hannah's two worlds collide, and she falls back through time to ancient Pompeii. A place where her ancestor is a physician to gladiators engaged in mortal combat, where riotous mobs run amok and where a ghost from the past returns to haunt her.

Will Hannah and her loved ones manage to escape the devastation she knows is coming, before the town is engulfed in volcanic ash?

Will she ever find her way back to Max the love of her life, waiting not so patiently millennia away? Or will echoes be all that remain?

Embers of Destiny

Hannah's Heirloom - Book Three

AD80 - Hannah and Maxentius must embark on a new journey to Northern Britannia. This harsh frontier is far from the comforts of Rome and danger lurks where least expected; a garrison of soldiers, some unhappy with their isolated posting; local tribes, outwardly accepting of their Roman occupier, but who may still resent the seizure of their lands.

Millennia away, Hannah Vallier finds a familiar item while working in a museum near Hadrian's Wall. It is the pomegranate; carved by Maxentius on Masada. Before Hannah can discuss it with Max, disaster strikes! Believing her husband has been killed, Hannah retreats into the past, her soul melding with that of her ancestor, but with little idea of what they could face. Is the risk from the conquered tribes, or much closer to home?

As rebellion threatens to shatter a fragile peace, Hannah's heart whispers that just maybe Max isn't dead and that he is calling her home. Can she trust her heart, or will she remain caught out of time, her destiny floating away like embers on a breeze?

Etched in Starlight

Hannah's Heirloom - Prequel

Maxentius - a Roman soldier fresh from the battlefields of Armenia, arrives to take command of the military outpost of Masada, Herod's isolated citadel in the Judaean desert. A seemingly mundane posting after years of warfare, Maxentius finds it more challenging to maintain a focused garrison than to face the wrath of the Parthians across a disputed frontier.

Hannah - a young Hebrew physician spends her days dealing with injuries from street brawls, deprivation, disease and loss. As her beloved Jerusalem plunges into chaos; her brother — who belongs to a band of rebels determined to drive out their Roman occupiers — tells her of their plans to storm a desert fortress and steal the weapons stored there, persuading his reluctant sister to go with him.

Masada - following the ambush, Hannah finds and treats three badly wounded Roman soldiers. In the aftermath and against impossible odds, Hannah and Maxentius realise that they are more than healer and captive, their fate already etched in starlight.

Prelude to Fate

For Lucia, staring into the jaws of an horrific death, escape seems impossible.

Rufius Atellus, a veteran Roman soldier, is appalled when he recognises one of the victims about to be executed. Surely this is a ghastly mistake?

A ferocious she-wolf, anticipating a tasty meal, suddenly finds herself under a human's control.

In an unexpected twist, and as danger threatens, the lives of all three become inextricably entwined.

Was it chance brought them together in that theatre of bloodshed, or simply a prelude to fate?

Once Upon An Earl

Linen and Lace - Book One

When Fate saw fit to intervene in the life of Giles Trevallier, the very respectable Earl of Winchester, by dropping a female — soaked to the skin and with no memory of who she is or how she came to be there — literally at his feet, no one could have predicted the outcome.

While uncovering her identity, Giles realises he is falling hopelessly in love with his mystery guest, who unbeknownst to him, is succumbing to similar emotions; but, when the heart is involved, a thoughtless word or gesture can thwart even Fate's best-laid plans.

Faced with misunderstandings, whispers of scandal, secret documents and foreign agents, their chance at a happy ever after seems elusive, but fairy tales often happen when least expected, and love — however inconvenient — usually finds a way to conquer all.

To Unlock Her Heart

Linen and Lace - Book Two

Abused by a duke, and shunned by Society, relief seems at hand when Grace Aldeburgh is bequeathed a house in a small village, far from malicious gossips.

Once there, a tentative friendship blooms between Grace and Theo Elliott, the local doctor, who has already resolved to be the man to unlock her heart.

Just when happiness appears to be within her grasp, her erstwhile tormentor once again stalks Grace. After a failed kidnap attempt, the duke's quest culminates in an acrimonious confrontation, and the reason for his venal pursuit becomes agonisingly clear.

Love on a Winter's Tide

Linen and Lace - Book Three

Every day, Helena disappears into a world few acknowledge, helping the poor, downtrodden, and abused. A husband is the last thing she can be bothered with.

Busy managing his shipping line, Hugh Drummond sees no need for a wife, whose only joy is dancing and frivolity. If — and it was a huge if — he ever married, it would be to a woman as capable as he, not some giddy society Miss.

Then, Hugh meets Helena and despite their resolve, fate, it seems, has other ideas. As their attraction deepens however, treachery threatens to tear them apart. Will they uncover the perpetrator in time, or will their love be swept away, lost forever on a winter's tide?

A Love Unquenchable

Linen and Lace - Book Four

Jessica Drummond, a bright and cheerful young woman, rarely gives romance, let alone love, a thought. Long hours working in her brother's shipping office affords little chance of her ever meeting an eligible bachelor.

Duncan Barrington, veteran of the Napoleonic Wars, believes himself wounded in both body and soul. He has no intention of inflicting his demons on anyone, certainly not a beautiful and, in his opinion, irresponsible city lady.

One cold and snowy morning, the plight of a bedraggled puppy throws Jessica and Duncan together and, as a spark of something indefinable yet wholly unquenchable begins to burn, it is unclear who rescued whom.

A Hidden Rose

Linen and Lace - Book Five

After witnessing his mother's grief at the loss of his father, Nick

Drummond resolved never to cause someone he loved such distress. Even the happiness of his siblings would not sway him – until he met Rose.

Rose Archer was almost content assisting her doctor father in a tiny fishing village in the north of Yorkshire. To experience the world beyond, a tantalising dream – until she met Nick.

Unexpectedly, the impossible becomes possible, and the renounced – desired above all things, but the shipwreck that brought them together, may yet tear them apart. Will Nick learn to trust his heart, or will his love for Rose remain forever hidden

The Daffodil Garden

Horrifically scarred during the war, William Harcourt - Marquis of Blackthorne - prefers to spend his days in the quiet of his daffodil garden; plants do not pity, turn away, or judge.

Lucy Truscott, whose life is far removed from that of the *ton*, has no idea that by saving the life of a young woman, to whom she bears an uncanny resemblance, her own will be placed in mortal danger.

A chance encounter leads to something more. William begins to trust that Lucy sees the man beneath the scars, while Lucy is persuaded that love might actually transcend status.

Unfortunately, before their courtship has really begun, someone has every intention of ending it - permanently.

The Unconventional Duchess

Refusing to suffer the humiliation of her husband flaunting his mistress at Society events, the newly married Duchess of Wallingstead, Ella Lennox, takes control of her life. She leaves London for the family's country seat in remote Yorkshire.

A woman alone, Ella spends the next four years turning a cold, grim house into a home, and transforming the fortunes of the estate. Not afraid of hard work, she soon earns the respect of those around her with her determination and unconventional attitude.

Out of the blue, the duke arrives. Resigned to another arduous visit, Ella is stunned when it seems he is attempting to court her.

Impossible!

Could her dream of a happy marriage be about to come true?

Everything hangs on a snowstorm, a herd of cows and an uninvited guest!

His Fiery Hoyden

A Novella

Livvy has no respect for the nobility; they let her down when she most needed them. Why should she accede to their demands now?

Philip, Lord Harrington, is stunned to discover the young heir to the dukedom lives a stone's throw away in a ramshackle cottage, and resolves to restore the child to his birthright.

They meet in a clash of wills, but just when it seems Livvy might surrender, the victory Philip desires, may not taste all that sweet.

A Regency Duet

Luck be a Pirate

Luck wasn't something retired pirate Kennet Alexson believed in – good or bad. However, even he had to concede that landing a job at Trentams shipyard, and meeting Lynette Collins, was more than coincidence.

Fortune it seemed, was smiling on him for once.

As Kennet adjusts to life on dry land, his friendship with Lynette deepens into something far more enduring, and what once seemed elusive now becomes possible.

Unfortunately, fate has other plans, and Kennet's good luck is about to run out.

The Highwayman's Kiss

Surrendered Hearts – Book One

Nothing exciting had ever happened to Juliette St Clair. Her days were spent assisting her father or calling on friends, wandering art galleries, taking constitutionals or, and more preferably, escaping into her books. Her evenings her evenings — an endless round of balls, where she preferred to remain invisible.

Until the day she was robbed by a highwayman.

A Regency Christmas Double

Heart Rescued

Four years since Jasper lost the woman he was hoping to marry. Four years since he closed his heart and withdrew from Society. He has no idea his reclusive existence is about to be shattered.

Enter his sister's best friend, Harriet, a flame haired beauty, who needs his help.

Reluctantly he agrees and as they spend time together, it is clear their feelings run deep. Although Harriet affects Jasper in a way no woman ever has, he believes her to be out of his league ~ but it's Christmas and she might just be the one to melt his frozen heart

Catch a Snowflake

Romance often blossoms in the most unlikely of places - but in a ward full of wounded soldiers - surely not?

When Lucas Withers comes face to face with Jemima Parsons - a young woman who blames him for her brother's injury - falling in love is the last thing on their minds. What neither of them anticipated, was the magic of snowflakes.

Fate is Curious

Happily, ever after? No such thing! Bereft, following her beloved husband's sudden death, Lady Charlotte Sherbrooke has lost her belief in such romantic nonsense.

Successful shipping merchant, Zacharie Romain, is no stranger to loss; his business can be hazardous. Moreover, his wife died in childbirth and even though it happened a decade ago, he has no mind to expose himself to such sorrow again.

They meet in less than joyful circumstances but, as the year turns and grief diminishes, the woes of a small boy become the catalyst for something wholly unexpected. Can Charlotte and Zacharie trust what Fate has in store or will past heartbreak prevent them from taking a chance on love?

A Christmas Prayer

with Ashlee Shades

A Short Story

An entreaty from a frightened child.

Orphaned and only nine, Caroline Thorne has to grow up before her time. She is doing everything she can to keep what is left of her family together and out of the workhouse but is terrified her prayers are not being heard. Or maybe they are…

A petition from a woman desperate for a family.

A chance meeting with three orphaned siblings, tugs at Elizabeth

Barrington's heart strings. Thus far, she and her husband have not been blessed with children and, as Christmas approaches, a plan begins to form - one which might just be the answer to her prayers.

Two Christmas prayers, as different as they are the same.

Will they hear and, more importantly, heed the answer?

The Lady's Wager

Surrendered Hearts- Book Two

A Novelette

Ged Mowbray will do anything to avoid being married off to the suitable prospects his parents insist on parading in front of him.

Melissa Bouchard is under no illusion her sizeable dowry is the attraction to suitors, not her.

An overheard conversation leads to an offer too good to refuse, but what happens when a lady's wager, becomes a gamble on the happily ever after, you did not even realise you wanted?

Winning Emma

Surrendered Hearts - Book Three

A Novelette

Randolph Craythorpe — earl, covert operative, and occasional highwayman — believed his dalliance with Lady Felicity Hartwich would lead to marriage. It did, but not to him! The arrival of an unwelcome guest, however, provides the perfect opportunity to indulge in a little retaliation.

Emma Newbury accompanies her cousin, Lady Charity Anscombe, to London for the Christmas season. Once there, she comes face to face with the three men who witnessed the humiliating aftermath of her father's disgrace — one of whom, to her irritation, has taken up residence in her dreams.

Their infrequent encounters only serve to confuse but, while winter tightens its grip on the city, what was inconceivable becomes the one thing for which they both yearn, yet bound by Society's rules, cannot admit.

As the snow falls, Randolph begins to understand that to win Emma, he will have to surrender.